THROWN

Also by Sara Cox

Till the Cows Come Home (2019)

THROWN

SARA COX

CORONET

First published in Great Britain in 2022 by Coronet
An Imprint of Hodder & Stoughton
An Hachette UK company

1

Copyright © Sara Cox 2022

The right of Sara Cox to be identified as the Author
of the Work has been asserted by her in accordance with
the Copyright, Designs and Patents Act 1988.

A CIP catalogue record for this title is
available from the British Library

Hardback ISBN 9781529373837
Paperback ISBN 9781529392494
eBook ISBN 9781529373844

Typeset in SWIFT LT Std by by Palimpsest Book Production Ltd,
Falkirk, Stirlingshire

Printed and bound in Great Britain by Clays Ltd, Elcoraf S.p.A.

Hodder & Stoughton policy is to use papers that are natural, renewable
and recyclable products and made from wood grown in sustainable forests.
The logging and manufacturing processes are expected to conform to the
environmental regulations of the country of origin.

Hodder & Stoughton Ltd
Carmelite House
50 Victoria Embankment
London EC4Y 0DZ

www.hodder.co.uk

Dedicated to all NHS staff and key workers. Thank you.

In memory of Alice Procope (1978-2021), who walked by in the sunshine as I wrote this book.

1

Becky

Becky stood in the Inventors' Estate community hall with her hands on her hips, absent-mindedly squeezing the extra bit of flesh that had taken up residence over Christmas and had made itself so at home that it seemed set to stay through Spring.

It actually felt quite nice between her fingers and thumb, rolling the little lumps like dried peas just under the surface. *Must do something about that*, she thought, though it'd been an age since she'd been to Zumba.

The wire from her bra had escaped into her cleavage – that'd teach her for bunging them in the machine instead of hand washing them. The bra also felt very tight – surely at forty-two she was too old for a growth spurt? Today, like most days, her curves were covered with a baggy T-shirt and black leggings that'd gone saggy at the knees – this she considered her work uniform. Her bottle blonde hair was chucked up in a scrunchie, and she'd nicked her son Elliot's old red Converse. He'd just turned 26 and had towered over her since his teens, though that didn't take much. 'All good things come in small packages' mum always told her.

The bra wire was currently jabbing her left breast every time she breathed in and, today of all days, she'd need to take some deep breaths.

The scene before her was like one of those immersive theatre experiences, with Becky the unsuspecting audience member suddenly surrounded by the cast as the drama unfolded. Eight large wooden workbenches were grouped in a corner like a herd of cows spooked by an over enthusiastic sheepdog. Next to them was a stack of metal stools, leaning over at an alarming angle.

A block the size of a huge fridge was squatting on a pallet surrounded by nine slightly smaller blocks. All were wrapped in thick white plastic with wedges of polystyrene cradling the corners.

There were currently three men in various poses positioned around the blocks. The first delivery man, wiry and beige of skin, hair, tooth and overall – a pouch of rolling baccy poking out his top pocket – was on his hands and knees, peering underneath the biggest pallet.

He sat up – 'I'd like,' he said, slowly stroking his chin as if about to reveal an earth-shattering prophecy 'to get this beauty into position before unwrapping her.'

His colleague, a chubby lad with raspberry cheeks and gelled black hair, stopped wrestling with the plastic on one of the smaller packages and looked up. 'I bet you would boss,' he gurned.

Becky looked over to Jack for support. He was standing a few feet away, scratching his head.

'What you thinking Jack – you look confused?'

'I'm thinking . . .' Jack stopped scratching. 'I've got nits again from Elsie – little buggers love me, treat my scalp like an-all-you-can-eat-buffet they do.' He chuckled. 'I've told Elsie they like her 'cos she's delicious.' Even when describing an infestation of lice, Becky marvelled at how his eyes shone whenever he mentioned his granddaughter.

Becky had a real soft spot for Jack – he'd been caretaker at the centre ever since it was built in the mid-seventies, and had always been lovely to her mum when she'd cleaned there. He was sturdy, topped with a generous crop of salt and pepper hair, and had a kind face that hinted at a rugged handsomeness in his prime.

'Brew?' he asked, smiling. 'Come on Becky, you look like you could do with one, let's put kettle on for these lads too, I'm spitting feathers here,' and he held out his forearm for Becky to take, as if leading her into a grand ballroom, not a cramped community centre kitchen.

Becky hopped up onto the unit next to the sink and watched as Jack dropped teabags into four large mugs. She could feel the air thicken with silence like it did when he was building up to a pep talk, and braced herself. 'Now then Becky, you inherited a lot of things from your mum – her height for starters, 'cos she was a short-arse too.' Becky laughed, but noticed the slight wobble in Jack's voice. 'Not to mention her lovely smile. However, her tremendous self-belief seems to have skipped a generation. Young Elliot has it in spades; you though missus, you need to believe in yourself.' He stirred milk into the tea and looked at her, eyes shining. 'Your mum would be so proud of you Becky. This old place might be a bit tatty round the edges, but you're doing your best to breathe life back into it, and more importantly, bring people together – and that,' he waggled the teaspoon at her, 'is exactly what your mum was all about.'

'I know Jack, it just feels like I've bitten off more than I can chew.'

'Nonsense.' He frowned. 'You can handle this – it's a pottery class you're organising not a military coup. It's a positive thing, people will love it. They need something like this to bring them together a bit.'

Becky sipped her tea. 'It's just . . . I'm worried people will be too nervous to come along; people don't know each other like they used to – when I was little I reckon ninety-five per cent of the estate was counted as either an aunt or an uncle even though mum was an only child!'

Jack smiled warmly. 'I've lived in Lennington all my life Becky – what makes this estate special is the people. I used to ride my bike in the shadow of the munitions factory right here where we're standing now; I saw the estate spring up, fill with families. This place,' he pointed to the floor, 'was the heart of it then, and it can be again. You just have to have faith.'

2

Louise

Louise watched the rise and fall of Danny's chest and noticed a tiny bubble of spittle inflate then pop at the corner of his mouth, like a toddler blowing raspberries. Except Danny was no toddler; he was a forty-two-year-old HGV driver, fast asleep at two in the afternoon having driven home through the night after delivering pallets of paint around Cumbria.

The smell of his breath hung in the air, a sour yoghurty whiff that seemed to make the already small room close in on Louise even more.

She tiptoed across the carpet and gently pulled back the pink curtain to crack a window. A flash of sunlight spilled into the room, dazzling her and illuminating the trail of dried dribble on Danny's stubbled chin. He shifted in the bed, scratched his balls, and farted softly.

This is it then, thought Louise. *This is my life.*

She didn't know what was wrong with her today or why she suddenly felt a surge of frustration towards Danny. She loved him, she knew that much, but looking at him now she felt an irritation – a heat simmering below the surface. What was fuelling this fire?

Glancing at his football trophy gathering dust on a shelf of nick-nacks, she thought back to the moment she'd first clapped eyes on Danny.

He had been down the pub, still in his muddy footie kit after a game of five-a-side with his mates. She'd felt like she already knew him – that he was the one designated for her and their meeting was a mere formality.

He was built like a big rugger boy, thick blond hair cropped short so it stood up like the bristles on a yard-brush.

For such a big bloke she discovered he was surprisingly shy once they got chatting, but he had the most beautiful dark blue eyes and, as it was summer, a few freckles were scattered over the bridge of his snub nose, peeking out from a smudge of dirt left over from the game.

He looked Scandinavian and in another life he could've been a Viking he was so big and blond, and she told him as much as they talked at the bar and he offered to buy her a drink. He laughed a deep, throaty laugh when she said that, and blushed. She clocked, slightly weak knee'd as he passed her a glass of wine, how big his hands were.

He returned the compliment, and said she could be Cleopatra with her black bobbed hair and 'amazing green eyes'. She remembered saying, 'A Viking warrior and Cleopatra – quite the power couple,' blushing again, but he'd held her gaze and said, 'Cheers to that' and they'd clinked glasses.

That was knocking on for seventeen years and two kids ago.

Louise appreciated that Danny worked hard to support her and the girls, but she missed just hanging out with him. She missed the laughs they used to have – he was never showy with it, but had a wicked sense of humour. She loved how he used to make her laugh with a sly aside, a well-observed quip about someone in their company (a barman, a fellow bus-passenger, his mum) sometimes leaving Louise with, as she called it, the 'assembly giggles', when something inexplicably set you off mere feet from the headteacher – a word, glance or nudge from your mate.

There had been so many good times with Danny that the doubts she was feeling now stood out and sat starkly in her conscience like a black bear on a snowy landscape.

It was a feeling that nestled in the pit of her gut. Most of the time it lay dormant, but when it raised its head she felt sick and ashamed . . . It was an undeniable yearning for . . . more – more what, she didn't know. And it was getting harder to ignore.

Louise shook herself free from her thoughts, and rubbed her arms – she suddenly felt chilly, as if her coolness towards Danny had made the temperature dip in the room. She smoothed down her skinny jeans and caught her reflection in the full-length mirror on the wardrobe door. She still looked good for forty-three – petite and slight, her thick black hair cut sharp in a bob at her jawline. She rarely wore make-up, but with her large, almond-shaped green eyes and thick black lashes she didn't need to.

She glanced back at Danny and felt a contradictory swell of love for him. She gently closed the curtains again and tucked the duvet around his bare shoulders, trying not to wrinkle her nose at the crop of springy blond hairs that sprouted there.

Downstairs in the kitchen the dog watched her with sad eyes. She put the kettle on and tried to savour that no-man's land between getting in from work and the kids' arrival home.

Sixty precious minutes all to herself – what should she do with it? She had a meditation app she liked, maybe she should do that? Or sort a sock drawer? The dog could do with a walk judging by the way his tail slapped hopefully against the lino every time she glanced in his direction. By the time she'd made a brew and run through all the possibilities, she felt overwhelmed. 'Paralysed by potential' is what she'd heard one of the mums at school call it – so much she could be doing but not really knowing where to start, so not starting.

She could always draw.

One of Louise's passions was art. Her parents had given her the nickname Doodles when she was little as nothing was safe from her sketching and drawing; she'd filled book after book, and when she had run out of paper she had drawn inside her reading books, even absentmindedly on her bare arm and legs, earning her a telling off. Even the pale blue wallpaper by her bed had succumbed to her doodling; covered in the dozens of circles she had tried so hard to perfect, it was as if the bed had sunk to the ocean floor and was surrounded by bubbles.

She was always hunched over, her tiny frame curled around a sheet of paper, pencil gripped as if her life depended on it, her black hair falling like curtains over her face, the tip of her tongue poking out of the corner of her mouth.

Sometimes she was hardly even aware she was drawing. The endless circles she tried to perfect.

She'd wanted to be an artist when she grew up, and as much as her parents had encouraged her to draw, as much as her art teachers had given glowing reports of her talents at parents' evening – it had still been seen as a pipe dream; the sort of creative job that all young girls fantasised about – dancer, actress, artist, singer – before real life kicked in. Which it did.

Louise didn't get out her sketchpad. Instead she sat down at the kitchen table with her cup of tea and looked at her phone: two WhatsApps from her mum, two texts from her mum informing her that she'd just WhatsApped her, a text reminder from the dry-cleaners, and another one offering a 2-for-1 pizza deal.

Her emails bore even less exciting fruit: something about the school fair and some bumf from the bank on how to recognise fraudulent emails.

There was the latest neighbourhood newsletter, *The Inventors' Inventory*, which was compiled by the local community centre committee, and sent out every other Thursday. It was usually worth clicking on just to chuckle at the randomness of some of the stuff on there.

The estate really was a hotbed of activity.

First nugget of news was that Martin and Sheila on Harrison Lane had a cross trainer for sale – £150 ono. It was 'an unused impulse buy' plus, Sheila confessed in the ad, she now 'preferred Zumba'.

The flotsam and jetsam of peoples' lives floated past her eyes in the rest of the for-sale section – from second-hand breast pumps to a good-as-new sheepskin jacket.

On Tull Avenue, Jameela and Simon had screen-grabbed from their smart doorbell an image of a man in a white coat selling dodgy fish, and wanted to warn others not to be 'reeled in by him', as they put it.

A comfort to know they could joke despite their trauma.

Louise barely knew any of these people, apart from seeing their names pop up occasionally in the newsletters. The Inventors' Estate (each road named after a famous British inventor) was a friendly enough place, but the residents led busy lives, and, apart from a nod and smile en route to and from school or work, most people kept themselves to themselves.

Louise got up and dug out the cheddar from the fridge, slicing off a chunk and nibbling absent-mindedly at its corner before flopping back down at the kitchen table.

Twenty past three – definitely too late to start learning a new language or trying out some ashtanga yoga before the kids came tumbling through the front door disturbing her downward dog.

Every day after school, Jodie and Jemma would arrive home giddy with freedom and demanding snacks, chicks in a nest squawking relentlessly at mummy bird.

Louise glanced back at the newsletter; that's when she saw it: GO POTTY! it shouted in big red capitals.

3

Sheila

Over at 12 Harrison Lane, Sheila was also looking at the newsletter, checking to see that her cross trainer advert was in. It was. Sheila smiled to herself.

The cash from the cross trainer would go straight towards their Spain fund. For a few years now she'd been saving her pennies and daydreaming about moving to the Costa Blanca. She watched rerun after rerun of *A Place in the Sun*, and was learning conversational Spanish thanks to an app. She was pretty confident she could shoot the breeze with the locals in Playa Flamenca about the weather and the time as she bought *los panecillos* at *la pastelería*.

In the kitchen she kept a Spain mood board; neatly pinned articles snipped out from the Sunday supplements about people who'd made the leap, overlapped with photos of potential properties printed off the internet, along with recipes for authentic paella – if she couldn't quite yet live amongst the Spanish they could at least dine like them. 'It's all part of the transition,' she'd tell Martin.

It was Martin who had spotted the metre-square board in a skip outside the grey block of offices they were knocking down in town.

Despite an awkward journey home on the bus with it where

he'd twice knocked a baby's buggy when the bus braked and had
been trapped in the jaws of the bus's doors as he got off, he'd come
home absolutely buzzing; chucking his door keys on the table in
the hall whilst kicking off his shoes and shouting, 'Sheila! Sweetheart!
Where are you my angel? I've found you some treasure!'

Sheila, who'd been lying on the couch with a banging headache
listening to her Michael Ball album, slowly peeled off one of the
cucumber slices from her eyes and watched the door suspiciously.
She silently coached herself, *Don't snap, Sheila, you should be grateful
he loves you so much*, while out loud she shouted, as enthusiastically
as the axe currently nestled in her frontal cortex would allow, 'In
here my love!'

Martin loved 'up-cycling', as he called it. Sheila referred to it as
'scavenging' when she was in a bad mood, and 'salvaging' when
she wasn't.

No skip was safe from Martin's keen eye. Wicker chairs, curtain
poles, and even a box commode had found their way onto the bus,
and home to Harrison Lane.

The wicker chair (having survived a dousing of anti-bacterial
kitchen spray at Sheila's insistence) was in the conservatory
with a couple of John Lewis cushions on it, and the curtain poles
had been sanded down and painted white, and were up in the
spare room. Sheila had drawn a line at the vintage commode
– she felt squeamish at the thought of over a century's worth
of bottoms that may have perched upon it – so it was relegated
to the back garden. Martin had given it a lick of sealant and,
after a trip to the garden centre, some shiny leaved Bergenia
now grew quite happily in its chamber pot, and Sheila secretly
liked it.

On first spying the proffered cork board, Sheila had found it
hard to summon up much enthusiasm. Martin had said, 'It's for
shopping lists, vouchers, receipts – anything really,' but since Oliver,

their son, had left home there was less need for shopping lists. Though Sheila still bought his favourite crisps most weeks. A peek into the snack cupboard would be enough to make you think she had the inside scoop on an international beef Hula Hoop shortage and was stockpiling.

Sheila, despite her headache, smiled. Since taking early retirement from his role at Ross Cereals, Martin had been on what would, in reality TV shows, be called a 'journey'. Sheila thought 'breakdown' was a more realistic term.

If the raisin shoot became blocked or the oat dispenser stopped turning, Martin was the man they summoned. Overnight he went from the guy responsible for the smooth running and maintenance of the machinery that manufactured four of the country's most successful mueslis to being, in his eyes, just another man knocking sixty and ready for the scrapheap.

When he left they made sure that after forty-three years of dedication, starting as a spotty teen with a mullet, sweeping out the loading bay and brewing up for the drivers, he was well rewarded with a pension as juicy as the Turkish sultanas he added to the premium muesli. But Sheila knew Martin felt lost – she confided to a friend that his get up and go had gotten up and gone and hadn't left a forwarding address.

Sheila thought he'd love retirement – 'No more 4 a.m. alarms!' she'd reminded him on numerous occasions. But for the first year after he'd hung up his hairnet she'd often wake up before 5 a.m. only to find him sitting at the kitchen table, face and pyjamas creased, nursing his third cup of tea.

'The body clock is very cruel,' he'd say, smiling weakly, 'been wide awake since four.'

He was plagued with terrible nightmares. Sheila would shake him awake as he thrashed around in the bed. 'Martin! Wake up!'

He'd burst awake, gasping for breath, and sit up, Sheila switching on the bedside lamp and noticing the sweaty imprint he'd left behind on the bedsheet.

'I was drowning Sheila,' he'd pant, bottom lip quivering. 'I was at work, wading through honey, trying to find my work phone, then sinking in the linseed silo – thousands of seeds sticking to me like a *Crackerjack* game. I was caked in it; it was so realistic. I was being dragged down into the silo's guts.' He'd touch his face as if to check it really was a dream. 'The seeds were in my nose . . .'

Sheila would comfort him as best she could, fetching a warm towel to form a barrier between him and the damp patch as he lay staring up at the ceiling. 'My heart is hammering, feels like it's going to tear through my chest.'

'Well if it does, keep it in your lap and away from that new carpet,' she'd joke to distract him.

Over breakfast he'd apologise, and she'd reassure him, 'It's a big adjustment Martin, you'll get there.' But secretly she'd wish he'd pull himself together. Sometimes she'd add, 'Look at Joe – he's having a whale of a time now.'

Joe was Martin's old boss, who had retired a few years earlier. He, along with his wife Wendy, had fully embraced their leisure time. Sheila had noticed bitterly that his Facebook page was, as she'd pointed out to Martin, 'Like a Saga brochure.' Shoving her iPad under his nose she'd pointed with a lilac painted nail at the photos. 'If he's not on a long weekend at a Tuscan vineyard with Wendy, he's hurtling round on Segways with the grandkids. I mean, Wendy is nice enough, but that helmet really brings out the round-ness of her face. Who wants to see photos of every spit and cough of their lives?' she'd said, poring enviously over the pictures.

Now Martin spent most of the time moping around at home, which drove Sheila barmy. She fretted that her love for him was becoming akin to a fondness one might have for a neighbour's old spaniel – nice to pet occasionally but you wouldn't want it under your feet all the time.

She was frazzled too, what with first battling her menopausal night sweats, which she brought under control with tablets and sticky patches that mainlined the nectar of oestrogen into her, to sweeten her mood and her sleep. Hot on the heels of her menopause came Martin's insomnia, which had him thrashing around in the bed every night as if he was trying to wrestle a bear. Martin's issues were proving trickier to solve; shame there wasn't a magic patch that offered a different HRT – husband replacement therapy – once you stuck it on, a Michael Bublé lookalike appeared and your every wish was his command. She could dream, but in real life she reckoned she had at least three new wrinkles that were entirely caused by this past year.

She wasn't a vain woman, but she liked to look after herself. Back in 1984 she'd been crowned Miss Silk, by the makers of the face cream of the same name. Her mum had seen an article in the local paper about the search for young women who 'had that silk glow', and had sent in a pretty passport pic of Sheila without her knowing.

In the pic Sheila was grinning out from under a soft perm and, even under the shadow of her flick it was obvious she had a clear, bright complexion. 'Peaches and cream,' her mum had said, and her motherly pride had been rewarded with a photo shoot and a mention in the local paper.

The first few weeks of Martin's retirement had not been wrinkle-inducing – in fact it had been a novelty having Martin around. But it had soon worn thin – there were only so many garden centres to visit.

As time went on Martin became anxious, the man who'd held court with all the lads, cracking gags and cracking the whip with equal confidence, suddenly wouldn't say 'good day' to a goose, never mind 'boo'.

Six months in, Martin had not only lost his mojo, he had lost his appetite and dropped a stone. He stopped shaving, and didn't leave the house for days at a time.

Sheila's heart ached for the man he once was, and she tried to help by encouraging him to come out with her for a walk, a bit of fresh air or a mooch down the high street, but the reply would always be the same, 'Not today She, maybe tomorrow,' and he'd smile a watery smile, the panic in his eyes as clear as the whiskers on his chin.

In the end, as a last resort, Sheila booked a fortnight in Spain. She knew Martin wouldn't let a holiday and all that money go to waste. He may have been depressed, but he wasn't a mug – he'd have no choice but to join her in Playa Flamenca.

She'd popped to the high street, and Denise at Anderson's travel had found her a lovely last-minute deal.

When she arrived back home she shook the rain from her brolly, gently kicked the front door to, and shouted for Martin, 'Sweetheart, guess what?' He made her jump as he appeared from the lounge immediately, like an actor pre-empting his cue.

Sheila smiled at Martin, who was in his uniform of joggers and T-shirt, with a towelling robe over the top, like a bargain basement Hugh Hefner.

She babbled because she was nervous. She could hear her voice getting higher as she rattled through the details '. . . need a break . . . walking past Anderson's . . . special offer . . . spoke to Denise . . .' She could see herself in the hall mirror, her eyes wide and pleading, coral lipstick bleeding into the creases around her mouth. Martin had held up his hands in surrender and agreed some sunshine would be nice.

The holiday was a new focus, and made Sheila determined to help Martin. The family GP, Dr Khan, prescribed Martin a course of tablets, smiling kindly over her jazzy bifocals as Sheila dug around in her handbag for a tissue for Martin to dry his eyes on.

Spain was a success. The combination of the medication, the sunshine, and the change of scene meant that hour by hour, day by day, the old Martin started to come back. This wasn't a tampon advert from the 80s – he wasn't rollerskating, skydiving, and high five-ing strangers – but the despair that had lingered in Martin's eyes was replaced by hope, even an occasional brightness.

Long swims in the sea each morning invigorated him and gifted him a raging appetite – he tucked into pastries, boiled eggs, fruit and strong coffee on their little balcony overlooking a cobbled courtyard. They cat-napped and sunbathed and read by the pool. Strolls to the local street market to look at the stalls selling leather goods, olives, and fabric, and to eat the delicious freshly fried doughnuts became longer walks inland to Flamenca Gorge and cliff-top rambles to Punta Prima.

They held hands like newly-weds, and sometimes words weren't needed – Martin would squeeze Sheila's hand and she'd know he was feeling alive again.

On their last evening they sat, sun-kissed and relaxed, watching the sunset. Sheila, perhaps a tiny bit tipsy from a generously measured gin and tonic, turned to Martin and said, 'Imagine, we could live here,' and Martin had laughed, then when he realised she was serious, his face fell.

'She sweetheart, what about Mum? We couldn't just up and leave her,' and with that, the bubble burst and Sheila had suddenly felt very sober.

4

Jameela

The rain came as a welcome relief to Jameela, cooling her down as she rounded the corner onto Newton Pass towards home, pushing hard to sprint the last few hundred yards, her garden gate the finish line.

A vision in purple lycra, she crossed the road, leaping over a large puddle, almost skimming its oily surface with her trainers.

She knew as she approached the community centre that her running playlist would fade, Calvin Harris piping down momentarily to allow the well-spoken lady on her app to announce into her earbuds 'six miles completed' – she ran this route every other day, and she averaged 8-minute miles.

She loved the precision of her pace, the predictability of the run – the route, the timings. Her job as a partner in a small but successful local law firm required her to be in control and methodical – she approached running in the same way.

Past the precinct she sped, dodging the two old dears coming out of the post office trying to shake an umbrella into life, and deftly side-stepping the door of a car as it swung open into her path, Arctic Monkeys blaring from the stereo.

At the 'six miles completed' announcement she slowed to a jog and noticed a large white van parked slightly askew across the tarmac path that led to the front of the community centre, 'Kiln Bill', emblazoned in red lettering across its side.

The rain was really coming down now, making it even trickier to see what was happening, so she sped up again. Her black fringe stuck to her forehead and her feet slapped against the wet paving stones as she neared her goal, leaping the last few strides. She stopped by her gate. Someone had shoved a crumpled Red Bull can into her privet. She gingerly retrieved the can, popping it into the wheelie bin under the car port, where she sheltered to catch her breath and stretch. The rain was starting to lose its enthusiasm, and slowed to a drizzle.

Jameela took out her earbuds, placed both palms on the side wall, and straightened each leg in turn to stretch out her calves. To the untrained eye it looked as if she was attempting to push over her house.

As she stretched she thought about the can, and although she was obsessively house-proud and kept the garden looking equally perfect, she smiled to herself.

'What goes around, comes around,' she muttered to the wall as she grabbed her right foot, cupping it and standing like a flamingo, breathing deeply and sighing with pleasure as the lactic acid slowly drained from her quads.

It only seemed like yesterday that she had been the one shoving pop cans into neat garden bushes on the way home from school with her little sister Reju.

They were separated by twenty months but were more like twins – sharing everything from the way they laughed and sneezed to the way they smiled and cried. They were both blessed with huge round eyes the colour of cinnamon, long dark lashes, and glossy black hair that hung out of the way in a single waist-length plait like a length of tarred rope.

They'd been as thick as thieves back then. Dawdling and messing about all the way home – the longer they took, the less time they'd have to help Mum prepare the dinner.

As well as tossing their empty Pepsi cans onto neat lawns, a favourite game had been 'Mind that bush!', which involved shouting that warning whilst shoving each other into the beautifully mani-cured greenery that bordered the gardens they passed.

It was on one of these walks home that Jameela had told Reju she'd started her period that day halfway through Geography. 'Oh my GOD Jam,' Reju had squealed. 'You basically became a woman as Ms Watson handed out a worksheet on Drainage Basins!'

And it was where, aged fourteen and thirteen, they'd shared their first (and last) cigarette.

They'd stolen it from the inside pocket of Uncle Amol's brown leather jacket lined with purple paisley that he hung in the hall when he visited. Attempting to smoke it had prompted such a coughing fit that their eyes had watered, and they had laughed so much at each other's agony that they had tumbled through the front door with tears streaming down their cheeks, still green around the gills and guffawing.

Jameela chuckled as she remembered how she and Reju had caught their breath, only to dissolve into hysterics again when Mum had popped her head into the hallway brandishing a potato peeler and asked if they'd seen her box of Cook's matches.

Of course they didn't tell her the matches had been lobbed, along with a half-smoked ciggie, over a fence on the way home. Mum had retreated to her spot, cross-legged on the lounge carpet, a small mountain of peelings before her, as if she was paying her respects at a root vegetable shrine. 'Those girls are crackers,' she had clucked to herself, reaching for a large carrot.

A rumble of thunder shook Jameela from her daydream and her smile faded as she thought about the current state of her relation-ship with Reju.

She fished out her door key from the small slit in the waistband of her running leggings and went indoors.

She tugged off her soggy trainers and, taking care not to drip on the hallway carpet, headed upstairs for a hot shower.

5

Becky

The Inventors' Estate consisted of four roads that ran parallel to each other and, between two of them, Faraday Road and Newton Pass, sat the community centre and the precinct. Topping and tailing the four roads of three-bedroomed mid-sized terraced houses was Bell Way at the bottom, and at the top, the curiously named Watt Way.

Sitting atop Watt Way, like a rainbow over the two roads furthest from the community centre – Harrison Lane and Lovelace Lane – was Tull Avenue, a semicircle of larger, more expensive four-bedroomed homes, each with a car port, garage, and smart patio. The close curve of the avenue made it look on the original plans at least (a framed copy of which now hung on the wall of the community centre) like Tull Avenue was a bowler hat worn by the two lanes, with Watt Way the rim.

Built on the outskirts of the small town of Lennington, just north of Manchester, the estate hunkered down between upmarket Fenton with its mock Tudor mansions and private roads housing footballers, soap stars and bankers, and on the other side, the moors of windswept Howlesden, whose sheep-dotted hills welcomed weekend walkers to its low-beamed pubs hidden amongst the valleys' crevices.

The old farm buildings and low slung hostelries that once

welcomed coaches and horses travelling over the Pennines had become mostly gastropubs serving traditional fayre, craft ales, with a dog biscuit chucked in for any accompanying mutt.

Whatever happened on the estate, the first to know about it was the estate committee that met monthly at the community centre, made up of the retired, the community-minded, and those who enjoyed the power of a luminous tabard and clipboard when stewarding an event.

Jack the caretaker (who fell into the first two categories) was on it, as was Sheila (who definitely fell into the third).

Back in the main room, the delivery men drained their mugs of tea: 'Lovely that, thank you very much – my stomach was just starting to think my throat had been cut,' said the older one.

Becky had brought out a plate of Jammy Dodgers, and he was still brushing the crumbs from the front of his overalls as he spoke. 'I remember this place – my old mum used to come here for dress-making classes. They all chuffed away on their ciggies as they gossiped at the machines – my mum's best mate once stitched her finger to a skirt 'cos she was so busy gassing. Mum said she'd never seen so much blood.'

'Ouch,' Jack grimaced, 'you're going back a few years with that class. Since then it's been all baby yoga and pilates.'

Becky smiled at the memory of half a dozen babies gurgling on mats as their mums bent and stretched around them like willow trees. 'Unfortunately thanks to the cracks in the windows and our boiler having the temperament of a supermodel we lost a lot of the classes – it was so cold in the winter I half expected to see an arctic fox trotting across the frozen tundra of the main hall and through the circle of Gamblers Anonymous chairs.' The men laughed. 'I'm not even joking. The pilates group were fed up of wearing bobble hats. We tried attracting new classes. Remember "Footie Fun Crew" Jack?' Becky laughed.

'Oh Jesus don't.' He grimaced. 'Fifteen under tens and a string net of footballs – I still wake in the night screaming, thinking I can hear the sound of breaking glass.'

'It's a shame though,' said the younger delivery lad through a bite of biscuit, 'be sad if this place goes.'

'Excuse me,' huffed Jack in mock offence, 'this place isn't going anywhere, not with the new pottery class about to start. In some ways, it's only the beginning.' He clutched a clenched fist to his mouth and looked dramatically off into the distance.

'Very poetic Jack. I admire your confidence,' said Becky, collecting up the empty mugs. She was suddenly serious again. 'A few names have signed up online, but that takes seconds; we actually need them to turn up or the whole thing'll be a washout, and I'll be up for the high jump for frittering away council grants.' She felt her stomach flip at the thought.

'Nonsense,' said Jack. 'Have faith.'

She grunted, unconvinced. 'Anyway, there'll be no class to put on if we don't move all this kit, so tea break is over. That,' she said, pointing to the biggest pallet, 'needs to follow me to the stockroom please.'

6

Sheila

It was late morning when the doorbell rang and Sheila just about jumped out of her skin. It was a Friday, the day she liked to pamper herself with a long bath and face pack, ready for the weekend. Not that they had many plans these days; her best pals had moved away and she even found herself missing the socials organised by Martin's work back in the day.

Sheila was sitting daydreaming at the mirrored vanity table in her pale pink kimono, the fabric straining slightly over her ample bosom, stretching the pattern so the white cranes looked thicker set, like geese about to crash land on her belly.

Perched on the velvet stool, leaning close to the mirror, she'd been pushing the flesh back from her temples, her skin tight over her cheekbones, pouting in the mirror. 'Pretend you're blowing out a candle Sheila love' – that's what the photographer at the Silk Cream shoot had told her all those years ago.

She couldn't remember his name, but could see him clearly, the way his tongue constantly flicked out over his lips like a snake tasting the air, black leather trousers squeaking as he lunged towards her, taking shots from all different angles as if he was shooting a *Rolling Stone* cover rather than a promo shot for face cream.

As she pouted in the mirror now she thought about what April had said last week. They'd been in the back room of the food bank sorting through donations, the shelves of the former sports shop now groaning not with Reebok trainers and football boots, but tinned meat, tuna and vegetables.

They were chatting about ageing. 'You know,' April had said, picking a bit of protein bar out of her teeth with a long manicured nail, 'for three grand you could lift all of that.' She used the packet of basics spaghetti she was holding as a baton to draw a large oval in the air in front of Sheila. 'My sister-in-law went to Prague for a few days, came home looking thirty-five again – full face lift.' She smiled. 'Although,' she breathed, leaning in so close Sheila could smell the heady combo of Elnett hairspray and instant coffee that was April's signature scent, 'it can go wrong – my neighbour Jo had a brow lift at a clinic in Luton, and now her eyes don't fully close when she sleeps. She looks like a zombie apparently – stuff of nightmares.' Her eyes had widened for a second as the image sank in. 'Right. Pasta's done, noodles next I reckon.'

When the doorbell rang, Sheila let go of her face and the soft crêpe pillows of flesh settled once again by the outer corners of her eyes.

She could see the figure through the glass in the front door bobbing up and down as she made her way down the stairs.

She opened the door to a woman who looked like she was warming up at the start line of an olympic sprint, skin-tight purple crop top revealing a smooth brown tummy above matching purple leggings that encased every muscle, of which there seemed to be plenty.

She reminded Sheila of a sleek racehorse with her long plait swishing from side to side.

She sprang up from her squat position and thrust a hand towards Sheila, smiling broadly. 'Jameela,' she said, 'I emailed about the cross trainer for sale?'

Upstairs the cross trainer was hidden by last week's clean washing pile waiting to be sorted and ironed, Martin's jeans flung across the handlebars, and Sheila's sturdy bras – her boulder holders. No pretty little spaghetti straps for her, no flimsy lacy numbers – no, her breasts had been handed down through generations of buxom women.

It felt like overnight she'd sprouted bosoms, and it seemed something in the behaviour of others changed as a consequence. There had been a melancholic confusion in her dad's eyes, as if his little shed buddy had betrayed him by blossoming from the tomboy she once was. She had noticed subtle differences, like her male teachers trying to keep eye contact, to the not so subtle – builders, whistling and swinging from the scaffold like horny apes at the zoo.

During games at school the boys had gawped at her chest like cartoon dogs eyeing a string of sausages. Self-conscious, she had hung up her hockey stick and found solace in chocolate. Her curves grew and, although she was no Diana Dors, she was at least Miss Silk.

Sheila swooped her arm under the pile of clothes and chucked them on the bed. Jameela stood in the spare room, arms folded, head tilted to one side as if looking at a sculpture in an art gallery.

Switching on the main light Sheila quipped, 'Let's shed some light on the subject,' then immediately cringed at herself.

Why did she feel so nervous around this person? She went to the window and opened the wooden blinds. Minuscule specks of dust lifted into the air and Sheila made a mental note to whip around with the hoover later.

Maybe she was intimidated by Jameela because she wasn't used to being in the company of other women, especially one as dynamic and focused as Jameela.

She looked to Sheila like one of those women who 'have it all'. She'd read about them in the weekend supplements; women with five children, a sleek blow dry, rippling abs, a six-figure salary in the city, who still finds time for the charity work helping refugees, as well as enjoying regular knock-out sexual gymnastics with their equally high-powered husband.

'Your house is lovely by the way,' said Jameela, moving her gaze from the cross trainer to Sheila. 'I love this room – the colours are very . . . soothing.'

Sheila glanced around her spare room, the oatmeal carpet and pale wheat walls reflecting the glow of the late morning sun. 'Well, we like it. It was our boy's room,' she corrected herself, 'I say boy, he's nearly thirty. Though I'm pretty sure I can still smell his rugby socks in here.' She smiled sadly to herself. 'We re-decorated after he moved out – we left it a couple of weeks in case he came back, but him and Charlotte seem very happy.'

It's wasn't that she disliked Charlotte – a junior doctor with swishy blonde hair and a passion for triathlons – it was just that Sheila felt relegated.

At the beginning of their relationship, as Oliver's love for Charlotte grew, it felt to Sheila like his love for her withered. His texts to her during the day dried up, and she found herself, stomach churning, constantly checking her phone for messages from him like some lovesick teen rather than a middle-aged mum.

When he did get around to ringing her she acted bruised and brittle. 'Hello stranger,' she'd say in a tight little voice she didn't recognise, and hated herself for it. The phone calls would follow a similar pattern: embarrassed by her needy opening line, she'd then prattle on, determined to sound busy and fulfilled now she had more time for herself since he'd moved out – like a heartbroken divorcee chatting to the ex she still pined for.

Oliver sounded bored by the whole charade, and trotted out the usual questions 'How's Dad? Things OK at the food bank? How's the Spain fund coming along?' Ticking each query off the list before making his excuses to get off the call.

Now Sheila reckoned she'd settled mid-table in his affections, behind Charlotte, their rescue cat Cleo, Xbox, and all things rugby.

Jameela tinkered with the control buttons of the cross trainer, then climbed on, placing a foot on each ribbed pad and grabbing the handles. She began to move, slowly at first like a skier making her way through a snowdrift, then she picked up pace – the LED lights on the screen burst into life, moving through green to amber to red as she increased the resistance and upped her speed. Her arms were moving like pistons, her legs pumping away as if she were being chased by some invisible monster. Jameela stared straight ahead, jaw clenched. Sheila stood and watched, mouth slightly agape, in awe at seeing her former clothes rail actually being used as it was supposed to be.

After a few seconds, like a wind-up toy, Jameela gradually slowed down and then stopped completely – frozen in position, arms still holding the handles, eyes slightly glazed, only her chest moving in and out from the exertion. Then she snapped back to reality and turned to Sheila. 'I love it,' she panted with a grin.

'Great,' said Sheila. 'Fancy a brew to celebrate?'

After a quick change from kimono to jeans and a nice Breton striped top, Sheila was now standing on her little kitchen step to reach the very back of the cupboard where the nice cups were stashed. As she rummaged, she could see Jameela leaning in close to the kitchen doorframe and running her finger gently over the little notches in the wood, moving slowly, as if, like butterflies, the marks would take flight if she moved too fast and startled them.

Each notch had a date and an age written next to it – from two years at the bottom, all the way up to fifteen, which was level with Jameela's own head. Over a decade of life recorded on a doorframe. About halfway up, in wobbly blue felt tip, it said 'Ollie'. Jameela touched the name and glanced up to Sheila with her eyes glassy.

Sheila set down the teapot and smiled at Jameela. 'Ollie,' she said, nodding at the door, 'my son. Every birthday it became a tradition – even before he'd opened his pressies, his dad would stand him up against the doorframe in his pyjamas and scratch out his height. He sprouted so quickly, his grandad used to joke that he must've been sleeping in a Gro-Bag.'

She took a tiny sip of tea, still looking at the door, seeing Oliver standing there, age two in his dinosaur jamas, through six in his Superman ones, all the way up to his fifteenth birthday, when he stood towering over Martin in his boxers and a Beastie Boys T-shirt, sleepily rubbing his eyes and protesting he was too old for such 'soppy shite', but still letting his dad make the mark one last time.

'He ran out of patience by his mid-teens – he towers over me now,' said Sheila, still looking at the lowest notch. 'They're not "yours", your kids.' Sheila sighed. 'You're just loaned them for a while – took me a long time to learn that. In a way I'm still learning.' She gazed through the window at Ollie's old rope swing. 'The more I look at the notches, they're almost like a sad countdown to the time he started to grow not only upwards but away from us.'

'No. It's lovely,' Jameela said, her eyes welling up again. 'It's the sort of thing I would've loved to do with my own, but it wasn't meant to be.' She sipped her tea.

Sheila felt guilty about her presumption that the woman before her definitely 'had it all'.

'We've been trying for years, but we only ever get so far,' said Jameela, studying her nails, 'and before we knew it we became something we swore we never would – "ovulation slaves".' She gave a forced laugh. 'And as time went on we came to think that surely if we were determined enough and did everything right we'd succeed?'

Sheila felt bereft for this poor young woman. 'Did you manage to get pregnant?'

'Yes.' Jameela gave a small nod but didn't look up. 'Seven is a lucky number for some, but not for us.' She sighed. 'And I think with each loss we grew further apart – so much grief does terrible things to a marriage.'

Sheila smiled gently. 'You've both really been through it love, but there's still time surely? You're young and obviously look after yourself – it'll happen when you least expect it.'

'Well,' Jameela gave a joyless chuckle, 'it'd certainly be unexpected if it happened now, it'd be a bloody miracle. I'm sure he'll be back, but at the moment my husband's not even living under the same roof as me.'

'Ahh,' said Sheila, 'that is tricky. I got a D in my biology O level, but I'm almost certain you need to be in the same room to get pregnant.' Sheila busied herself placing some biscuits on a plate. 'Look Jameela I don't know what's going on with you and . . .?'

'Simon.'

'Simon, but I do know that marriage can be tough. It's a marathon, not a sprint – and sadly you don't get a medal for it, though sometimes I've felt I deserved one.' She smiled grimly. 'Martin and I have hobbled along through some rough patches, but it's worth it if,' she looked skywards for inspiration, 'if, to really stretch the analogy, you know you've found the person you want to cross the finish line with.' She took a bite of a Viennese whirl and put the rest on the plate.

'I thought I had,' said Jameela. Sheila could tell she was trying to hold back tears, and the effort caused Jameela to hiccup and gulp, spilling tea on the table. 'Oh God, sorry,' she said, as Sheila handed her a fistful of kitchen roll for the table and grabbed the box of tissues from the side to dry her eyes. Jameela blew her nose and looked at Sheila apologetically. 'You were only offering a cross trainer, not a counselling session.'

7

Becky

Becky was nervous. In her fifteen years as the manager of the community centre this weekly pottery class was the biggest challenge she'd ever undertaken; she'd been given a grant for half of the equipment, but she'd blown the rest of her rainy day budget on the extras. The rainy day cash was literally just that – the centre was in disrepair and the roof sprung leaks wherever it fancied during a downpour so a more sensible business decision would've been to save some money for emergency repairs. However, she didn't want the community centre to limp on like a wounded giant, she wanted to breathe new life into it, and this pottery course would stretch through the whole summer, and if it was a success, could extend into the next year with a promise of more funding.

She felt as if an invisible force was pushing her to get people together and try to bond a community that had in recent years drifted apart. Becky knew why she felt like this. Her mum was a huge believer in bringing people together again, and it was nearly the anniversary of her mum's death. Thirty years gone, so much life missed, so many moments that Becky had wanted to share with her, but instead had had to make do with a sad glance skywards, searching the clouds for a sign her mum was out there somewhere, looking over her through all the highs and the lows.

A devastating date marked in her phone with a single red heart emoji. Becky wanted to make the pottery class a success for her mum in this watershed year, and that only added to the pressure. She daren't say it out loud to Jack or to her son, but she didn't want to let her mum down.

Jack appeared with a mop and bucket. 'That leak's come back over the stage,' he said, holding up the bucket like a charity collector. 'By 'eck you look very stressed – not like you at all; your mum used to say, "If our Becky was any more laid back she'd be horizontal".'

Jack had a knack of mentioning her mum whenever she felt down, like he was a messenger, a sign sent by her mum. Some people believed feathers or rainbows or robins were their dead loved ones appearing – Becky's mum had seemingly sent a man in his seventies with a bucket.

'Eeh I miss your mum, always so smiley. I miss how colourful she was – she was like a tropical bird with her outfits.'

Becky smiled broadly. 'Yeah, everyone was wearing peach, cerise, and turquoise in the eighties, but not everyone wore them all at once. Her dressing gown was the brightest pink, with a satin trim. I used to lie curled up on the sofa watching telly with my head in her lap and stroke the fabric like it was a furry animal.' Jack chuckled softly. 'Mum used to say we must've been bears in past lives because come the winter we loved to hibernate, cuddling up. I'd lay my head in her lap and Mum would stroke her fingers through my hair, and in those moments Jack,' she met his gaze, her eyes bright, 'I felt a bliss I've never known since.'

Jack clamped his lips tightly, like he did whenever he felt emotional. 'You were a team of two, you and your mum, you were like her little shadow when you came here with her.' He busied himself swapping the bucket to his other hand, and cleared his throat. 'Right, I'd better get on.'

Becky watched as Jack went to patch up the leak. She had paperwork to be getting on with, but found it hard to focus. Her mind travelled back to a happier time, watching *Taggart* and *The Bill* with her mum, and *Cagney & Lacey* re-runs on a Saturday night – all these shows had cemented in Becky's mind the desire to be a copper one day. Something else that had gone by the wayside.

Mum's dressing gown had smelled like the rest of the flat – a mixture of cooking, an occasional sneaked cigarette and Impulse body spray – a scent that Becky loved as it smelled of home and warmth, feeling secure and cosseted. Every year Becky had saved up the pocket money she got from her nan to buy Impulse for her mum's birthday.

Becky had occasionally tapped up her dad for cash when she was lucky enough to spot him darting between the bookies and the pub. She would usually collar him for 50p, but if his horse had come in she'd sometimes get a pound, accompanied by a beery kiss. 'You're a good girl Becky,' he'd say, one eye on the door of the Lamb to Slaughter, already tasting his celebratory pint. 'Tell your mum I'll be round to see her next week.' But they both knew this wasn't true – it was his way of putting a full stop on their conversation. Becky didn't care. It was peaceful without Dad – whenever he came he brought chaos, and upset Mum. It was just her and Mum, and Becky was happy with that.

Becky knew Mum loved the body spray because the first time she'd bought it under the blinding strip lighting in Cohen's chemist and smuggled it home and into her room, using half a mile of Sellotape to secure the home-made gift wrap around it, Mum had cried when she opened it.

Becky nipped to the kitchen to make another brew for her and Jack, and remembered the packet of chocolate biscuits she'd bought for the occasion on the way in that morning. She grabbed them from her bag and gently tipped them out on to a plate. She couldn't help laughing when they turned out to be snowman shaped. 'Jesus,' she said out loud, 'our esteemed guest is gonna think I'm a right oddball.'

Jack, who could hear a kettle boiling from the moon, popped his head around the doorway and spotted the biscuits. 'Season's greetings,' he said. 'Old Christmas stock then?'

'Yup,' said Becky, 'in my defence I was in a mad rush, though I did wonder why they were half price.'

Jack laughed. 'I seem to remember your mum liked a bargain too, remember her whoops surprises?'

'Oh God Jack, don't remind me!' She laughed, and left him in the kitchen drinking his tea. She checked over the main hall (still a bit dusty despite her efforts) and smiled at the memory of the whoops surprises.

Mum would wait till just before the supermarket closed to do her shopping so she could hoover up all the last-minute discounts. She'd invent new dishes named after the yellow "whoops" stickers that were stuck to the reduced stock. Jack had been lucky enough to come around for tea on a couple of occasions, and had sampled one of Mum's startling concoctions cobbled together from the bargain bin.

Becky wasn't a fan. Slamming the bright orange door to their little flat after school Becky would shout, 'I'm back . . . what's for tea?', and groan half in fear and half in anticipation when Mum replied, 'It's your lucky night Becky-boo! surprise – and this one is really special.' Occasionally it'd work – knocked down gammon (80p!) with pasta and melted cheddar slices (15p!) was a highlight, but a sort of jambalaya with mackerel (66p!) and a badly dented tin of pineapple (4p!) was the worst. Becky's mum fancied herself as a bit of a renegade chef – 'I'm experimental, Becks,' she'd say, as Becky picked through a chicken (72p!) lasagne as if she was performing an autopsy. 'Mental, more like,' Becky would reply.

Becky's mum had been a cleaner at the community centre – the very floor where Becky now stood, eating a snowman biscuit in April and avoiding her paperwork, had been polished by Mum using an industrial vacuum cleaner that dragged her around the hall like a hulking mastiff taking its owner for a walk.

She'd stagger past Becky, almost at a run, holding on with one hand, waving comically with the other to make Becky laugh.

What would her mum think of her now, manager of the place she'd cleaned? Maybe she'd say, 'Get you, Ms Bosslady!', or would she be sad Becky had never followed her dream and joined the force?

From the day Becky had spotted the position advertised in the *Lennington Echo* she knew the job was hers and in a weird way, she felt closer to her mum here. Now, as Becky stood in the hall, slightly panicking about the impending meeting with the pottery teacher, she wished more than ever before that her mum was here too.

She smoothed down her top and checked the clock again – any minute now Sasha the teacher would arrive for their initial meeting. Becky hoped everything was up to her expectations. They'd chatted briefly over email, and she'd said she just needed to check the equipment and layout before Tuesday's first class. 'And of course,' Sasha had typed, 'meet the big boss,' referring to, Becky presumed, her.

She had wondered if Sasha was being a little bit sarcastic with that last comment. As if running a community centre didn't take much effort or hold much responsibility. Maybe Becky was being paranoid. She was already intimidated by Sasha, and imagined she'd be beautiful and serene and would float in like she'd been caught on a breeze – slender hips encased in a flowing skirt, with waist-length hair. She didn't have any evidence to back this image up, but she'd spent an inordinate amount of time creating a back story for Sasha. A gap year split between travelling in south-east Asia and helping to build an orphanage in Malawi, before returning to finish her art degree. Becky had decided to be slightly in awe of this woman, and also to strongly dislike her.

8

Sheila

Sheila was having a fabulous afternoon with her new friend Jameela. She was pretty sure she could call her that; they'd covered quite a few topics over the last hour, and Sheila was just pouring the last drops of a bottle of pale rosé into Jameela's glass and getting to the punchline of a story, 'So I just left the broken trampette in the middle of the class and walked out with my head held high,' when she heard the front door slam and Martin's usual mating call ring out from the hallway.

'Sheila! Sweetheart! Where are you my angel? I've found you some treasure!'

Jameela looked startled and they both stifled a giggle. 'What did I tell you?' whispered Sheila, who'd been regaling Jameela with stories of Martin's finds.

'Oh hello,' said Martin, who'd taken off his boots and now stood in his socks holding what looked like a dirty biscuit tin under his arm. 'I didn't know we had company.' He smiled at Jameela, and Sheila noticed his moustache twitch as he spotted the wine, which he'd been saving for the weekend.

'We're putting the "yay" into "Friyay",' said Sheila a little too loudly.

'Yes, you girls look like you've been having a lovely afternoon.

I'm Martin,' He gave a small wave, then immediately looked embarrassed.

'I know,' smiled Jameela warmly, 'I'm Jameela, and I've heard all about you and your magnificent finds.'

'Ah, I bet you have.' He glanced at his wife, and Sheila smiled beatifically. 'Victorian,' he said to Jameela, holding out the tin. 'Found down on the canal towpath, it'll clean up a treat. Thought it'd be nice to keep bird seed in Sheila.'

'Wow Martin, thank you. I'm one lucky woman. The good news just keeps coming today – Jameela is buying our cross trainer, we thought we'd toast her new bit of fitness kit.'

'Yes, so I can see,' said Martin.

'It's a beautiful day to sit out. You've made a lovely space out here Martin,' said Jameela, 'not often we get the sunshine up here. Just wait for Spain – you'll be bathed in the warm sun every day, Sheila's told me about your exciting plans.'

Sheila saw Martin's face drop at the mention of Spain and appreciated he at least quickly tried to prop it back up with a bright smile. 'Has she now?'

A small silence which neither woman made an effort to fill followed. 'Well, I'll get this cleaned up, nice to meet you Jameela,' and Martin was gone.

'Do you see it?' asked Sheila. 'The sadness in his eyes?' She'd been telling Jameela about Martin and his poor mum – the dementia that was currently riding roughshod over her once brilliant mind.

'It must be awful – for both of them,' said Jameela.

'Well yes, it is, of course it is. At least when someone dies you can grieve, move on. His mum hasn't died, but also she's not really there any more. Sometimes she's no idea who he is even.' Sheila felt a lump rise in her throat at the injustice of it all – she didn't know who she was most upset for, her husband, his ill mother, or herself. 'Spain is where we should be, but whenever I try to make plans Martin says, "How can we expect Mum to understand the concept of us emigrating when she can't grasp the concept of how to put on her cardigan?"'

Sheila knew Martin only saw Spain as a fling, a holiday romance.

He'd made it clear that he'd rather visit every year – they didn't have to move there. Sheila had her volunteering and committee work, but she no longer had any real friends locally – they'd scattered, moving for work reasons or to be closer to their grandkids. She wanted a fresh start, but Martin insisted going to Spain was just running away – loneliness, boredom, getting older, all these things would still follow them to the sunshine.

'Oh God,' said Jameela, 'it's so sad. When was she diagnosed?'

'Last year. She'd started to get a bit "dotty" as we called it – losing her keys or her purse, sometimes finding them in the fridge. We put it down to the quirks of getting older and didn't really worry, or maybe in truth we knew but had been papering over the cracks.' She shrugged. 'Then we popped round and she was struggling to put her niece's birthday card in its envelope. She was turning the card and the envelope this way and that, like she was holding two completely unrelated items – a sock in one hand, an egg timer in the other.' Sheila paused to sip the last of her wine. 'Martin was in bits. We had to pull over on the drive home so he could be sick. The fact is, she was sinking before our eyes.' Sheila shook her head as if to empty it of the sad thoughts 'She's in a care home now. She has a ground-floor room overlooking the gardens – she loves to sit listening to the bird-song. It's very peaceful and calm there. That's where we were, on one of the garden benches, the time Martin tried to get her to put her cardie on – honestly Jameela, she looked at him like he'd asked her to change the gearbox on our car, not slip her arm into some knitwear.'

Sheila knew Martin hadn't been sleeping well since that day.

She'd wake when he got up to go to the loo and could almost hear the cogs turning in his brain as he then lay in the dark, his worries playing on a loop. 'He told me he felt like dementia was a monster and it was in no rush, but had his mum in its sights, and he couldn't protect her.'

'Have they always been close?' asked Jameela.

'Oh yes, a little too close, I used to think. When we were first married I found it quite suffocating, like she knew stuff about him I didn't. It's hard to explain; there was a "knowingness" about their relationship. He just said, "She knows me better than anyone and loves me no matter what".'

'Right,' said Jameela. 'Sure that reassured you.'

Sheila laughed. 'Well, I just learned to accept it over time, and now as a mother myself I feel guilty it bothered me at all. She's gone from this slightly intimidating English teacher to sometimes being childlike. When she was first ill she'd be able to describe it so clearly it would break your heart: "Marty, it's like the thought I need is on a shelf that's just out of my reach – I can see it, but no matter how hard I try I just can't reach it."'

'It's a very cruel disease.'

Sheila and Jameela sat quietly for a moment as the sun came from behind a cloud and flooded the garden with golden light.

Sheila sighed. 'Sorry. Not a very cheery subject.'

'No,' said Jameela, 'don't apologise – sometimes it's healthy to put your own troubles into perspective.'

Sheila stood up a little unsteadily and said, 'One for the road?' And went inside for another bottle of wine, ignoring Jameela's half-hearted protests.

When she returned Jameela was looking at the printed-out news-letter.

'If it wasn't for this we wouldn't have met.' She smiled. 'Did you see the advert for the pottery class on here?'

'Not exactly,' replied Sheila, pouring the wine. 'Martin spotted it though, and said I should go – think he hopes I'll find new interests to distract me from Spain.' She rolled her eyes. 'To be fair I've always fancied having a go at pottery. *Ghost* is one of my favourite films. But I'm not going on my own, and Martin says he's too busy restoring his various bits and bobs to come.'

'I could be up for it.' Jameela nodded, sipping her wine. 'I saw it and felt the same – I was always a bit envious of the arty crowd at school in their Doc Martens and eyeliner. But it'd be too awkward to go alone. Also, I feel like I barely know anyone on the estate, I don't know if it's an age thing or 'cos I feel "all work and no play" at the moment, but I'd like to get to know more people round here.'

Sheila cocked her head on one side and said, 'It can't be an "age thing" because you're still annoyingly young . . . are you sure it's not a "wine thing"? I can just see us both signing up, then you getting cold feet when you're sober.' She laughed. She was absolutely thrilled that Jameela might be up for it, and the fact it was her new friend's idea and not Martin's somehow took the pressure off.

'If we sign up I'll not chicken out, you have my word as a lawyer,' said Jameela solemnly, 'but if you chicken out, I'll sue you.'

9

Louise

Louise watched as Danny used the bread to mop up the yellow slick of egg yolk that was making its way across the plate.

She wanted to talk, but also knew he was in his 'happy place' – eating. She perched, still as stone, his mum's words to her when they first met seared for ever into her memory: 'Keep him well fed and he'll be happy.'

His plate was resting on his lap, on a tea towel. The *One Show* was on, and Alex Jones was asking Charlie Dimmock about a new garden makeover show.

'I know you want something,' Danny muttered without looking up, 'but I have to prioritise this delicate operation – I need to intercept the yolk before it reaches the baked beans, because if it merges with the beans, going that rank peach colour, it'll be game over. I would not want you to have that on your conscience, especially as you were the one who cooked this delicious meal just for me, the love of your life.' He said all this as he deftly folded a slice of buttered bread in two to create a dam in front of the beans before dabbing at the yolk expertly and demolishing the bread in two bites.

Despite herself, Louise smiled.

He chewed slowly, eyes half closed, his focus softened. 'You know the best bit? The sensation of the thick, salty butter mixing with the warm yolk.'

'Well yes, I do know all about thick things Danny . . . I am married to you after all.'

His eyes sprang open, and through a mouthful of food he said, 'Rude, just rude.'

She reached for the remote and muted the telly.

'Danny,' Louise gave a weary smile and tried not to let the irritation she felt sharpen her tone, 'I'm loving your whole *Masterchef* schtick, but I need to talk to you about something, and I need you to actually listen.'

He'd always been able to make her laugh, but recently she found his clowning around annoying, especially when she was trying to talk to him about anything meaningful, like their relationship, their future, how she felt they were in a bit of a rut.

The more serious she became the sillier he seemed to act.

Now at last, she thought she'd found something that could help her feel better and would give them a chance to spend some time together.

Danny gently placed his knife and fork down on the plate and looked at her. 'I'm all yours. Every inch of me, which at the moment, is quite a lot. So if this is about me having a little extra junk in my trunk let me say A: I've already texted Duffy about a game of five-a-side, and B: there's currently just even more of me to love.'

'No Danny, it's not about that, though obviously I'm pleased you're thinking about looking after yourself a bit more.' She smiled patiently. 'You know I've been saying for a while that me and you need to get out more, do new things, meet people?' She paused at this point, eyes wide, lips pursed waiting for a response.

'Yes . . .' replied Danny warily.

'And,' she continued, 'perhaps most importantly, have something for us that is just for US and not connected to the girls?' As if on cue Jodie and Jemma came tumbling into the room, a tangle of pre-teen limbs wrestling over an iPhone.

'GIVE. IT. BACK!' shrieked Jodie. 'MUUUUMMM TELL HER,' she yelled, as Jemma clung on to the phone for dear life.

'Out,' said Louise calmly. So calmly in fact that it spooked both the girls and they quit their wrestling and looked at their mum and dad in turn. 'Me and Dad are talking, so out. Now. I won't ask again,' said Louise quietly. Out they went, closing the door behind them – even they seemed surprised by how quickly they obeyed the instruction. They could be heard squawking and giggling as they thundered up the stairs.

'So, as I was saying,' said Louise, then paused as she clocked that Danny had used the girls' appearance to sneak another slice of bread and was now nudging the last of the beans around his plate.

Danny looked up with a bashful grin. 'Go on,' he said, through a mouth full of beans.

'Go Potty – it's a pottery class, it starts next Tuesday at the community centre. Remember Becky? Who runs it? She used to be there when we took the girls to toddler groups? Blonde girl, pretty. Anyway, according to the newsletter she got an arts grant, so it's free to join, and we're going.' She smiled excitedly, as if she expected him to whoop with joy. No whoop came, so she continued, rattling through the details. 'I've put our names down. I know you're on an early on Wednesday, but we'll be home by ten. Please Danny.' Her eyes widened, weakening any resolve he may have had to refuse. 'I need this Danny. WE need this.'

10

Becky

Becky paced the hall at the community centre, repeatedly glancing at her watch. She hoped Sasha wasn't going to be late; she had the leftovers of a veggie lasagne, half a bottle of rioja, and a new Netflix dating show waiting for her at home. She did one last lap, weaving in and out of the eight workbenches. A single sack of clay was out ready for Sasha to inspect – *If*, thought Becky, *she ever graces us with her presence.*

The door banged. *Oh God, she's here.* Becky felt weirdly nervous – she hated meeting new people, especially arty types in flowing skirts. She pulled self-consciously at her T-shirt, trying to straighten it.

'Helloooooo,' a voice called out from the hallway. It was a man's voice. Becky felt instantly irritated – the last thing she needed was to be dealing with a local nosing around asking about room hire when Sasha made her grand entrance.

Becky headed towards the voice and, as she rounded the corner, she found a tall man standing looking at the noticeboard by the front door. She didn't recognise him from the estate. He had dark wavy hair tucked behind his ears, wore a denim jacket, and when he turned to her she was caught in the beam of the bluest pair of eyes she'd ever seen.

They settled on her and twinkled as he smiled broadly. 'You must be Becky,' he said, in a sweet Scottish burr.

'Yes?' she said, still no idea who this handsome stranger was.

'Ah grand, I'm Sasha, nice to meet you at last.'

To say Becky was shocked was an understatement. The emails they'd exchanged had been pretty humdrum – dates, times, that sort of thing, so nothing to really give away the author's gender.

She'd just presumed from the name Sasha that she was dealing with a woman. Sasha, followed everywhere by the gentle tinkle of the dozen or so thin gold bracelets she wore along her delicate wrist that she'd bought on her travels. Not this frankly gorgeous bloke with a kind face and a smile that could melt an icecap.

Becky realised she was making a terrible first impression – her mouth was gaping open. Plus, in the usual pattern of a civilised conversation, it was now definitely her turn to speak.

'You're a man,' she stated, matter-of-factly.

Sasha looked down at himself as if it was also news to him. 'Oh my God! I am! How did THAT happen?' he asked incredulously.

Becky was relieved when he broke into another broad grin that made her stomach flip; so he wasn't offended at least. She was sure she could feel her pupils dilating as she drank him in.

She tried to get a grip. 'God, sorry – you must think I'm mad.' She laughed a laugh that she hoped sounded confident and carefree. 'I was expecting . . .'

'A woman?' Sasha finished her sentence. Becky felt herself blush. 'Don't worry, it happens a lot. When my mum was expecting me she saw Sacha Distel on the *Val Doonican Show* and loved the name.' He smiled. 'She winged it with the spelling though, hence the S. I like it now, but I wasn't so keen growing up in Leith in the eighties – I just wanted to be called Craig or Mark like my mates,' he stopped. 'Sorry. I'm waffling now.'

'No,' Becky said, 'I like it, I mean, I like the story, and your name.' She smiled. 'Right, most important business first, tea?'

Becky made two brews in the tiny kitchen, which suddenly seemed overcrowded with Sasha's broad shoulders in there. Then they embarked on the 'not so grand tour', as she called it. She felt self-conscious about the scuffed doors, the creaky floorboards. Sasha didn't seem to notice – and listened intently as she gave him the lowdown on the place. 'Hard to imagine now,' she said as they walked along the tatty corridors, 'but in its heyday this place threw the best street parties for royal weddings, and even had a funfair that ran the length of Newton Pass on the eve of the Millennium – it was so exciting for the kids who lived on the street. Teacup rides and hook-a-duck stalls all lit up under their bedroom windows? It looked magical.'

'Yeah it sounds it. Remember on the stroke of midnight waiting for planes to drop out of the sky?' smiled Sasha.

'Oh God yes! The bug! I'd forgotten about that. I remember the next day I was feeling rather delicate and found Jack sweeping up the car park – dozens of those gold paper "2000" glasses where your eyes peeped through the first two zeros. Stylish!'

'Bet you looked lovely,' said Sasha, and even though he was clearly joking, Becky felt herself redden. 'Who's Jack?' he asked.

'Ah well. None of the events would've happened without the committee here raising the money – the community centre was like the beating heart of the estate, and I guess the beating heart of the community centre is our caretaker Jack, wait till you meet him.' She smiled as she pushed open the doors to the small hall. 'Every hinge and bulb in this place has been tinkered with or replaced by Jack. He's officially retired, but he loves the place – he says he has a special connection to the centre because they're both "a little weather beaten and worn", and that's why he'll never give up on it.'

Sasha laughed. 'He sounds quite the character.'

'Oh he is,' said Becky. 'Out there,' she nodded through the fire escape doors towards the car park, 'we have our German Christmas market.' Becky could almost smell the steaming glühwein, which always loosened the inhibitions and purses of the locals enough for them to buy frankincense candles and decorations made from cinnamon sticks. 'And every year Jack is Father Christmas. If the pottery goes well you might still be here – he'll give you a pressie if you're a good boy.' Becky cringed – what was she on about, all this talk of Christmas and being a good boy? But Sasha laughed, the corners of his eyes crinkling deliciously.

'It's a nice place, the Inventors' – lots of good, hard-working people.'

Sasha frowned. 'Where does the name come from? Is the local area awash with inventors?'

'Ha . . . no. I used to think it was when I was little – hoping to bump into Caractacus Potts trying out another flying car. I now know it's probably just because all the other themes were used up – there's a racecourse estate, and an authors' estate on the other side of Lennington. Still, I thought that we could reflect our creative name by doing something creative like a pottery course. I just didn't think we'd actually pull it off.'

At this Sasha smiled. 'Well you have. I hope you're going to join us?'

Becky laughed. 'Me? No way!' Sasha looked crestfallen so she rushed on. 'No, I mean, I'm just not very artistic, and I'm clumsy as hell – health and safety nightmare if you let me near a spinning wheel and lumps of clay. Besides, I work here, I'll have other responsibilities to take care of.'

'OK,' he held his hands up, 'either way, you should be proud of yourself. What you've done so far is really impressive – winning the grant from the council, to pay for all this kit. I think together we can make these classes really special.' He studied her as he waited for a response.

There was an intensity to him that unsettled her – it was the passionate way he spoke combined with his honest, open face. A contrast to Tony's face, with its sharp features and eyes that could never be trusted. Why, during such a nice moment, did the ghost of her ex have to creep into her thoughts? She shooed it away.

Sasha was still watching her, and she looked at the floor shyly – it'd been a while since anyone had said anything so encouraging to her, and when it came to accepting praise she was out of prac-tice. She batted it away. 'Well – we'll see – there's still a few days for people to chicken out. I mean, going by the response online we should have a full house, but we need people to actually turn up.' She was doing her best to sound businesslike.

'They will,' said Sasha firmly with a slight nod, as if any other outcome was completely ridiculous. 'You'll see,' he added, and he strode on ahead as if searching for something. 'Where is she then?' Sasha shouted back over his shoulder.

'Who?' Becky said, suddenly worried they were about to be joined by a third person she'd not heard about – had he expected an assistant?

'The kiln of course.'

'Ah, OK, this way.' Becky tried to ignore the rush of relief she felt that some hot young assistant wasn't going to rock up; she had to admit she was loving having Sasha to herself.

The kiln was bigger than Becky had expected and, as it was the last thing off the van, it'd made a grand entrance, like a buxom opera singer being wheeled centre stage. It was cream coloured and the size of an overweight phone box. It now squatted in the corner of the old stockroom.

The space used to be filled with everything from catering sacks of teabags to boxes of ping-pong balls, and props from the play-group's nativity shows. There was still a shepherd's crook made from an old walking stick and gaffer tape lurking behind the rolls of yoga mats in the corner. Every time she spotted it she hoped the grandparent who'd loaned it to their toddler shepherd had made a miraculous recovery and no longer needed it.

Sasha slowly approached the kiln, reaching out and gently caressing its side like a vet trying to soothe a nervous horse. 'She is . . .' he said, turning to look at Becky '. . . a BEAUTY!' He grinned broadly. 'We're gonna have some fun us three,' he said with a wink, and Becky felt her insides liquefy again.

Once he'd finished inspecting the kiln, opening and closing the door, studying the temperature gauge, he headed back out and strode along the corridor, Becky at a light jog trying to keep up.

She caught up with him at the doorway to the main hall as he peered through the door's narrow window. 'And here, I presume,' he said as he flung open the double doors theatrically, 'is where the magic will happen?' He looked around the room.

Becky cringed at the loud creak of the hinges, then took in the high, dusty sills she could never quite reach, the floor with the odd mismatched board where Jack had done an emergency fix-up job, and the stain on the ceiling from when the roof had leaked during Storm Hilda, and grimaced.

'It's perfect – excellent little set-up.'

This time she was certain Sasha was taking the mickey, but if he was, his face gave nothing away.

He strode over to the first workbench, then weaved his way around the others, ending up at the back where all the rest of the equipment was stacked up neatly. He gently rummaged through the trays, checking over the tools – holding each one with reverence as though they were ancient artefacts. Next he perched momentarily on a stool to try it out, then dropped to one knee to get a closer look at one of the wheels – it was exhausting just watching him. He moved nimbly – Becky could barely focus on him before something else caught his eye and he sprang towards it.

Eventually he stayed still. 'What you've done so far is spot on,' he said. 'By Tuesday, each wheel should be on the left of the benches as we're looking at them, with a stool next to each. Please.' He put his hands on his hips and bit his lower lip gently as he considered his next instruction. 'That's it – knew there was something – all the cables need to be taped down. I can come early on Tuesday and help out, so don't worry too much.' As he spoke he held a small sculpting knife in his hand. 'You've got aprons yeah?' he said over his shoulder as he headed back between the rows of benches towards his wheel at the front.

'Yup,' said Becky, pointing at the thick beige cotton aprons hanging on three hooks by the door.

'Perfecto!' he shouted into the heavens, making Becky laugh. *God he's a loon*, she thought to herself.

She caught up with him at the front just as he pulled open the bag of clay next to his teaching wheel, an action Becky could tell he'd done a thousand times before.

'So where have you come from Sasha?' Becky asked, moving closer. She could smell the earthy scent of the clay escape the top of the sack.

'What's a nice potter like me doing in a place like this you mean?' He smiled. She laughed, waiting for him to answer, but he didn't.

'This,' he said, now on his haunches and tugging off a small conker-sized lump of the grey, damp mixture, 'is straight from the earth, there's nothing purer than this,' and Becky blushed again as she watched him manipulate the clay in the palms of his hands, his flesh and the clay almost becoming one as he rolled and squeezed the lump. Becky didn't in that moment care that she didn't know where Sasha had sprung from, plenty of time to find out his story. For now, she was lost, imagining him kneading and grabbing at her waist, her thighs, her hips, with his strong hands . . . He looked up at her with a nod. 'It's nice and wet too,' he said, and Becky smiled politely. *It's not the only thing*, she thought to herself.

Inspection over and times arranged for Tuesday, Becky waved Sasha off and locked up, leaning her back against the closed door like a teenager after a first kiss. He was . . . gorgeous. Her nerves about the following Tuesday were now mixed with a much sweeter antici-pation about seeing Sasha again. The four days were going to drag, she knew it.

11

Jameela

On Tull Avenue, keep-fit fanatic Jameela wasn't feeling particularly fit. In fact she still felt rough after her unexpected boozy afternoon with Sheila.

She stood in front of the mirror in the small dressing-room next to her bedroom, getting ready for bed. She'd made herself a sandwich and had grabbed a packet of crisps and a large bottle of Evian from the fridge in the garage.

Tonight she planned to break all her own house rules, and dine in bed whilst watching something thoroughly trashy on her iPad.

Sipping wine in the spring sunshine had been a welcome distraction and it felt great to laugh, but she was regretting it now. A faint headache was gathering like storm clouds on the horizon. Never would she have imagined getting on with someone like Sheila. She'd seen her on various occasions organised by the estate committee, and Sheila was always in the thick of the action, from policing sparkler etiquette on bonfire night, to selling cupcakes at the summer fair, to adjusting the Union Jack bunting at the last royal wedding, up a ladder, feather fascinator quivering in the breeze. Jameela had wrongly assumed Sheila came with an inbuilt points system mechanism, the cogs of which never stopped whirling around as she mentally added or subtracted approval points depending on peoples' behaviour. From a too loud laugh here or a raucous child's slight misbehaviour there, to a chic skirt or new shiny Volvo parked outside – nothing went unnoticed, as Sheila registered everything, measured it against her own social standing, and points were deducted or added accordingly with brutal efficiency.

Jameela had wondered before now if her own brown skin had counted against her, presuming Sheila, with her Shires blow-dry, Breton stripes, and general whiff of *Daily Mail* reader wouldn't really approve of someone like Jameela.

Over the course of the afternoon though, Sheila had shown her true colours, and Jameela felt ashamed at how quick she'd been to write her off. It turns out she was warm and caring – and very funny, and when she mentioned her volunteering at the food bank it wasn't virtue signalling but a means to set up a funny story about her co-workers' eccentricities.

Sheila had also revealed she'd kissed a boy called Ishmael when she was at school. A clumsy way of showing Jameela she was broad-minded and multi-cultured. Usually this sort of thing irritated Jameela, but the way Sheila said it was so sweet, waxing lyrical about how she'd written in her teenage diary about his 'glossy black quiff', that she'd forgiven her. Perhaps the wine helped.

They'd spent a large part of the afternoon laughing, but also forming a bond, so when they discussed the pottery class Jameela had been touched by Sheila's vulnerability in wanting her new friend to join her. And she was equally pleased to have someone to go with. She didn't need anyone to hold her hand, but joining something sociable and learning a new craft was different, and she was relieved she wouldn't be arriving alone.

Jameela's work world was one ruled by facts, clauses and contracts – perhaps it'd do her good to try something looser – to see if she had any creative juices she could let flow. It'd also be nice to have a focus beyond work, running, and her faltering marriage.

Perhaps her bravado was bolstered by the Sancerre too. 'No going back now,' she'd said as she and Sheila filled out the forms online. Jameela added the date into her phone as 'Clay Day!!!' alongside a vase emoji, then waved goodbye to the couple on their doorstep saying 'OK . . . cross trainer delivery at the weekend – thank you Martin,' who doffed an imaginary cap, 'and then Tuesday is pottery!' and headed home for a cat nap she regretted the moment she woke up.

Reviving herself with a quick shower turned into a rather longer, more luxurious pampering – she used her favourite hair conditioner and, whilst it got to work, she spent a few minutes masturbating under the warm jets of water. She missed Simon, she missed the sex they used to have when they first moved in together – his hands on her as soon as he was through the door from work, a kiss hello turning hotter, him pulling down her knickers roughly, pushing his fingers into her – his long, searching fingers – he'd always known just where to touch her. It was these moments she thought of in the shower.

Before long and in keeping with most of the things she did, Jameela came quickly and efficiently, then rinsed her long hair and stepped out of the shower.

She'd opened the wardrobe to grab a sweater, but found herself drawn to the furthest hanger on the left. She felt a surge of nausea. 'Don't,' she said to herself, but she couldn't help it, she had to look.

There, to the far left, hanging like some kind of ghoul, was a top, unworn, its labels still attached.

It was flouncier than her other clothes – dusky pink and A-line, designed to cover a growing bump. But the bump never quite appeared, not really.

*

The one thing Jameela and Simon wanted more than anything in the world was a dream that was dashed by the arrival of blood – a tearfully unexpected period or a sudden doubling over in a shop, a sharp pang in the night, a twisting dragging twinge in bank holiday traffic.

Hope ending there and then in the most mundane of situations, while all around them normal lives continued in the other cars. People sang along to the songs on the radio, bored kids squabbled, and dogs poked their heads out of windows for air – whilst Simon and Jameela's hearts broke and they felt they might suffocate with the sadness of it.

Jameela blamed herself; she was a failure. What purpose did she have if she couldn't fulfil the most basic human function?

The last miscarriage had been the worst one yet, further along than the others, so she'd dare to let herself begin to hope. All faith had been shredded by then, but still, surely they deserved a glimmer, no matter how pale and fragile . . .

The next day Reju had called round and, as Jameela opened the door, her little sister had thrust forward a gift bag held on one hooked finger by the expensive cream ribbon that served as a handle.

In that first split second Reju had clocked too late Jameela's tired face and swollen eyes – the skin underneath dark and papery – and recoiled, trying to retract her arm. But already Jameela had taken the bag and was peering inside. It was the maternity top.

'What's this?' asked Jameela, an accusatory edge to her voice. She'd always been superstitious, and was scrupulously so now – never daring to cross the threshold into Mothercare or John Lewis to dreamily touch the soft fabrics of the babygros and blankets, to browse the buggies and car seats – surely that would curse an already damned wish even further?

She was a rational woman, but when Reju replied, 'It's nothing, it doesn't matter, it's just when we spoke the other day you sounded so happy and then I saw a top . . .' Jameela felt a fury rise in her. Of course she knew that losing the baby and Reju buying a maternity top were in no way related, but like a wounded animal she attacked.

'Well I won't be needing it thanks. And you know what Reju? I can't believe you even bought it. Why would you do something like that?' Reju opened her mouth to answer, but Jameela cut through with an incredulous high-pitched laugh as if she'd just stumbled on the answer. 'I know – I think you're actually trying to hurt me. That's it. Or actually is this your weird twisted way of reminding me just how useless I am?'

Reju's face crumpled. 'Jameela, please, stop,' but Jameela couldn't.

Years of pain and jealousy and resentment came pouring out. 'No I won't stop, Reju. Not all of us can pop a kid out when we fancy it. You've even said yourself the only thing your fat dopey husband is good at is getting you pregnant!'

At this, Reju's eyes filled with tears, but the mauling continued.

'Well done Rej, you've made a shitty day even shittier with your thoughtlessness.'

Reju started to turn and walk back towards her car, stumbling on the path through her tears, but Jameela wasn't quite done.

She wanted to hurt Reju, one of the people she loved most in the world – maybe if she hurt her, some of the unbearable pain would seep from her own bones, providing momentary relief from this agony. She delivered her final blow, heard her own voice rise and become shrill as she shouted down the path at her retreating sister, 'You've always been jealous of my drive and my ambition, so you have to rub it in my face that you've spent your entire twenties barefoot and pregnant mopping up after your stupid husband and bratty kids.'

Jameela slammed the front door behind her with such force the frame splintered slightly. The spewing of so much fury felt like a release, but, as she leaned with her back against the door, her legs gave way and she sank to the floor, spent. Then the horror of what she'd said washed over her. It was as if she'd been floating above, watching two women – the smaller one cowed and silent, the other screeching and wild.

What had she done?

She scrambled to her feet, wobbly now, and ran to the downstairs loo to be sick. Then she curled up on the floor, feeling the cold tiles against her face as the tears came.

She'd managed in a matter of minutes to rip open old wounds that had healed years ago, or if not quite healed, scabbed over sufficiently.

The times Reju had said she was proud of Jameela and her career, how she was envious of her neat, stylish house . . . but it was always with a smile that showed she was pleased for her sister.

All through school, Jameela had been the bright one, and captain of every sports team. At their family home, Jameela's old sports trophies were still on display, but now they jostled for space next to framed photos of the grandchildren. Jameela hated it – it was as though the trophies were her only achievement until she could have kids, and the medals would be taken down and replaced at long last with photos of her baby.

When they were teenagers their mum used to reassure Reju that she was just as special and just as loved, but Reju didn't need the reassurance – she was proud of her big sister. Nowadays it was Jameela their mum offered words of comfort to: 'It'll happen for you one day my love. It's not easy for everyone.'

With Jameela's cruel words she had shattered the trust that gentle Reju had in her.

Jameela knew it had taken a lot for Reju to confide that things weren't perfect in her marriage – she'd told Jameela all about her frustrations with her kind-hearted but lazy husband Tariq.

Jameela winced at the irony. She'd screamed Reju's secrets about her husband back in her face, when in fact Jameela really liked Tariq and had always told Reju as much – that he wasn't perfect, but he was funny and kind and a brilliant dad to the three kids.

Jameela loved her two nieces and nephew with all her heart – and they loved their auntie JamJam back, always throwing themselves at her, sticky mitts and lolly-stained lips plastering her with love and cuddles. They weren't remotely 'bratty'.

What the hell had she done? She could feel her mouth slacken and relax and allowed her eyes to blur as sleep edged closer, offering escape from her thoughts. It was then, as she stared, eyelids heavy, at the skirting board, that she saw the long strand of brown hair stuck to it, curled in a figure S. The only other person to have been in the house for weeks was Karin her cleaner, and she had short hair, dyed pillar-box red. She followed the hair's shape – S – was it a clue? She was delirious, she felt almost drunk. She must've fallen asleep because the next thing she knew it was dark and she heard the familiar rattle of Simon's key in the door.

Jameela pulled the top from its hanger and tossed it on the floor – it was time she had a clear-out. No point that top hanging in there like a skeleton in her literal closet – ready to taunt her with the memory of the day she had screamed at her sister. She could play back each second of the argument in her head – each bitter syllable she'd spat at her sister became more pronounced, ready to be replayed again and again.

It'd been nearly three weeks since that day, and still Reju was refusing to take Jameela's calls.

Jameela surveyed the gaping spaces in the wardrobe, left when Simon had hurriedly grabbed his clothes just a week after the sisters' fight and scarpered to the empty flat above the dentist practice.

'Not bad Jameela,' she muttered to herself grimly as she rifled through the neatly hung clothes. 'You managed to lose another baby, your sister, AND your husband in the space of a fortnight.'

The empty hangers danced noisily up and down the rail as she exhumed an armful of clothes at once. It felt good. She shoved the huge mountain of clothes into two bin bags then climbed into bed with her sandwich.

12

Sheila

The day of the first pottery class had arrived and Sheila couldn't get home from her Tuesday afternoon shift at the food bank quickly enough. She found Martin reassembling the parts of a Victorian toy car at the kitchen table.

'Can I rant while you tinker please?' And before Martin could answer Sheila launched her attack on her fellow volunteer April. 'Madam is clearly very jealous of my new hobby,' she said, plonking her bag next to the pile of parts, sending a couple of washers spinning. 'I only mentioned the class a couple of times while we were sorting the knobbly veg boxes, and she insisted on regaling me with a horror story.'

Martin gently laid down his paintbrush on a piece of kitchen roll. 'Hmm,' he said, gathering the washers, 'I get the feeling I'm about to be regaled too,' and sat back in his chair.

'Yes, well,' Sheila smiled tightly, 'that's what husbands are for Martin. Listening. Anyway, apparently, a friend of April's mother's was an experienced potter at the wheel and was working away on a vase and got so carried away she didn't notice her silk scarf had fallen loose, and before she knew it, the scarf got caught in the workings of the spinning pottery wheel and she was almost garrotted! Apparently they had to cut her free! And,' she paused dramatically, 'it was a Liberty scarf!' Her eyes widened at the thought of a designer scarf being sacrificed in such a cruel way. She continued, 'April said the poor woman had welts around her neck for weeks and never fully recovered from the mental impact. She said she couldn't speak for a year 'cos she'd almost been throttled, and had traumatised her voice box in the process!'

Martin laughed. 'Imagine the peace and quiet for her husband though!'

'Very funny Martin,' Sheila snapped.

'Hey, come here.' He stood and gently pulled her towards him, his arms around her waist. 'Ignore April, she's just jealous. Let me make you a mochaccino while you go and get ready, and just to be on the safe side my angel,' he added, 'maybe don't wear a scarf.'

An hour later Sheila had finally settled on an outfit. She wanted to look slightly bohemian for the pottery class, so she plumped for a tangerine jumpsuit she normally saved for holidays. It was made from soft velour and was very flattering, with its pulled-in waist and deep V-neck. She paired it with a chunky, wooden blue necklace, again from the holiday drawer, and tied her hair up in a loose pony-tail. 'Not bad,' she muttered to herself as she looked in the mirror. She wouldn't look amiss wandering the corridors of Central Saint Martins with a canvas under her arm and a pencil behind her ear.

'Not bad at all,' said Martin, appearing genie-like. He slid his hands around her from behind and rested his head on her shoulder, looking at them both in the mirror. 'You feel like a warm peach,' he said, tracing his hands along the arm of the soft fabric.

Sheila smiled at him in the mirror – he looked like quarry she was carrying back from a hunt, slung over her shoulder like a slain muntjac deer.

'What are you going to get up to while I'm gone?' she addressed Martin's reflection in the mirror.

'Up to? Not much, thinking I might pop to visit Mum. Either that or I'll sit at the window waiting for you to return like a spaniel missing its mistress.'

'Hmm,' replied Sheila, slowly rotating her head around like an owl to look him in the eye properly. 'You're giddy – do I detect a twinkle in your eye Martin? Are you planning to crack open a little bottle of something as soon as I'm out the door?'

'Well Tuesday's the new Friday, as nobody ever said. Anyway, enough about me my little tiger shark – are you looking forward to seeing Jameela?' he asked. 'She seems lovely – she was so grateful when I took over the cross trainer. You excited?'

'Yes Martin, a bit, and a little nervous – fear of the unknown and all that. Yes Jameela's lovely, I just hope it wasn't only the wine that made us get on.' She tucked a strand of hair behind her ear as Martin continued to nuzzle her neck. His breath was warm and he felt a little too close, but she tried not to tense up – she liked it when Martin was playful and was careful not to reject him even casually in case it dented his confidence.

His blue moods were less and less frequent at the moment, and she didn't want to jeopardise what she saw as progress.

'To be honest, I'm glad you got on with Jameela, it'll do you good to have a pal who lives nearby,' he said.

Yes, thought Sheila, *especially if a new best friend makes me less eager to up sticks to Spain.* Honestly, Martin was as subtle as a tonne of bricks.

Out loud she said, 'Yeah you're right, it's also nice to know we're not the only ones with problems,' and immediately regretted it as his face crumpled. 'Not that we have "problem-problems",' she rushed on. 'I guess I mean one never knows what goes on behind closed doors.' At this Martin raised his eyebrows, interest piqued. 'Whenever I'd seen Jameela out running she looked so calm and focused and in control. I always thought she looked a bit . . . smug.'

Sheila looked ashamed. 'Turns out she's had a tough time of it –
poor girl has been struggling to have a baby, she's nearly forty so
you know, the biological clock is ticking, and by the sounds of it
her husband isn't man enough to deal with the stress of it all.'

'Crikey,' said Martin. He began stroking her again, lightly tracing
his fingers along the soft curve of her hip, but now she felt hot
and bothered, and gently shrugged him off.

'Right, I need to get a wriggle on – these masterpieces won't
create themselves.'

As she left the room in search of her holiday pumps, she noticed
Martin reach out and gently stroke the royal blue silk scarf she'd
left thrown over the wardrobe door. He gazed at the fabric and
rubbed it between his thumb and finger.

13

Becky

Sasha had arrived a couple of hours early as promised, and he and Becky were now sitting on the mini stage at one end of the hall, surveying their work. Pottery wheels, aprons, tools and workbenches all laid out expectantly.

'I guess you must be used to this feeling – the pre-class butterflies?' she said as she sipped her tea.

Sasha nodded. 'Oh aye, it's the best bit. I've taught all over the world – Berlin, LA, private schools up in Edinburgh, a kibbutz in Israel, you name it, I've probably made a small vase there.' He smiled. 'But the feeling before the first class is always the same – that feeling of, I dunno, promise? Like anything can happen.' At this he waggled his eyebrows and she groaned inwardly at the weird coquettish giggle that seemed to be coming from her.

'Well, that all sounds very glamorous, I didn't realise we were dealing with a global superstar potter.'

Sasha laughed. 'Yeah well, man can't live on glamour and excitement alone – that's why I'm here with you.'

'Sure. Well you've added a certain chicness yourself,' she smiled sweetly, 'Not many men round here can pull off double denim, not since the mid-nineties anyway.'

'Ouch!' He looked wounded.

'Seriously though,' she searched his face, 'why *are* you here?'

Sasha shrugged. 'My mum says I need to settle down, to put down roots, and I guess she's right. I just need to find the right place I guess, and the right person.'

There was a brief silence. 'And is this the right place?' Becky asked.

Sasha looked around him and nodded. 'I like it here.'

'Good,' she said boldly. 'Well, maybe you'll find the right person too . . . if not, you'll have fun looking!'

'Cheeky! Aye, well we'll see. I've been in love before, but not for a long long time.' He picked at the specks of dried clay on his hands.

'Oh really, who was the lucky girl? Or are there too many to remember their names?' Becky knew she was being nosey, but she didn't care.

'Absolutely, I just use a simple cataloguing system for all my exes, alphabetical order and all that.'

She laughed. 'Sure. It's the only way.'

'Enough about me, how about you?' said Sasha, adopting a Lothario voice. 'What's your story?'

'Ah well,' said Becky, 'I never dreamed I'd one day reach the dizzy heights of community centre management – in fact I always wanted to be in the police, but it wasn't meant to be.' She smiled. 'But I'm happy – I have got my son, who is pretty much everything to me.'

She told him about Elliot, her beautiful boy who made her world go round.

Becky couldn't help noticing how she was opening up to Sasha more than she ever normally did with new people. He was a great listener; he asked so many questions, and whenever she paused he didn't push or interject, he let her gather her thoughts. She wasn't used to it. Tony would always just talk over her or belittle her when she did speak. She couldn't really bring herself to meet Sasha's eyes – they were so searching that she feared that to look into them would expose too much of her. Years with Tony had taught her to build a hard shell around her heart to protect it from any more damage.

She paused and sipped her tea.

Sasha said, 'You sound smitten – does Elliot have you wrapped round his little finger?'

'Ha! Sometimes – when he wants something, usually hard cash . . . But to be fair we're more of a team really. Look at me, blathering on.' She drained her tea and winced as the tepid liquid hit her tongue.

They both stood up from the stage and dusted themselves down.

'Tell me to mind my own business, but is Elliot's dad on the scene?'

'Ah, him,' she said as they began walking across the hall. Where did she begin with describing Tony? The chipped tooth that at nineteen was rugged, but now just looked rough? The dark hair that flopped over his eyes making the fifteen-year-old Becky weak at the knees? Maybe she could regale Sasha with tales of their charming courtship – cider flavoured kisses and stoned sex in his car when she should've been at school? Or later, the screaming arguments, the slaps, the bites, the bruises?

Instead she said, 'He's very much not on the scene thanks to currently being detained at Her Majesty's pleasure.'

'Ah, OK,' said Sasha. 'That must be tough?'

'On him maybe, not on us; life is much calmer for Elliot and me when he's in prison.'

As Becky unlocked the main double doors to the centre, Sasha ducked into the office.

The early evening sun dazzled Becky momentarily and she closed her eyes, remembering as clearly as if it was yesterday the moment she had had to tell her nan she couldn't go to sixth form – all thoughts of A-levels and a police career on the back burner as her belly swelled on her slender frame.

And now here was the cause of that swelling walking across the patch of closely-cropped grass in front of the community centre.

Elliot had always had terrible timing – three weeks early coming into the world, and now rocking up minutes before she was due to open the doors for the first Go Potty class. She was touched he'd come to support her though, and he'd promised to take part, even if only for the first class.

Her face softened as he approached. Cheekbones you could slice ham on, big round light-grey eyes, and pale wavy hair clipped short at the sides and long on top in a style that made him look elfish – like one of Peter Pan's lost boys. He wore skinny jeans and a faded Madonna Material Girl T-shirt. He was tall and skinny and was twenty-six, but looked more like nineteen.

'Hiya Mumski,' he said with a grin, then stopped and pursed his lips dramatically. 'Oooh what's going on? Why are you looking all pink and pleased?'

He knew her better than anyone and now he was studying her, just inches from her face, just like he used to as an inquisitive toddler, when he'd hold her face with his sticky little paws on both her cheeks to get her full and undivided attention.

Now, he leaned down so their noses were almost touching, and they both went a bit cross-eyed.

'OK, so Becky darling,' he loved calling her by her name to wind her up, 'I'm working on a strictly need to know basis, and I need to know immediately why you're looking like the cat that got a gallon of cream?'

'Oh shush you muppet!' Becky laughed. 'I'm actually hot and bothered because this pottery class is about to start and if no one turns up apart from you I'll have filled my hall with thousands of pounds' worth of equipment for no reason, and I'll be up for the high jump with the council.'

'Mum,' said Elliot, gripping her by the shoulders, 'repeat after me: "I am brilliant, it'll be OK".'

Becky laughed. 'OK . . . I am —'

'BRILLIANT!' shouted Sasha as he appeared through the door from the office, making Elliot and Becky jump, 'and it WILL be OK Becky,' he said, 'and you,' he said as he reached them, holding his hand out, 'must be Elliot? Hiya, I'm Sasha.'

Elliot smiled sweetly as he shook Sasha's hand, but his eyes were on Becky, who suddenly seemed to be studying her own socks.

'Oh I see,' said Elliot, 'you're the pottery teacher! Mum had been dreading a woman who whiffed of patchouli oil and self-satisfaction, so you must've been a lovely surprise.'

Sasha laughed. 'Well, there's a compliment in there somewhere, so I'll take it thanks. Becky, I will leave you and Elliot on crowd control – I'm just going to open the clay sacks,' and he turned and strode up the corridor.

'I knew it!' Elliot hissed gleefully in his mum's ear. 'You're in a tizz for the hot Scot! I don't blame you, he's gorgeous. Pleeeeeease can I be the bridesmaid?' He laughed, grabbing her and twirling her around.

'Oh now, that's enough,' Becky said, 'and as for crowd control, I don't think we'll be needing tha—' but as she turned she saw a small gaggle of people heading towards the community centre.

Once in the hall the group stood around nervously and the whole thing had an air of a school open day.

Becky knew some of the faces. 'Hi Sheila,' she said.

'Hello Becky, how are you doing? It's lovely to see you looking so well,' Sheila said, her voice dripping with sympathy, head cocked on one side.

Becky had known Sheila for years through their involvement with the community centre, but they'd never been particularly close. Sheila's main pastime was gossiping, and Becky knew that Sheila was probably referring to how Becky used to look in the bad old days when her ex Tony was on the scene – worn out and sad, like a teddy strapped to the front grill of a lorry.

'Thanks Sheila,' Becky smiled through lightly gritted teeth.

The older woman reached out and squeezed Becky's forearm. 'Good for you. You deserve buckets of happiness after . . . everything.' Sheila scanned the room, brightening. 'Wow! Look at all this equipment, how exciting! The whole committee is very impressed – well, the ones who manage to stay awake in the meetings.' She sniffed. 'Honestly, the combined age of the male members make the Rolling Stones seem like thrusting young guns!' Sheila half-turned to the woman next to her. 'This,' she said with a flourish, 'is my friend Jameela.'

'Hi Jameela, welcome – I think I've seen you running at high speed around the estate?'

The woman nodded bashfully. 'Yes, that's me, you did well to recognise me with my clothes on – or rather, with normal clothes on instead of lycra.' She looked around. 'Amazing that you've organised all this.'

Becky beamed, but before she could answer, two hands grabbed her shoulders from behind and she spun to see Jack, looking pleased as punch in his best navy jumper.

'Nice turnout Becky!' he said.

'Thanks Jack, You look very dapper.'

'He does rather, doesn't he?' The voice came from a petite lady next to him, around his age, and wearing a mischievous smile and a yellow jumper.

'Why thank you,' said Jack, gruffly.

Becky saw Jack begin to panic and decided to save him. 'I

normally see him in his overalls as he's caretaker here. I'm Becky, lovely to meet you, and this is Jack.'

The lady grinned. 'I'm Pearl – lovely to meet you both too.' Her eyes shone as she looked up at Jack. 'I moved onto the estate last year when my husband passed away. I've seen you a few times Jack – you always seem so busy fixing stuff up a ladder.'

'Well, there's a lot to fix here.' Becky saw he'd regained his composure, puffing out his chest a little. 'Plus, as you probably know, being a widow, it's important to keep busy. I'm a widower myself so I like to keep my mind occupied – even if it's just clearing out some guttering.'

Pearl nodded. 'Well, I must say I was very nervous coming here, but I feel I've already made a friend in you Jack.'

The door banged open and a striking couple strode in holding hands. Becky knew the petite woman with the shiny black bob from the toddler groups a few years back – Louise – but she'd never properly met her husband, who was a handsome barn door of a man.

After a few moments everyone settled in a sort of semicircle, and all eyes turned expectantly to Becky. She froze, her eyes widening and her lips settling somewhere between rictus grin and grimace.

Shit, she thought, *I need to say something!* She'd been so busy torturing herself with visions of an empty hall and tumbleweed blowing through the deserted corridors she hadn't thought about what her opening gambit would be. She hadn't dared hope there'd be so many eager faces here ready to 'Go Potty'.

She opened her mouth, but just a small croak came out. Luckily Sasha stepped forward to speak.

14

Louise

'Ladies and gentlemen,' – the guy at the front was tall and good-looking, and had a smoky Scottish accent – 'welcome, welcome – it's amazing to see so many potential potters here.' He smiled, and Louise glanced sideways at Danny, who was dressed in his best jeans and pale blue polo shirt. He'd even had a shave. She noticed that as this bloke had started speaking, Danny stood up a little taller and had sucked his belly in.

'In a moment I will give out stickers so you can make a little name badge each, very naff sales conference I know, but it means you can concentrate on the clay and come together from the off, plus,' he paused, 'I'm shocking with names, so you'll be doing me a favour.' Everyone smiled. 'But before we start anything, it's crucial we give a loud round of applause to the woman we have to thank for winning the funding in the first place and arranging this whole thing – the fantastic Becky!' The group applauded politely, though there was one man who whooped wildly, which made a few people laugh. *That must be her son*, thought Louise, *he's the spit of her.*

Becky went slightly pink and glared at the whooping man. 'Elliot!' she hissed, but it was obvious she was chuffed.

Louise's older sister and Becky had been at the same school, though Becky was a few years older – the scandalous spectre of a pupil's pregnancy lingers for a long time over a school's reputation. Louise could remember all the mums gossiping about it – hushed chats over tea and custard creams, biscuits dunked, voices lowered whenever any kids came in the room.

Louise soaked up snippets: 'poor girl, losing her mum and having a deadbeat dad'; 'never stood a chance'; 'it was inevitable really'; 'fell in with that wrong 'un'; 'that lad's entire family probably has loyalty cards for prison, the dole office and the pub – it's the only three places they ever go'.

Louise knew Becky lived with her nan after her mum had died, and things must've been tough. The council had given her a little flat, but being alone with a baby at sixteen? Louise couldn't think of anything worse.

Louise also kind of knew the baby's dad Tony, as he had sometimes sold the odd bit of weed to her big brother. He always seemed dodgy, weaselling around, fancying himself as a big-time gangster when in reality he still lived at his mum's and was known to the local constabulary for knocking out anything from pills to stolen trainers.

Becky and Louise's paths crossed again when Louise had brought the twins to the Bouncy Bugs toddler group at the community centre.

Becky had always been really pretty – Louise thought she looked Scandinavian, with her bright blue eyes, creamy skin and blonde wavy hair – but sometimes she had a deflated look about her, as if life – or if the rumours were true, Tony – was slowly knocking the stuffing out of her.

Tonight though, thought Louise, *she looks glowing*. Maybe it was thanks to the Scottish potter, who Becky was now watching intently as he chatted to the group, hanging on his every word.

He introduced himself as Sasha and was now going through a

few of the rules and safety procedures. As he talked, Louise looked around at the rest of the class. There was a middle-aged lady who had a look of Bette Midler, wearing a bright orange jumpsuit that clung to her impressive curves. She was with a tall lady with a beautiful long ponytail who stood with her hands on her hips like some kind of computer-generated warrior.

Next to them stood Becky's son, then a tiny older lady in pale lemon jeans and a yellow fluffy sweater, looking like a newly hatched chick, standing next to a smartly dressed older gent, who Louise recognised as the caretaker who'd been a familiar feature on the Inventors' Estate for years. *He scrubbed up well*, she thought.

Clocking Jack looking smart, Sasha seemed to direct his next point towards him, 'You'll find an apron on each workbench to protect your clothes.' Sasha winked at him, and Jack rolled his eyes and chuckled.

Louise grinned to herself. It was good to be out of the house, away from her daughters, and surrounded by so many friendly faces – she was really excited to be trying something artistic again.

She'd always hoped to have a career that involved something creative, until life got in the way. But her love of art remained.

A weekend job at a large printing firm became a full-time summer job during her uni years, and then after uni, even though she'd toiled hard for her art and history of art degree, she couldn't get a foot in the door of any galleries, private dealers, or auction houses. An internship was a luxury only affordable to those with wealthy parents who could support them.

Louise's parents weren't in a position to fork out, and she couldn't live on fresh air, so she decided to return to C&J Commercial Printing just until something else turned up. But there she still was, fourteen years later, now as a part-time manager.

A steady job with decent maternity benefits and flexible hours once the girls arrived was hard to walk away from, plus her colleagues were a good bunch.

Still, she dreamed of more. Louise still occasionally sketched – especially on holiday. As toddlers, the girls would have a siesta, sun-kissed and sleepy, their pink arms entangled as they napped in vest and pants, and she'd draw them. The blonde downy hair on the base of their backs, the pink fleshy earlobes and sandy toes – all the details were drawn in the low light, white curtains pulled against the glare of the Spanish sun, the murmur of the air conditioning and the girls' soft breathing the only sounds. She would study every centimetre, like she used to when she breastfed them. Some primal instinct to drink in every detail so you'd for ever be able to spot them from a distance in a large flock.

'Right,' said Sasha, shaking Louise from her thoughts, 'each of you needs to choose a workbench and go and stand behind it. Aprons on, sleeves rolled up, hair tied back, let's go potty!'

Louise stood behind her bench and looked at the tools all laid out neatly like scalpels in an operating theatre.

'Imagine stone, sand and clay as all the same family – with planet earth the mother,' said Sasha, holding up a hazelnut sized ball. 'This is clay. Grab a small lump like this, roll it on your fingers. Go, on.' He raised his eyebrows expectantly and paused while everyone reached into the sacks of soft clay by their workbenches. 'Let's chat a little about the material you're about to use – where does it come from and what is it made of? Perhaps most excitingly – what can it become?' He smiled like a cult leader addressing his followers. 'Clay incorporates all the elements – earth, air, water and fire – it is of the earth, the air dries the water away, and the fire transforms the clay to ceramics.

'Sniff it,' he said, looking at Danny, who was on the bench behind Louise. She turned to see his surprised expression and almost got the giggles. 'Pinch it,' he said to Elliot, who was now sporting an apron tied at the hip with a stylish bow. He was stationed at the front bench, seeing as most of the grown-ups (apart from the smiley lady who'd come dressed as a traffic cone) had been too scared to go to the front. 'Roll it in your hands.' He smiled at Louise now.

Everyone kept rolling their little chunk of clay as if working prayer beads.

'Ceramic is the transformation clay goes through once it has been fired at over 600-700 degrees centigrade, and during our classes each week we will definitely see transformations – we will go from strangers to friends, and the clay will go from a moist, soft lump to something beautiful, something useful and, if we're really lucky – a bit of both!' Sasha looked around the room. 'While I've been talking, you've each been holding your small piece of clay. When you first pulled it from the sack you could probably feel the water in it; the ratio of moisture to solid matter in clay determines whether the clay is soft or hard; notice how different it is now your hands will have taken out some of the moisture – it will feel more crumbly and dry.' The class studied the clay in their hands. 'The water acts as a lubricant between the particles, enabling you to manipulate the clay – understanding this basic behaviour means already you're on the right path to understanding the material you're working with.' He smiled. 'Now, they say it takes two thousand hours to become good at something and ten thousand hours to become a master,' the potters glanced at each other in mock alarm, 'and seeing as we just have a couple of hours, let's get cracking!'

Louise glanced over her shoulder at Danny, who was engrossed in rolling his clay. He'd had practice – he used to spend hours with the girls and their Play-Doh, making little animals or dozens of tiny cakes. He was always better than her at playing with the girls – he was a natural, whether it was rough and tumble on the trampoline, or lying still while the twins took a hand each to perform a sparkly manicure.

There was no doubt that he was a great dad, and that was very attractive. He worked hard for his family. But still Louise had the same unsettling feeling she used to get when she escaped the twins as babies and had a couple of hours of freedom – that nagging feeling that something was missing.

She still fancied Danny and he had a twinkle in his eye for her, but she wished he was a little more ambitious. He seemed happy to settle, to not push for more out of life. She'd started to think they were on different pages. His lack of drive was turning her off him.

'Right,' said Sasha, 'I know you're all desperate to give it the full on Patrick Swayze at the wheel, but for our first session we're going to build with coils.'

Louise was relieved, and knew Danny would be too – the night before, the twins had shown them YouTube clips of TV reporters on local news trying to use a pottery wheel and accidentally creating a huge comedy clay penis they had to grapple into submission. 'Oh Jesus! I bet I'd do that!' Danny had shuddered.

Sasha continued, 'It's a traditional but really easy way to build something. And as some of you look like rabbits caught in the headlights,' Louise thought Sasha had glanced fleetingly in Danny's direction as he said that, 'it's best to start with something that is relaxing and that we can all do without being shoved in the limelight.'

'Wow!' whispered Danny just loudly enough for Louise to catch. 'He's sexy AND a mind-reader.' She stifled a giggle.

In his hand Sasha held up a lump of clay about the size of a grapefruit. 'Righty-ho. Here we go folks, this is going to be the start of a beautiful relationship – you and clay. From a piece this size, you should be able to make six or so small balls, then one at a time, simply roll each ball into a long worm . . . these will become your coils.'

15

Jameela

Jameela took a slug of her water and got down to business. It was really nice seeing Sheila again – there was no chance of any awkward silence because almost immediately after a hug hello, Sheila had launched into a story about someone being throttled by a pottery wheel. No danger of that tonight with the rather more sedate coiling. Right on cue, Sheila sidled up to Jameela's bench. 'I could've worn a scarf after all,' she muttered.

'I did think that,' Jameela said.

'Sasha's dishy isn't he?' Sheila whispered, looking back over her shoulder at the teacher, who was currently chatting to Elliot.

'Really?' smiled Jameela innocently. 'I hadn't noticed.'

'Course you hadn't Jameela. I know we're both married women, but there's no harm in window shopping so long as you don't open your purse,' and with that Sheila was gone.

Jameela began rolling the cool clay and felt a calmness descend and her shoulders drop; it was hypnotic, pushing the coils away and bringing them back towards her, her fingers straight and long and in control of the movement; she watched as the ropes of clay became thinner and longer under her touch, all of it dependent on the pressure she applied.

She had to remember to breathe. Sometimes when working out

she'd be so focused on a certain move that she'd hold her breath, only realising when her eyes began to swim.

She breathed now, in through her nose, hold 2-3, out through her mouth, 2-3 . . . this was a method she'd learned from a one-off therapy session – when the world threatened to crumple in on her, when shadows start to fall, if she could just remember to breathe, it would pass.

'Great technique Jameela,' said Sasha passing by. 'They're looking very even.'

At least she'd taken something away from the therapy session – she hadn't wanted to go, but did it to please Simon.

'It could help,' he'd said in that slightly patronising tone he saved for his dental patients.

He had come in from work to find her lying on the bathroom floor. Hearing his key in the door, Jameela had tried to sit up, but her arm had gone dead and she couldn't. She called out to warn him, but the earlier sobbing followed by the mouth breathing whilst lying on the cold tiles had made her throat dry. She suddenly felt parched and not a little silly.

Simon had gasped finding her there curled up like a prisoner in a tiny cell. He'd gently gathered her up in his arms and helped her to the sofa, where she curled up again. He brought her a glass of water and some sweet tea.

'I'm sorry,' she whimpered. 'I had a huge row with Reju and now I've upset you – not very nice coming home on your birthday to find me like this.'

He'd been kind – had stroked the hair from her forehead and watched her. That's when he'd mentioned counselling.

'It's not therapy I fucking need Simon,' she'd whispered sadly, 'it's a baby.'

He hadn't replied.

She'd felt a shift in him, a cooling – all in that split second. Maybe it had been building for months. Whatever it was, the atmosphere had hardened, as if she'd pushed through a one-way door and there was no way back. She felt a snapping in the air of a final straw.

'I'll go open the wine,' he said.

A week later, to make up for how dismissive she'd been about the counselling, she'd spent an expensive hour in an expensive leather armchair chatting to a lady with an expensive blow-dry. At least she'd learned to breathe.

'Penny for them?' It was Becky. Before Jameela could answer, Becky gave her a kind smile. 'Don't worry, you're not the only one in a trance-like state, must be the therapeutic nature of the clay, seems to be soothing people.'

'Yeah, it must be,' Jameela said, her voice cracking slightly. 'I'll take whatever help I can get at the moment.'

Becky lowered her voice. 'Look, if these classes offer some respite from the stresses of daily life as well as producing a couple of vases along the way then it's definitely worth doing. Anyway, I'm taking orders for tea or coffee if I can tempt you?'

'Tea, please,' said Jameela, and watched as Becky worked her way around the room.

Jameela had just one more coil to roll and she absentmindedly formed an S shape with it, reminding her again of the strand of hair she'd spotted from her prone position on the bathroom floor. It was too light to be hers, and she thought of it quite often, but managed to sweep it to the back of her mind; she hadn't mentioned it to Simon for fear of sounding deranged.

She tortured herself that it was the same shade as Belle's – his young, pretty dental assistant. Surely Simon wouldn't be such a cliché . . . would he?

Jameela had insisted on throwing a dinner party to make up for Simon's disastrous birthday evening, when they'd shared a bottle of wine and a delivery pizza before she'd gone to bed at 9 p.m., fragile and exhausted from the afternoon's drama.

Simon wasn't keen. 'It's too much for you,' he'd said, 'and we're not really in the right frame of mind for entertaining.' But since that night Simon had been working late every night, and Jameela was afraid he'd somehow moved away from her emotionally.

She had to stop her marriage from derailing. Little did she know then that the dinner party would simply push them even further apart.

Jameela rolled the final coil; all eight were the same length and thickness, which was ridiculously satisfying. She smiled. She felt more at peace today, rolling out clay with a bunch of strangers, than she had done in ages.

16

Louise

Louise had rolled eight perfect coils too. She couldn't help take a quick glance around the room, and could see Jameela looking very pleased with herself. Perhaps she would be her main competition for teacher's pet.

'Are you finished already?' Danny hissed from behind her. The room was library quiet and Louise could tell it made Danny nervous. She turned and looked at his coils – clearly when it came to clay, as in life, what Danny lacked in finesse he made up for in enthusiasm. A couple of the coils were fat at one end and tapered at the other like carrots. One poor specimen looked like he'd strangled it. 'They're good babe!' she said. 'You've only two more to do, then you can start the pot.'

He didn't look convinced. 'Hmm . . . they're not as good as yours.'

'There's no good or bad Danny, it's your own creation. Your pot will have loads of . . . character.'

Turning back to her bench, Louise carefully wound the first coil into a tight spiral, creating a flat base, before building up the walls with more of her coils. The clay moved beautifully while moist, and would bend and curl – you could manipulate it and push it into position. She found herself in a space where her mind emptied of the usual worries to do with work and life. Somehow, concentrating on the clay created a distance from her cares so that when a thought bubbled up she was able to keep perspective, and calmly study her emotions like a scientist observing a specimen – not deny her worries, bat them away or let them flood over her, but just . . . 'be' with them. It felt peaceful.

The whole class was silent. Sasha was observing the room whilst sitting cross-legged on the stage at the front like a denim-clad Buddha. Once in a while he'd walk from bench to bench, tucking his hair behind his ears to lean in, quietly murmuring a few words of praise and guidance.

There was stillness to the room, a reverence, like being alone in an empty church.

Louise worked, she breathed, and she watched the clay almost come to life under her fingers. Suddenly she was aware of someone within her orbit, hovering closer. It was Sasha.

She could sense he was trying not to break the spell, but she didn't mind.

'You've created an almost oval shape there – strong yet delicate,' he whispered. He watched her gently winding the coils to build up the walls around the base.

Sasha smiled and nodded appreciatively. 'Great technique Louise.' He bobbed down to get level with the pot, then straightened and peered into it. He moved his fingers to stroke the inside of the walls gently, and their wrists accidentally brushed against each other. 'Sorry,' he whispered, 'I'm just checking the walls aren't too thin. We need this lovely thing to survive the firing.'

Louise carried on coiling, but she must've looked worried by his warning.

'It's fine,' he reassured her. 'It'll be OK; when you smooth over the ridges inside, just make sure you're thorough so there's no wee holes the heat can get into and expand – that's where the trouble starts.'

She nodded and watched him as he made his way to the front of the class. When their wrists had touched she'd hidden her blushes by keeping her head bent low, concentrating on the coiling until she felt the heat in her cheeks dissipate as quickly as it had arrived.

She felt ridiculous – only their wrists had touched, this wasn't Victorian England for God's sake. How had something so innocent made her react like that? Was her irritation with Danny now making her respond differently to random scraps of attention from any passing male?

Sasha now stood at the front, soothingly addressing the class as if gently drawing back the curtains on a room of slumbering children

'OK potters,' the group exchanged pleased looks at their new name, 'before the clay begins to dry and while it still wants to play ball with us,' he smiled warmly, 'you now need to use your thumbs to smooth over the ridges between the coils, gently blend the coils together – however,' he paused dramatically, 'these are YOUR pots. How smooth and sleek you want the walls is up to you. You may want your pot to be like life itself: with all the lumps and bumps. You may want your pot to look raw, manhandled.'

Elliot theatrically raised an eyebrow. 'Ooh, now you're talking,' he said saucily, which raised a few chuckles.

Sasha continued, 'Just know that the thicker your piece, the more you're throwing yourself at the mercy of the kiln gods. Beware,' he growled, 'of damp, thick bottoms; they may seem dry, but moisture can lurk deep inside. If you touch them to your cheek—'

'Which cheek?' piped up Sheila.

'Your face will do,' said Sasha primly. 'If it feels cold, it's not really truly dry.'

The class lifted their coil pots and gingerly touched them to their cheeks.

'There may be pockets of moist air waiting to be turned to steam by the ferocious heat of the kiln.'

Everyone looked suitably alarmed.

'The kiln gods can be kind, but they can also be merciless.' He widened his eyes and in his best 'Here's Johnny' voice said, 'And that's when things get explosive!'

'I like a big bang,' said Elliot, just loudly enough for everyone to catch. Becky glared at him, but the class laughed and got to work.

The time was flying by and Louise was loving it. She had purposely chosen a workbench parallel to an occupied one, so Danny was forced to take the bench behind her. If he was in her eye-line he'd be constantly looking over to her for approval or to make her laugh.

Whether it was choosing restaurants, his outfit for a family wedding, or even booking holidays, Danny deferred to her. She knew it was a compliment that he trusted her judgement, but lately she'd started to resent it; she didn't want the pressure of always knowing best – being in charge was exhausting. They were supposed to be partners, but it felt to her as if he relied on her opinion so much he'd forgotten how to have one himself. She wished he could shoulder some of the responsibility for their lives together, then she could focus a bit on herself and her next move. She had to struggle free from this rut. Was the problem her life with him or her life at work? She needed space to decide. Coming to this class had felt like a chance to bring them closer as a couple by doing something together, whilst also allowing them both to find themselves a bit.

She pictured the bewildered look on his face if she tried to explain it to him. 'Hey, we need to reconnect with ourselves before we can truly reconnect together.' That wouldn't exactly be the encouragement he needed to attend the class. Instead she'd prom- ised him a romantic stroll home via the chippy.

She smoothed the inside walls of her pot, gently dragging the tip of her thumb along the grooves until they gave way to her touch and melted into each other.

Sasha addressed the room again, 'Remember potters: part of the skill is knowing when to stop.'

At the end of the lesson the class scraped their initials on the underside of their creations with their potter's needles, and left them to dry on the wide wooden shelves in the corner of the storeroom.

Everyone clocked the kiln squatting menacingly in the corner – Sasha's talk about kiln gods made them eye it cautiously, as if magical powers lurked behind its thick steel door.

Louise was scraping the clay from the tips of her tools when Sasha appeared by her bench – he had a habit of seemingly materialising out of thin air.

She concentrated on the guilty pleasure of feeling the still damp clay filling up and compacting in the space under her nails as she scraped.

'If a tidy bench is a tidy mind, yours must be immaculate,' said Sasha with a grin.

'What? Oh hi, *haha*, yes,' she said, scraping quicker with her nails. 'Well actually my mind isn't as clean as this . . .' she trailed off. 'Not that it's dirty, I didn't mean that. Obviously,' she ploughed on. She could feel Danny watching them chat, and glanced over her shoulder at him.

If Sasha noticed her blushing he didn't show it. Instead he said, 'Before you go, I just wanted to tell you that for a first coil build yours is really something. You're clearly naturally very artistic. Can't wait to see how you're going to glaze it.' He smiled encouragingly.

She was taken aback. 'Thank you. That means a lot,' she said.

'I actually did my degree in art about . . . ooh 150 years ago now, but never really put it to good use.' She started to untie her apron strings, just for something to do because suddenly, horrifyingly she felt like she might cry.

'Until now,' said Sasha gently. 'It's never too late Louise – I'm looking forward to watching your art shine through in the next few months,' and with that he was gone.

17

Sheila

Sheila was very pleased with her pot, and she'd had a lovely time. It was good to reconnect with some familiar faces from the estate rather than just communicating through the newsletter. It was nice to see Becky – she'd clearly put on a couple of pounds but it was heartening to see her looking so buoyed by the whole occasion, and Jack too. Recently at committee meetings he'd looked deflated since losing his wife, but tonight he seemed much chirpier. Sheila wondered if that lady Pearl had put a bit of the colour back in his cheeks, he looked rather taken with her. Once she and Jameela had found their coats and bid their farewells, they set off walking home.

'I really enjoyed that Sheila,' said Jameela, squeezing her arm. 'I'm so glad I looked in that newsletter – a cross trainer, and a pottery class, and of course,' she paused, 'a new friend.'

They walked on in a comfortable silence.

'Hey,' Sheila said suddenly, 'talking of that newsletter – you never did tell me about the dodgy fishmonger incident. I remember reading your warning to the other residents. How did he manage to dupe someone as clever as you?'

'Ah, yes, that.' Jameela looked embarrassed. 'Flattery. He was a bonnie lad, mid-twenties, ruddy cheeked and windswept, like he'd just docked his fishing boat at the end of the road. I wanted to make things up to Simon with a nice dinner party.' The evening breeze was picking up and they both pulled their coats tighter. 'Long story short – it was a perfect storm: I'm a sucker for a Geordie lilt, add to that a promise of some cut-price halibut, and,' she paused, 'he told me I reminded him of someone.'

Sheila stopped walking and cocked her head, studying Jameela's face to see if she could work it out. 'Who?' she asked.

Jameela looked mortified, but at least she was smiling. 'Nicole Scherzinger!'

Both women roared with laughter.

'I know, I know,' Jameela groaned. 'He said we could be sisters. Next thing I know his van was long gone and I'd paid £130 for about a tenner's worth of, according to Google images, river cobbler.'

The two women were still laughing as they rounded the corner onto Sheila's street.

'What's Martin up to tonight?' Jameela asked. 'Still working on that biscuit tin?'

Sheila groaned. 'He said he was going to pop to see his mum; he's worried about her, she's got no appetite, but she'll eat a little something to please him. He was also hoping to polish his bottles.'

'Pardon?' laughed Jameela.

Sheila looked at her in the half-light. 'He goes mudlarking in London with his friend Mike – they met on "Treasure finds" forum.'

Jameela laughed. 'Mudlarking though – I read a piece on that in the *Guardian*. It's all the rage, digging around by the river for gold.'

'Well, Martin's been doing it for years, he's found all sorts – nineteenth-century codd bottles with marble stoppers, dozens of coins, even a war medal.'

'Wow,' said Jameela.

'Yup.' Sheila smiled. 'He comes back from London having spent the weekend picking through seagull poo and wet wipes on the banks of the Thames a completely new man. Revitalised.'

Jameela laughed again. 'Aren't you ever tempted to join him? Pop to Harvey Nicks while you're down there?'

'Never been invited. I don't mind – I quite look forward to having the house to myself. I can do a face pack and wash down a weepy movie with a nice bottle of wine. You should join me next time.'

'I'd love to,' said Jameela.

Sheila glanced up and saw the light in the spare room snap off, the red brick around it suddenly dark. Martin must've been putting his bottles back.

The two friends said their goodbyes and, once through the door, Sheila kicked off her pumps – they were pinching her toes, but it was worth it to top off the outfit. Her orange jumpsuit had certainly received a few admiring glances.

'What are you up to?' she called up to Martin as he appeared at the top of the stairs with just a towel wrapped around his waist. Sheila squinted one eye, studying his face in mock suspicion.

He didn't laugh though – if anything he looked a little cross. 'Not up to anything thanks very much, Miss Marple,' he said. 'In fact you made me jump – I didn't hear you come in.' He looked hot and bothered, and his hair was wet.

Sheila smiled. 'Sorry, love, I was joking, I didn't mean to sneak in on you . . . have you had a bath? You look all pink.'

Martin pulled an indignant face. 'Yes. Well, no. A shower . . . I had a shower. Just now,' he said.

This weirdly stilted conversation was taking the sheen off Sheila's good mood, plus she was desperate for a brew.

'Why don't I put the kettle on while you get dry, you're dripping all over the carpet?' she said, and made her way to the kitchen.

18

Becky

'It was nice that Jack came – I barely recognised him all smartened up.' Becky was tidying away the mugs while Sasha swept the floor around each workbench, pea-sized bits of clay becoming fluffy with dust as they rolled along, gathering in a small pile.

Sasha didn't reply and kept sweeping, clearly lost in thought.

As Becky moved silently around the room she was careful not to clank the mugs together and break the spell. All evening she'd watched how his whole face lit up when he smiled. She loved the crinkles around his eyes when he grinned, which hinted at a life lived.

She liked the twinkle in his eye, as if he found everything a tiny bit amusing. But now he looked very serious and even more beautiful. His dark, jaw-length hair tumbled forward from its usual resting place behind his ear, making him look like a surfer dude in a teen photo story.

His chin had a hint of five o'clock shadow. Even his nose was handsome. Becky had always loved a strong nose, and his was big enough to stop him looking too conventionally handsome – he was imperfect to the perfect degree.

The way his hands gripped the broom handle made her stomach churn.

She barely knew the man, what was going on? Was this pure lust, or was it love at first sight, and today was just the beginning of their story? 'How did we meet? Well, it's a funny story actually – I was expecting a female teacher . . .'

'Sorry, what?' said Sasha. He stood by the pile of debris.

Now it was Becky's turn to snap out of it.

'Oh . . . I was just saying it was nice to see Jack here, all smart – he's usually in his caretaker overalls.'

'Oh yeah, yeah it was – he's a nice bloke.'

Sasha swept the pile into the dustpan and emptied it into the bin. 'I'm sorry,' he said sheepishly, 'I'm no good when I'm hungry and I'm absolutely starving.' He looked at his watch. 'Anywhere open now?'

Becky thought for a second. 'There's a nice Greek place on the precinct – should still be open if you fancy that?'

'Aye,' he said, 'perfect. Thanks.'

Sasha looked at her and grinned. *Jesus, that mouth*, she thought, *it's too much.*

'You must be hungry too?' said Sasha. 'Come on, let's lock up, and I'll treat you to some celebratory tzatziki?'

Stepping through the door of The Apollo was like falling back through time to the 1980s.

The tiny room was filled with tables and bistro-style rattan chairs that clustered around them like autograph hunters at a stage door.

On each table was a blue and white checked cloth and a candle wedged in an empty wine bottle – the neck of which sported a ruffled red cravat of dried wax. Plastic ivy climbed the white-washed walls, and the flickering candlelight made it cosy and welcoming.

The owner was called Apollo, like his dad and his grandad before him. It was the most senior Apollo who'd opened the restaurant when he'd arrived from Athens in the mid-seventies with, as family legend had it, nothing in his pocket but a few quid and his mother's lamb kleftiko recipe. All the generations were featured in faded photographs pinned to the 'Apollo wall of fame' next to the till. Smiling out in sepia tones were local rugby stars, a couple of newsreaders, and the quiz show host Henry Kelly – they all stood smiling in the friendly clutch of a grinning Apollo. The most recent was a snapshot of Jedward, flanking the current Apollo, smiling broadly.

Becky and Sasha were welcomed like old friends by Apollo and his wife Zoe.

They were a striking couple – both boasted ample chests straining under their white shirts, which accentuated their tanned arms, and glossy dark hair. Zoe's was clipped up in a messy bun, but some ringlets had escaped and fell loose around her face. They knew Becky because she sometimes brought Elliot in for lunch, but this handsome stranger was new to them. They exchanged curious glances, eyebrows working overtime.

Ignoring their protests that they weren't drinking, Zoe brought over a large carafe of red wine and plonked it down, alongside a couple of glasses and a tiny dish of fat green olives slick with oil and lemon juice and scattered with fresh oregano.

'On the house! *Yamas!*' she called, as she squeezed her buxom frame through the sea of tables and busied herself near the kitchen hatch.

'This is nice,' Sasha said, taking a long sip of his wine and sitting back in his chair. 'What a day!'

Becky thought he suddenly looked a little weather-beaten. 'It was great, I hope we didn't wear you out too much.'

He laughed. 'Och no,' he brushed off her concern, 'I loved it. They're a fantastic bunch of people, some real potential and some real characters too, especially the lady who'd clearly come straight from a high security jail,' he said.

They both laughed.

'Oh yes, Sheila. Bet you didn't know whether to give her some clay or ask where her warden was.'

They laughed again and drank more wine.

'Elliot is very funny,' he said, and she smiled proudly.

'I know. He's cheeky, but he's got such a sweet soul. He leaves in a few days to do a season in Ayia Napa.'

'Good for him – doing what?'

'Club PR – basically dragging tourists into bars to drink. He'll love it, though I feel sick at the thought of a summer without him. I've promised I will not sob till he's through departures.' She smiled and took another sip of her wine. 'Seeing as we weren't drinking, this is actually going down really well,' she said, nodding at her glass.

'Agreed.' He smiled that smile, touching his glass to hers. 'Think we deserve to toast our first day.'

Becky nodded, trying to tear her eyes from his mouth. 'Honestly though Sasha, I'm glad it went so well. You're a brilliant teacher.' She used one of the little cocktail sticks to spear an olive and popped it on her tongue. A tiny droplet of oil fell, landing on her top. 'Oh God!' She grabbed a napkin and rubbed at the greasy splodge, instantly spreading the stain. 'Oh well, at least I didn't wear my Gucci one, this is just Primarni. I'm so clumsy,' she gabbled. 'I get it from my mum. Her favourite saying was "a man on a galloping horse wouldn't notice", whenever one of us had slopped something down ourselves.'

Sasha laughed. 'It's a strong saying to be fair. Are you close?'

Becky's smile faded only slightly – she'd fielded this question many times, and over the years she'd perfected her tone to allow the information to be shared without making the asker feel bad for asking. But something about Sasha made her want to drop the barrier and just be honest.

'We were. Very close. Sadly she died, when I was twelve, stomach cancer.'

'Jesus,' Sasha said, studying her face. 'I can't imagine . . .'

'No, you can't,' she said quietly with a small grim laugh. 'It was . . . pretty much the end of my world. For a while at least. But,' and at this she looked him squarely in the eyes and held his gaze, feeling suddenly unafraid. Even talking about her mum made Becky feel strong, like she'd summoned her up by merely mentioning her. 'I feel like she's still with me in some ways. There are some things I do – how I hold my fork, how I laugh, how I spill things down myself,' she smiled, 'that are just "her". I can feel her in them. As if my movements are so similar to the way she moved they're echoes of her. That as long as I'm here – breathing, laughing, living – then she is too, somehow.'

Her eyes had filled with tears and she took a wobbly breath, blowing out through her lips, making the candle's flame dance and almost go out.

'Sorry – thirty years this October, and it still hurts like it was yesterday.' She sipped some more wine, her eyes now studying the flame.

'What was she like?' asked Sasha.

'Oh,' said Becky, 'she was a force of nature. Everyone loved her, everyone on the estate knew her. Walking down the street she'd be stopping chatting to everyone. She knew everyone's business, but only used that knowledge to help out – picking up people's prescriptions, minding the neighbour's dog, campaigning for more street lights. She was a grafter too. She was a cleaner, she even had shifts at the community centre.'

Becky had later learned from her nan that it was whilst hoovering at work that mum had felt that first twinge, across her tummy and back, which she tried to deny, but which eventually could no longer be silenced with paracetamol.

'I had no idea she was ill – she'd been a bit quiet, and I remember her legs had started to feel bonier when I lay my head on them when we cuddled up, watching telly. Then Mum's sister, Aunty Cath, came to stay, and they sat me down and told me Mum was very poorly.'

Sasha shook his head. 'Just beyond awful, I'm so sorry, you poor wee thing.'

Becky took a deep breath. 'She lasted three weeks at the hospice before slipping away. It's all a bit of a blur, there's snatches of memories: weeping visitors at the flat drinking all the tea, my best navy party dress that I wore to her funeral.' Becky stopped there and took a deep sip of wine

'I'm so sorry Becky,' said Sasha. 'What about your dad?'

'We've never been close,' she said, leaving out the more gory details – her dad turning up drunk to the wake in a skew-whiff tie and having to be shoved out through the fire exit by Uncle Charlie.

'Who looked after you after your mum died?' Sasha asked quietly.

'My nan. She was great, but you know, I was twelve with no mum, a useless dad . . . There was this ache in my stomach, like a pit of . . . emptiness. I thought it'd swallow me whole if I let it. I didn't think it'd ever go. It did eventually. It went when I held Elliot in my arms for the first time; I guess I didn't feel alone any more.'

Sasha was silent. Then he reached out and gently took her hand in his. 'You and Elliot are lucky to have each other. I think your mum would be so proud of the brilliant, bright woman you've become, Becky.'

Becky looked up and met his gaze.

'Souvlaki!' Apollo boomed, appearing from nowhere with a huge platter of griddled chicken and lamb skewers, chargrilled peppers, onions and tomatoes. 'And here, homemade today by my beautiful wife: warm pita.' Somehow he made all the dishes fit on the tiny table like crockery Tetris. 'This is your tzatziki, and here, your side of watermelon salad. Enjoy!'

An hour later, after settling the bill and enjoying bear hugs from Apollo and Zoe, who'd insisted they join them for a shot of sweet, floral mastika, Sasha and Becky left the restaurant. Becky felt suddenly giddy with tiredness and more than a little loose-limbed and lipped.

As they walked through the estate towards her little house on Harrison Lane, they turned into Watt Way. On seeing the name of the road, Sasha got the giggles, so much so he had to pause and rest his hands on his knees.

Becky loved the feeling of making him laugh – it felt like pulling off a magic trick. 'So of course, when we moved in, all my friends had a good giggle – 'Turn off what way? But what way is Watt Way?', and all that. I've heard them all. I reckon someone in town planning was working out their notice after a dispute, and rubber stamped the name as a way of cocking a snoot at their employers.'

Sasha stopped laughing and looked at her, attempting to straighten his face. 'Cocking a what?' he asked, head on one side.

'Snoot,' she said. 'Cocking a snoot,' only this time she sounded less confident.

This set Sasha off again. He made a snorting noise and his shoulders shook as he tried to hold in his laughter 'Isn't it snook?' he said.

Becky looked mock insulted. 'I have never used that phrase before, and have no idea where it came from, so either way, consider my snoot or snook well and truly cocked in your direction sir!' And with this she spun on her heel and flounced off along the dark street, the effect only slightly spoiled by her having to swerve to avoid a protruding privet bush.

Sasha caught up with her, still chuckling. 'I enjoyed that,' he said cheekily. 'It was an honour to be given a good snoot cocking by someone so beautiful.'

She laughed. God, they were actually quite drunk. The wine, the shot of liqueur, the tiredness, and then walking out into the fresh air had combined to make them both really rather squiffy.

'Play your cards right and I might do it again,' she said cheekily. 'Right, Watt Way, not a question, but the road is behind us and here we are, Harrison Lane and that there is my house.'

Sasha looked up at her neat red-brick terrace. 'OK, well, thank you,' he said. 'Thanks for a great day and a very fun dinner.'

Becky's heart started to thump. *Oh God,* she thought, *I want to kiss him.* She froze and, after what felt like a lifetime, leaned forward and instead pecked him on the cheek. 'Night,' she said chirpily, though her legs felt like liquid. *Just make it to the door Becky,* she told herself.

Sasha watched till she was inside, raising a hand silently as she pushed open the front door. She waved back and quietly clicked the door shut behind her so as not to wake Elliot. She needn't have worried – the hallway light was on and she could hear voices. *Oh gawd,* she thought, *I hope Elliot's mates aren't going to stay for long* – she had a busy day the next day and needed to get to sleep without a load of lads thumping around. But as she listened more intently she realised it wasn't lots of voices – just two. Elliot and someone else.

Some kind of instinct made her slow her movement towards the kitchen door. She strained to decipher the voices. There was a shift in the atmosphere, a cooling of the air, she could feel the tiny baby hairs on the back of her neck stand up. Danger. *Oh God no. It can't be.*

Her heart began to thump in her ears. Her instinct was to run, but her son was in there. She slowly moved towards the kitchen door, reached out her hand, watching it turn the handle. Taking a breath, she steeled herself and pushed open the door.

She saw Elliot first, and then turned to his companion knowing, from the look on Elliot's face, who it would be, that her worst fears were about to be confirmed. The room seemed to lurch a little.

'Hello Becks.'

It was her ex, Tony.

19

Becky

Despite his half smile, Becky could sense that Tony was braced – the forced casualness of his tone belied his nervousness at her reaction.

Becky turned to Elliot and felt the world shrink until she could focus only on her son's face. The colour must have seeped from her cheeks, as Elliot's voice sounded strained. 'Mum, are you OK? Maybe sit down . . .' Was he speaking underwater? No, she didn't want to sit down. She didn't want to be in a lowly position. Not in front of Tony – her abuser, her tormentor, the cloud that cast the longest shadow over her life. Here he was in front of her, instead of in prison, where he should have been rotting for another year at least. Another year of recovery, of building her resolve, of preparing herself for his release. He absolutely should not be here, in her kitchen. On the floor, at his feet, was a canvas sports bag.

At last she found her voice. 'What's going on?'

Tony cleared his throat. 'All right Becks. I know it's not ideal.'

'Not ideal?' Becky whispered. 'Not ideal?' It would've been funny if it weren't so tragic. 'You can say that again. We were starting to move on from the wasteland you left in your wake . . . the heartache – the lies.' She shuddered. 'The violence.'

'Mum.' Elliot came towards her.

'No,' she said, shaking her head, 'I can't pretend Elliot – he has to go, he can't be here, we were doing so well.' The tears burnt her throat with the effort of forcing them back.

'Come on Becks, it's not for long,' Tony said to the floor. 'I'm desperate. I'm out as part of a new pilot scheme, I've got an ankle tag on, I have to behave.' He twisted his foot towards her, the grey plastic band above his sock. 'Mum won't have me, not yet. I just need to prove to her I've changed.'

Becky snorted 'Right. You've changed have you?' He looked at her sharply then, a brightness in his eyes – the old glint never far below the surface. He bit his lip and she saw him flex his fingers against the work surface as if preventing them from curling into a fist or reaching out to grab her hair.

Becky wasn't stupid – she knew even with Elliot there she wasn't safe from Tony's temper. She knew how quickly he could snap. She suddenly felt very tired.

Tony softened his tone again. 'Just a few days Becks, please. No longer than a week. Then I'll be gone.'

Becky knew if she said no, both her and Elliot wouldn't be a match for Tony. They wouldn't be able to physically throw him out, and she had no appetite for a drama. She didn't want the neighbours' net curtains twitching as the street was bathed in blue lights – she'd been there too many times before. The only thing she could do was let him stay and pray his mum or some other mug took pity on him sooner rather than later.

She looked to Elliot, whose tiny shrug said, 'What choice do we have?'

'A week,' she said. 'You can have the sofa, but then I need you gone Tony, I mean it.'

A little while later she was changing for bed when she heard a small knock on her bedroom door. She tensed and clutched a towel to her.

'It's me Mum,' said Elliot, poking his head around the door. 'Can I come in?'

Becky put down the towel, furious that she wouldn't be able to breathe in her own home until Tony was gone.

'Course sweetheart.' She put on her pyjama top as Elliot perched on the bed, smoothing a wrinkle in the sheet.

'I'm not going,' he said finally, looking up at Becky.

'Not going where?' Then she realised. 'Oh no Elliot. You're not giving up Ayia Napa. No way. It'll do you the world of good to get away, get some sunshine, earn cash – you need to go and have some adventures.'

His eyes brimmed with tears. 'How can I? I can't leave you here with him. We can't trust him, you won't be safe.'

'Elliot,' she spoke firmly now, taking his face in her hands, 'listen to me. I will not let that man in there ruin one more thing for you. I will be OK. You are going, understand? I don't need you to look after me. It'll break my heart if you give up this chance.' She squished his cheeks gently to make him smile. 'I love you for looking out for me, don't ever stop being so bloody lovely,' and she pulled him into a hug before he could spot her own tears.

20

Jameela

Jameela loved running in the spring, ducking down underneath overhanging blossom, the white velvety petals tickling her bare shoulders. This morning she'd been woken by the sun streaming in, the sky already a soft pale blue by 5 a.m., so she'd got up and left nice and early for her morning run before work.

She arrived home on a wave of endorphins – just in time to see the rear of Simon's navy blue Golf pull away from the house.

She raised her hand in a half-wave, but he was gone.

If she was the cynical sort, she might think he'd timed his visit to coincide with her run – he knew she was a creature of habit.

Why had he been around? She stretched out her legs under the car port and tried to focus on steadying her breathing.

It'd been over a fortnight since he'd left, and they hadn't spoken – just exchanged a few frosty texts.

He'd said he wanted space, so she was giving it to him – he was welcome to it.

She was surprised by how little she missed him. She'd enjoyed her own company, and the house had been tidy and calm. She found she slept better without his bony ankles starfished out on the bed.

She let herself in to the house and noticed at once that the pan drawer was ever so slightly ajar. Jameela walked over slowly as if trying not to disturb an intruder, and, as she opened the drawer fully, she gasped. Some of the bloody Le Creuset pans were gone. 'Wanker!' she shouted, surprising herself. 'Bloody selfish grabby pan wanker!' She enjoyed the release of shouting swear words in the kitchen before breakfast.

The pans had been a wedding gift. He'd taken three of the set of six, but they belonged here, at their home. She wondered briefly if there had ever been a custody fight over a non-stick wok before.

Clearly Simon still needed space and for a while to come – it seemed as if he was setting up home at the pokey flat above his dentist's practice rather than just using it to crash in.

She'd presumed he'd be surviving on Pot Noodles for a week before coming home to clear the air.

Was he taking the pans because he was planning on entertaining? A romantic dinner for two perhaps? The thought made her feel sick, and she shooed it away. Still, she sighed with relief to see that the napkins and the table runner were still in the linen drawer.

Ten minutes later she knew Simon might never come back. He'd taken his smart suit, all his trainers, a framed photograph of his parents in the seventies, and his passport. As she got herself ready for work she noticed other little things that were gone – his shower radio, his tennis racquet, and sunglasses. Tiny gaps in their home that were once Simon-shaped. She felt strangely calm – a weird kind of adrenaline, like the thrill of picking off a scab and it hurting just enough to still be pleasurable. She felt almost excited, until she thought about her mum.

It was bad enough Jameela marrying a non-Hindu white boy in the first place, but divorcing one would be a double blow for the family's reputation.

Jameela knew the one person who'd understand – Reju. Her fingers lingered for a moment over her sister's name on her phone screen . . . maybe now she'd be ready to talk? Clearly not – after two rings it went straight to voicemail. Jameela winced, stung by the rejection. Instead she called Sheila.

An hour later Sheila and Jameela were sitting at a small glass table in The Coffee Place.

'Well this is very nice. Unexpected, but very nice,' said Sheila, blowing delicately at the froth on her cappuccino and looking around at the smart café, with its bare bulbs and exposed brickwork.

'Yes, I was hoping I could tempt you to a quick breakfast before work.' Jameela smiled

'Absolutely – you had me at "croissant". Anyway it won't do April any harm to start without me at the food bank. What's going on then?'

'Oh you know, the usual,' replied Jameela softly. 'Still estranged from my sister, who also happened to be my best friend, and I still have an AWOL husband who seems to have moved out completely now.'

'Ooh Jameela, I'm sorry. What actually happened with you two?'

'Oh, I don't know; well I do, but it's complicated. "Death by a thousand cuts" I guess – the last few years have taken their toll on us, and the last few months have been particularly miserable. The thousandth cut was when I got drunk at his belated birthday dinner party and – according to him – made a fool out of myself and him.'

'It can't have been that bad? You probably needed to let off a bit of steam after the time you've had,' Sheila said, tearing off a chunk of croissant and popping it into her mouth.

'Yes, I guess, but I went a little overboard.' Jameela cringed as she remembered the worried glances exchanged by the other couples at the dinner, as she downed her drinks and got louder and louder. She was already smarting after Simon had rejected her advances earlier that evening before the guests had arrived, and dousing her anger with numerous glasses of wine hadn't quenched the flames, but had instead reignited her resentment.

'I was in a bit of a mess. Simon had told me before the dinner that he never knew which Jameela he was going to get when he came in from work, whether I'd be weeping, chirpy, quiet, or, God forbid,' she widened her eyes in mock horror, 'wanting physical affection. He said the whole thing was "draining". All throughout dinner that word kept sliding into my thoughts.'

Sheila put her cup down and looked at Jameela. 'You know what? You are an incredibly bright, brilliant young woman, but you've had a tough time, and for him to say that your reaction to so much heartache is "draining" is, if you don't mind me saying, more than a little cruel.'

Jameela felt tears prick at her eyes. It was reassuring to be told it wasn't all her fault.

'Thank you Sheila, it's so helpful to hear that.' Jameela smiled and rolled her eyes. 'I know it sounds mad, but the week before I'd spotted a long hair on the floor of the bathroom and, in my darker moments, I'd convinced myself that it belonged to Belle – Simon's assistant at work. What with the "draining" comment and a few drinks, one hair had snowballed in my mind into a full-blown affair by the end of the evening.'

Jameela remembered the moment in little flashbacks – Simon and his fellow dentist friend had been having a work chat: 'Good assistants are hard to find and even harder to keep. Do you still have . . .'

And Jameela had interjected before Simon could answer, 'Belle.' She remembered now with fresh embarrassment the slight slur in her voice. 'He definitely still has Belle.' Simon had looked up then, confused. 'And I'm starting to suspect he literally HAS Belle, behind my back,' she'd said, and smiled at him darkly.

Sheila drained her coffee cup. 'Go on.'

Jameela took a breath. 'At the end of the meal, I drunkenly pointed out to our close friends that I couldn't blame Simon for having an affair with Belle, as her name was French for "beautiful" and that she WAS beautiful, if a little dumpy. I seem to remember I shouted the word "dumpy".'

'Oh Jameela,' Sheila whispered, 'what did Simon do?'

'He said I was making an idiot of myself – I said at least it made a change from me being draining.' She studied her nails, remembering how she'd accidentally smashed a glass as she'd lurched to her feet; snapshots again of their friends looking horrified, unable to tear their eyes from the drama, like rubberneckers passing a pile-up. Her friend Vic trying to steer her through the scattered glass shards on the floor. 'Fuck you Simon,' had been her parting shot – the edge taken away by a drunken hiccup as she swayed out of the room.

'It's all too mortifying – I was really out of control,' she said now.

'You were grieving,' Sheila said, putting her hand on Jameela's wrist. 'You still are. Grief does strange things to people.'

'Yeah, so does two bottles of Sauvignon Blanc and a shot of vanilla vodka,' Jameela laughed grimly. 'Anyway the next morning he went, saying he needed space, that it had been the last straw.'

Sheila spoke gently, 'Well you can't leave things like this – you two need to talk.'

'I know. But I need to work out what I want – if I even want Simon back, if things are worth saving. And the only person who can help me, who knows me better than anyone in the world, is my sister Reju, but she's still not speaking to me. I need her help if I'm going to try to fix this.'

21

Becky

On Harrison Lane Tony was watching morning telly whilst using the corner of a lottery ticket to pick his teeth. His body, lithe like a polecat, was draped along the sofa. A single duvet and pillow rolled in a ball and stashed down the side.

'So,' Becky began brightly, 'it's been three days now, Tony. Have you spoken to your mum?'

Tony didn't seem to hear, he was engrossed in Phil and Holly chatting to a psychic about her celebrity contact list in the afterlife. Becky could feel her pulse quicken as she worked out how best to proceed. On the plus side, Tony was currently sober and was on best behaviour in order to keep his place on the sofa.

'She's barmy this one.' He grinned, not taking his eyes from the screen. 'Reckons she can chat to Bowie and near enough has Sinatra on speed dial.' He chuckled to himself and carefully inspected the shred of pale bacon he'd extracted from his teeth. The bacon was now stuck on the gummy corner of the ticket. He saw Becky looking at the ticket in disgust. 'Don't worry, it's last week's, my numbers didn't come in – but when they do, I'll take you away from all this,' he gesticulated around the room as if making a speech to a crowd.

'I'm more interested in when you're gonna take yourself away from all this? I'm quite happy here . . . with all this.' She aped his gesture. She knew she was pushing her luck with his quick temper – but it seemed the two-year respite from him had made her bold.

Tony's conviction for numerous offences (a tatty list ranging from handling stolen goods, to possession of cocaine, to driving whilst disqualified, to assault – the latter happening in the bookies during a fight over a fruit machine) had resulted in him being detained at Her Majesty's pleasure for a five-year sentence.

The initial arrest for assault had led to his unravelling: a search warrant and a quick look around his bedroom at his mum's flat, and all the other charges quickly fell into place. The idiot had even driven illegally to the bookies, and had shouted, 'What about my car?' as he was escorted bloody-nosed to the police van – handing them another charge on a plate. Turns out though, that good behaviour in an already over-populated prison earns you early release with an ankle tag and a strict curfew.

The tag was still clipped just above his Reebok sports sock on his ankle, now draped over Becky's sofa.

Tony looked at Becky at last and smiled thinly. 'I told you. Three days, then I can move into my mate's. Mum won't have me back thanks to the police.'

Classic Tony; he wasn't accountable, of course, it was the police's fault – parking three squad cars outside, giving all the neighbours a good show, turning his mum's flat upside down. It took minutes to find the wraps of coke, the iPhones, laptops, and expensive watches, but according to Tony's mum, 'Those minutes took years off me.' She didn't know how she'd ever show her face at bingo again.

Naturally he was innocent – he was just holding the gear for a mate. Turns out that mate now owed him big time for not grassing him up and had offered Tony the use of his place while he and his missus went to their villa in Thailand for a few months to work on their 'import/export business'. Becky presumed that translated roughly as drug smuggling.

Becky sighed and felt her shoulders sag. Short of manhandling him out of there, which wasn't going to happen, she felt she had little choice but to keep her head down and get through the next few days.

Thank God Elliot had got off to Ayia Napa. She checked her watch – he'd be landing in the sunshine any minute now.

Elliot's trip had coincided beautifully with Tony turning up. Neither would've expected a cosy father and son reunion.

When she'd arrived home after the first pottery class she'd clearly seen the look in Elliot's eyes – as if he was trapped in a room with a snake and relieved to see her, but scared for his mum and what this might mean.

Growing up, Elliot had learned to dull down his natural brightness in front of Tony. It was a survival skill, like an animal using camouflage. When Tony wasn't on the scene, Elliot fizzed with energy and confidence.

Becky was so proud of her son. At school he was as popular with the girls as he was with the boys. He had a big heart and a sharp tongue, wittily batting away any snide remarks about his camper moments.

Arriving home from school to Tony, Becky knew Elliot shed his flamboyancy along with his blazer, leaving both in the hallway, ready to be put back on the next morning.

Becky knew what he was doing because he'd learned it from her, and the guilt of that killed her. The smaller Elliot made himself, the less chance Tony would notice him.

Depending on his mood and drink intake, Tony would either grab Elliot in an awkward rough and tumble wrestle, wrap him in a boozy emotional hug, or hungover, snipe at him for any minor misdemeanour. Elliot escaped by melting away into his bedroom, only emerging for his tea when Becky was back from work. Luckily Tony wasn't around for most of Elliot's late teens – he was either lying low having upset someone bigger than him, in prison, or round at his latest girlfriend's.

It seemed their conversation was now over. Tony had turned back to the telly and was watching a chef roll pork belly in a huge tray of herbs. Becky had a fleeting fantasy of doing the same to Tony, but he'd be too stringy and rotten.

Instead of cannibalising him, she clung to the hope that in a few days he would be gone. She'd enjoyed two years of freedom and hopefully she'd soon be able to breathe again when he left.

She picked up his empty coffee mugs and put them in the sink, teeth gritted. She felt drained, and a familiar misery had settled over her bones. The sheen had really been taken off the whole pottery thing. That first lesson would always be linked in her mind to Tony turning up. Any excitement she felt about Sasha had been squashed back down, a defence mechanism no doubt. How could she even think about a potential fresh start with a lovely new man, when her past had come back to haunt her in the shape of the cretin currently slouched on her sofa? She sighed wearily, grabbed her keys, and set off for work.

22

Sheila

After hugging Jameela goodbye, Sheila had gone on to the food bank where she found the front door unlocked but no sign of her co-volunteer.

'April?' she shouted.

Silence.

The lights were on in the front area of the former sports shop; there was the usual huge mural of Wayne Rooney screaming down at her, mid-goal celebration, but there was no April.

'What have you done with her Wayne?' Sheila asked the footballer out loud. The sound of her voice in the empty space spooked her.

Sheila was blessed with a fertile imagination and immediately pictured April bound and gagged in the stockroom, and all the food gone. But who would stage such an audacious robbery for the sake of some Super Noodles and tinned carrots? Sheila grabbed a can of fly spray from under the till desk to use as a weapon, and crept towards the stockroom. But as she did, she heard a snuffling from inside the loo. The door swung open and out came April, startled by Sheila, who was holding the can at arm's length like a cop holding a taser.

'Bloody hell Sheila! What are you doing?'

Sheila looked at her colleague, streams of blue mascara staining her cheeks, and lowered the fly spray.

'I've been shouting for you! Why didn't you answer? Why have you been crying?'

'It's Custard,' April said, a small sob bubbling up. For a second Sheila was confused and thought April was talking about stock. 'He's gone.'

'Oh no, sweetheart, I'm sorry.' Custard was April's ancient cat – older than God's dog, so it wasn't a shock he'd finally expired. 'He had a great life with you April – he knew he was loved.'

'What? No, he's not dead.' April blew her nose noisily on an already drenched scrap of loo roll. 'He's missing, for the fourth night in a row. This is out of character Sheila. I thought for the first couple of nights he'd found a new girlfriend but now I'm very worried. I was up till 2 a.m. stapling posters to trees.'

Sheila put her hand on her friend's shoulder. 'Well then, there you go. I'm sure someone will be in touch soon.'

'I hope so Sheila. I couldn't afford to offer a cash reward, so I put on the poster "a hand reading or tarot session for information leading to his safe return".'

Sheila slapped away a smirk before it reached her lips; April fancied herself as a bit of a mystic. If she really could see into the future you'd think she'd have seen Custard's departure coming. Sheila nodded supportively. 'Well done love.'

Throughout the morning, April kept bursting into tears. She was constantly checking her phone for missed calls which never came.

Sheila wasn't much of an animal person, so struggled to conjure up much empathy or sympathy – in fact she felt thoroughly pathy-free. By lunchtime Sheila changed tack and thought it best to help April manage her expectations. 'Maybe Custard has found a new home?' she offered, or, 'Perhaps he's "gone off to die" – don't animals do that in the wild so their carcasses don't attract scavengers to the herd?' She'd not actually intended to say the bit about carcasses out loud. Either way, whatever she said set April off again, who honked like a goose as she sobbed. April had a big cry for a small woman, each honk enough to make her fox-coloured curls tremble, her lipsticked mouth turned down at the corners like a toddler had drawn it on in pink crayon.

Sheila started to lose patience; April's honking was attracting curious glances from the users of the food bank, who clearly already had enough to worry about.

'You shouldn't have come in to work love,' Sheila said, but April shook her head and noisily blew her nose.

'No, Custard wouldn't want me to let people down,' she murmured.

Sheila thought it was unlikely an elderly overweight cat would give two hoots about the morals of not turning up for a volunteering shift, but kept schtum and instead patted April's shoulder, one eye on the donation bags that still needed sorting.

Sheila was relieved when 2 p.m eventually rolled around. She made a sharp exit in time to catch the bus to Tull Avenue, crossed over Watt Way and onto Harrison lane. As she passed Becky's house she heard the door open and slam shut. She knew it wouldn't be Becky, as she'd be at work by now. Sheila prided herself on being community-minded and knowing the comings and goings of most of the residents of her street.

It couldn't be Elliot – she'd bumped into him in town last week buying a new wheelie bag – he'd be abroad by now, Ayia Napa she recalled. Whoever it was was heading away from her towards Watt Way. Sheila's Neighbourhood Watch training kicked in, she got out her phone and, too late to take a clear photo of the man, instead discreetly recorded a voice note, pausing to watch the retreating figure. '14.25, suspect white male. Height, similar to Martin. Dark hair, unwashed. Build, skinny.' She kept her eye on the man, who seemed to slink rather than walk, keeping close to the shadows. Sheila clocked the security tag around his ankle as he retreated into the distance. She pursed her lips in disapproval. 'Tagged. Navy hoody, grey joggers.' At this point the man looked back over his shoulder and straight at Sheila. He grinned and nodded once. Sheila gasped and looked skywards as if fascinated by a passing cloud; she held her breath, and when she looked back, he'd disappeared around the corner onto Watt Way. She raised her phone to her lips again and breathlessly said, 'Suspect confirmed. Tony.'

He's back then, she thought, *blown in like a toxic cloud*. She did some quick maths. Wasn't he supposed to be in prison for another year at least? Poor Becky. She quickened her step, excited to feed this little nugget to Martin when she got home.

Approaching the end of the row of houses closest to hers, Sheila heard pounding music and scanned the windows to work out the culprit. She liked music – she'd seen Michael Ball perform five times after all – but no one needed to play it so loud. She realised with surprise it was coming from the upstairs bedroom of number 12, her and Martin's house.

It was Queen's 'Don't Stop Me Now', and as she put the key in the door she heard Martin singing out of tune '. . . I'm burning through the sky yeah – 200 degrees . . .' The door was sticking in the frame, so she gave it a good old shove and almost fell through the doorway and onto the mat, and there was Martin, roll-on deodorant as a mic, giving it the full Freddie Mercury at the top of the stairs.

'You're back!' he shouted over the music. He looked pleased to see her. 'Hang on!' he shouted, and ran to turn down the music that was booming out from their son Oliver's old stereo in the spare room. He returned and out tumbled a jumble of words. 'My little pickled cockle! I have sad news,' he grinned excitedly, 'I must depart these shores!'

Sheila forced a smile – she was more than a little irritated that her titbit about Tony's surprise return had been pushed onto the back burner by Martin's dramatics.

'I've nearly packed,' he waggled the deodorant, 'I'm off to London, we've nothing planned this weekend, and I thought you'd understand. A mudlarking trip. Mike called, he was in a right state, could barely get his words out.' Sheila wished Martin could be struck down with the same difficulty so she could get a word in edgeways, but he was having no such trouble. 'Turns out there's a magnificent tide, a "once in every forty years" event. Mike reckons she'll be churning out untold treasure long-hidden beneath her skirts,' he said, clearly enjoying the poetic sounding phrasing.

'She?' said Sheila.

'The Thames!' smiled Martin.

'Right. When exactly are you going Martin?'

'I'm meeting Mike at Piccadilly, and I've ordered a cab. I've chilled a nice Sancerre for you, and there's a tagine defrosting in the fridge so you're all set.' He spoke more quietly now. 'You don't mind do you my angel? I'm so lucky to have someone as understanding as you.'

Sheila softened at the compliment and the thought of the wine. There was a new Tom Hanks film she wanted to watch, so already her night alone was taking shape.

'Yes you are lucky. But so am I, to have you, there could be worse things for you to be fanatical about than trudging through manky seaweed looking for treasure. Go on, off you go, I'll survive.' Official blessing granted, Sheila was rewarded with a wet smacker on the cheek, which she discreetly patted dry with a tea towel once out of sight in the kitchen.

She made a cuppa while Martin grabbed the last of his things.

*

As the front door slammed ten minutes later, even the walls seemed to breathe a sigh of relief. Martin had been like a whirlwind, but now the house was quiet.

Ever since the cross trainer had gone, Sheila had meant to clean up the spare room. *Who knows*, she thought, *one day it might be my own pottery studio.*

After she'd drunk her tea, inspired by Martin 'rocking out', she grabbed her *Best of Michael Ball* CD, 'live from the Royal Albert Hall', and took it with her as she lugged the vacuum cleaner upstairs.

Sheila felt a sudden strange sensation as she pushed open the door to the spare room – as if there was something horrible in there. Maybe a pigeon had got in through an open window and was going to fly up into her face? She was being silly – Martin had been in there minutes ago. Still, she couldn't help holding her breath and bracing herself a little as she swung the door open.

She needn't have worried – the room looked as it always did: oatmeal carpets, pale beige walls. Without the cross trainer, the room seemed a lot bigger. 'Come on Michael,' she said, and carefully placed the CD in the little tray and skipped to the third song, his cover of 'Love On The Rocks' – her favourite. The applause faded, 'Love on the rocks, ain't no surprise,' Michael sang, 'pour me a drink, I'll tell you some lies.' Sheila felt goosebumps all up her arms.

She surveyed the room – there was still a pile of clothes on the bed where she'd shoved them when Jameela was around looking at the cross trainer. She gathered them up in one arm and with her other swung open the wardrobe door in one smooth motion. Immediately something caught her eye on the floor of the wardrobe. Black, silky, with a lace trim. Knickers, but not hers.

She froze. Only her eyes moved as she drank in every detail of the pants. They looked expensive. She stared, like one might stare at a partly concealed mine – scared to move, sure of its potential

devastation. Time slowed as her mind raced through the possibilities as to why there'd be another woman's pants in her house,
willing it to be some hilarious mix-up that would become family
legend, a story to be told and re-told at get-togethers. Her son
Oliver would start: 'Dad – remember knicker-gate? When Mum
found Charlotte's pants in my old room and thought you had a
fancy woman?'

Sheila almost smiled at the thought, but she knew it wasn't
possible. Oliver and his girlfriend hadn't been around for weeks,
and hadn't stayed over since Boxing Day. Sheila had been looking
in that very wardrobe yesterday, trying to find the pashmina April
had asked to borrow. 'I gave you my heart, I gave you my soul . . .'
Michael was still singing. She pressed Stop on the stereo.

She gingerly picked the knickers up by the black label. In swirly
scarlet lettering it said, 'Ruby Red's UK size 10'.

She wanted to get rid of them, burn them or fold them away
into a corner of her mind. If there'd been a rubbish shoot she
would've chucked them down there. Instead she slipped them into
the pocket of an old paisley quilted jacket she was thinking of
sending to charity. Maybe she'd send it, pants and all.

No, the knickers were evidence, and she'd need them to confront
Martin. She pictured her husband. His kind eyes, his unsure smile,
as if he'd borrowed someone else's mouth and was still getting the
hang of how to use it. With his slender build and round shoulders
he was hardly a thrusting Adonis. Was he really capable of being
so cruel and conniving to have an affair? It seemed he was.

The shock was starting to kick in. Sheila closed the door of
the wardrobe with a shaking hand. She studied her reflection
in the mirror on the outside of the door. Was this what a scorned
woman looked like? Would the trauma and betrayal ravage her
face? Would her bitterness consume her and suck the plumpness
from her cheeks?

April at the food bank had an aunt who'd wasted away and died of a broken heart just weeks after her husband left her for the village post mistress. The death certificate said she'd suffered a stroke, but, as April said, everyone knew the real reason.

Sheila turned to the side and smoothed down her shirt – it was blue gingham with a little white fringe across the collar bone, and this morning she thought it looked cute in a cowgirl kinda way, but through her new eyes it looked frumpy.

What was she like – the other woman? Had Martin succumbed to a midlife crisis and become a living breathing stereotype – falling for someone slimmer (the size 10 proved that) and younger than her? Maybe he hadn't fallen though? Maybe it was just a trip, a stumble. She could probably get over a one-night stand. *Oh God*, thought Sheila, *I don't know if I can bear the humiliation.* She gulped back a sob. And what were the pants doing here? Had the hussy been in her house, here in their lovely home?

She left the cleaning stuff where it was and slowly came down the stairs – her legs weak. It'd probably suit Martin if she fell and broke her neck, he could move that bitch in. She pictured her own funeral, his new 'friend' in a sexy black bodycon dress, veil and stilettos, 'supporting' Martin. The next day, he'd bin all of Sheila's things and in doing so, find the pants in the padded paisley jacket and know Sheila knew. Sheila, for her part, would do her very best to haunt them both.

She imagined all of this as she descended the stairs, then on the bottom step, she shook the thoughts from her head. She knew what she had to do first. She headed into the kitchen, opened the wine and poured a large glass. She needed to think, but for now, she needed to drink.

23

Becky

Becky enjoyed the feel of the sun on the back of her neck as she unlocked the community centre, the warmth soothing the knots that had settled there since Tony had turned up like a bad penny exactly a week before. Since then she'd only seen Sasha once. He had swung by to fire the dried coil pots from the first lesson, but she'd pretended to be busy on the phone in her office, waving but rolling her eyes as if on a long and boring call. He'd grimaced and waved back. Once the coast was clear, she'd said her goodbyes to the speaking clock and sneaked out on some, as she'd told herself, crucial errands.

She had continued to avoid Sasha all week, scared that the sadness that coated her skin like soot whenever Tony was on the scene would rub off on her shiny new friendship with him, smudging its brightness.

There was no avoiding him now though, as it was class day. As if on cue she heard a voice behind her.

'Beautiful day for a bit of creating don't you think?'

Becky spun to see Sasha, bathed in sunlight like a heavenly apparition in denim.

'You're keen,' she said, checking her watch. 'You're exactly eleven hours early.' She dipped her head away, avoiding eye contact so he couldn't see the weariness she felt was smeared all over her face.

'Early bird and all that,' he replied, as she swung open the door and hurried along the corridor. 'I've got a few bits to do. Plus,' he quickened his stride to keep up, 'I thought I'd catch you for one of your famously delicious brews before you get too busy.'

'Not a problem,' she said, turning briskly into the kitchen, hating herself for sounding so businesslike.

'Is everything OK Becky?' Sasha looked puzzled and a little hurt. 'I've not annoyed you have I?'

Becky got two cups out of the cupboard.

What could she say? 'No, my ex has annoyed me 'cos I really like you and want to snog your face till it aches, but I can't do that till I'm rid of him because his mere presence gives everything a sour taste including my blossoming crush on you. That's what's annoyed me'?

Instead she turned to him. 'I've just got a lot on that's all. Right, tea? Remind me, sugar?'

'Nope. I'm sweet enough,' replied Sasha, handing her the carton of milk.

Yes you are, Becky thought miserably.

The morning flew by – keeping up the pretence of being busy meant that Becky was getting loads done so when she heard a theatrical clearing of the throat and peeped around a mountain of paperwork to see Sasha there with takeaway coffees and sandwiches she couldn't help break into a broad grin.

'The way to a woman's heart is through a panini,' he said with a pseudo-seductive waggle of the eyebrows.

'I missed you this week,' he said as they ate their sandwiches. 'I wanted you to come crack the kiln with me.'

'I've had worse offers,' she smiled, then faltered. 'What do you mean, crack it? It's not actually cracked is it? If there's been some damage . . .'

'No no no, don't worry!' Sasha held up his hands. 'Once the kiln had cooled I opened the door a tiny crack – so we "crack" the kiln – allowing in a rush of cool air to collide with the heat could be catastrophic for the pots and cause dunting.'

'Right,' said Becky slowly. 'Dunting – isn't that a village in Kent?'

Sasha laughed. 'Dunting is when weak areas of a pot fracture with the shock of the sudden temperature change. Stick with me kiddo – you'll learn a lot.'

'Yeah, I'm beginning to realise that,' she said, sipping the last of her coffee. 'Well maybe we can crack the kiln together another time. So have you seen the coil pots? How are they looking?'

'Come see.'

Becky felt a wave of trepidation as they reached the storeroom. She hoped the pots had survived – during the first session Sasha spoke reverentially about the 'kiln gods' and their power. If all that remained was a pile of rubble it'd be a real bash to the fledgling potters' enthusiasm.

The faint smell of damp in the stockroom had been replaced by a baked, earthy smell. 'I cracked this a few days ago and fully opened it yesterday – I looked for you, but Jack said you'd gone to the cash and carry.'

Becky smiled ruefully. 'Teabags. Biscuits. Low on stock.'

Sasha nodded thoughtfully.

Becky felt silly – was he laughing at her? Maybe she was being paranoid – only she knew that there were already enough bags in the kitchen to fill an olympic swimming pool with tea.

All defensiveness washed away as Sasha signalled her to creep closer and peer into the kiln. Becky gasped gently.

Inside the small pots stood proudly and each one seemed to be in one piece.

'It's kinda magical,' she said, looking at him. 'Everything looks OK?'

'Yup,' he grinned. 'These beauties have survived their biscuit firing at 1001 degrees – I'm superstitious.' He smiled, looking a bit embarrassed 'I always add one on for luck.'

They unloaded the kiln – Sasha retrieving the pots and handing them to Becky, who tried not to twitch every time his fingers brushed against hers. Sexual tension plus transporting breakable goods was a potentially disastrous combination. She carefully placed the finished pots on wooden boards ready to be displayed in the main room. Becky held her breath as she handled each pot.

'It feels such a responsibility,' she breathed, 'like I'm holding treasure.'

He straightened up and moved closer to her so he was right by her side, hips almost touching, studying the pot she held. He smelled of soap and clay.

'To the potters it is their treasure, you can't put a price on your first pot, so they're literally priceless.'

'God you're cheesy,' she laughed.

'I know right?' he said. 'What can I say, pots bring out my inner philosopher. My inner cheese. *Urgh*, that came out sounding weirder than it did in my head.'

'Yeah it really did.' She grimaced, surprised to see a sweet blush develop high on his cheeks. 'I tease, but really I love how passionate you are, it's what makes you a great teacher.'

'Yeah well, I do my best.'

'Was it always your dream to teach?' she asked, studying the pots more closely.

'Not so much the teaching, that came later, born of necessity. I'd basically grown up watching my dad work every hour God sent as a painter at the shipyard in Leith then when that went, as a painter and decorator. He hated it towards the end, and he was always knackered. That spurred me on – I wanted to do something I loved.' He sniffed away the sentiment. 'Isn't that the dream? To turn your hobby or your passion into your work?' Becky nodded, and couldn't help thinking of her own wasted ambition to join the police force, to serve and protect. 'Plus,' Sasha smiled, 'I get to meet interesting people – mysterious blondes who make a good brew.'

Becky leaned into him, nudging him gently. She couldn't help noticing he felt toned under his T-shirt. Even his ribs were sexy.

'I was hooked the first time I tried pottery at school, and liked the thought of being an artist – popstars and royalty paying millions for my pieces – but I quickly found out it wasn't as easy as that.' He sighed. 'I sold quite a few pieces in LA at craft fairs, but that wasn't enough to keep me in spirulina smoothies over there, so I fell into teaching.'

'Right,' she said, 'all sounds pretty cool though – LA and all that.'

'Yeah, it was fun, but I was skint. I never met a fat artist over there, put it that way. Though to be fair I never met many fat people in LA.'

'Great you've found your passion though.' Becky kept her eyes on the pots, she felt too exposed looking directly at him, as if her desire for him was printed in gold leaf across her face.

'Well yeah, though a couple of times I fell out of teaching as quickly as I fell into it.'

Before Becky could get any more detail out of Sasha, Jack banged in through the door wielding a hanging basket overflowing with purple flowers and leaving a light trail of soil behind him.

'Petunias, for by the front door,' he announced to nobody in particular. He was breathing heavily and looked flustered.

'You OK Jack?' Sasha asked.

'I was,' said Jack, 'until I saw Tony crossing over the precinct just now Becky. Did you know he was back? I thought I'd better warn you because knowing him—'

'Yes,' Becky cut him off mid-sentence, not looking at Sasha. She could feel his eyes on her. 'I know Jack. Thank you though. Right,' she said, 'are they for the front Jack? They look lovely.'

Jack nodded – he looked confused – as if he knew he'd put his foot in it but he wasn't quite sure how. 'Everything all right Becky? You're doing the face June did when I bought her an iron for Christmas . . .'

'Everything's fine Jack, you crack on, I'll be out in a minute to have a look.'

'OK, well if you're sure,' and he was gone.

The swinging doors eventually stopped creaking and came to a rest. A silence filled the room. Becky moved to one of the benches and started to neaten up the already neat rows of tools. Her heart was thumping; she really didn't want to explain to Sasha how devastated she was by Tony's appearance, how it had derailed everything – including her hopes for maybe something happening between her and Sasha. What if she'd imagined the spark between the two of them – she'd look an idiot? No, she resolved, she must let one door close before opening another.

Sasha spoke first, quietly asking, 'I'm presuming Tony is Elliot's dad? When did he get back? I'm guessing that's what's kept you busy?'

Becky didn't look up 'It's . . . complicated, Sasha.'

He sounded hurt as he said, 'I don't know what's going on with you two and it's not my business, but . . . over dinner you said things were calmer when he wasn't around so . . .' he trailed off. 'I guess what I'm saying is if you need to chat, I'm here.'

'I know,' she almost whispered. She heard his soft footsteps cross the hall as he left. She didn't dare look up until the swing doors had fallen silent again, for fear he'd see the tears of frustration on her cheeks.

*

Becky busied herself for the rest of the afternoon. She was outside with Jack talking about litter when Sasha brought her out a cup of tea that was as welcome as the kind smile that accompanied it. The potters arrived, and Becky found comfort in their warm hellos to each other as they fastened their aprons, rolled up their sleeves, and checked over their tools.

Sheila came bustling over and, despite looking a little tired, was strangely animated; she had a bobby pin clamped in her lips as she adjusted her hair, which forced her to speak out of the corner of her mouth, giving her whisper a cartoonishly secretive quality. 'It's none of my business Becky love,' she said urgently, glancing over her shoulder, 'but,' she leaned in so close Becky could smell her face powder, 'I saw that Tony is back. I imagine he's as welcome as a hedgehog at a balloon factory. Now, firstly – are you OK, and secondly,' she slid the pin into her hair at the back and straightened, her lips now free to fully enunciate her concern, 'I'm afraid I had no alternative but to alert the rest of my Neighbourhood Watch team – a recently released felon is of course, deemed a Person of Interest.'

Becky took a breath, keeping her voice measured. 'I'm OK Sheila – thank you for your concern, but you're absolutely right,' she saw Sheila's eyes light up, 'it is none of your business.'

Becky smiled sweetly as Sheila's mouth formed a pink 'O' at her response. Becky turned on her heel.

'Right potters,' Sasha shouted, 'to your workbenches please!'

Becky perched on the stage behind him. She loved watching him speak to the potters, emitting pure hot teacher vibes.

'When you left here last week your pots were soft and damp. After a couple of days in a warm room they were dry and I then fired them to a thousand,' he looked over his shoulder at Becky, holding up a forefinger, 'and one. They transformed in the heat from bone dry delicate clay into hard ceramic.'

'Now that's magic,' said Jack in a squeaky Paul Daniels voice. Pearl giggled, and Jack beamed at his appreciative audience, this week clad in lilac mohair.

'It is magic Jack,' Sasha nodded, 'or at least that's what it feels like. The good news is your pots all survived this first biscuit firing and you're free to go and grab them from the display table ready to decorate.'

Becky felt weirdly emotional as she watched the potters making their way back to their benches, each cradling their creations. They were grinning – Louise looked particularly thrilled, as did Jameela. Sheila seemed deep in thought as she turned her pot this way and that, and Becky felt a little guilty – maybe she had been a bit harsh on Sheila earlier, and her comment had knocked the wind from her sails. Louise was looking at her husband Danny's pot, and seemed to be reassuring him

'Now, some of you,' said Sasha 'will notice the odd crack, but think of it as not a fault but an interesting feature with a story behind it, like a scar or an eyepatch. The digging up, shaping and baking of the earth below is the continuation of an ancient tradition, carried out for centuries by many hands – you showed respect to the clay and it's paid you back with pots that are all in one piece. Now it's time to make them even more beautiful.'

Sasha removed a hessian cloth covering a table at the front. Becky smiled at the theatrics, but it seemed to impress the potters who were wide-eyed at the reveal. *So that's what he was doing all afternoon*, thought Becky. The table was covered with numerous glass jars of coloured powder, and below, on the floor, sat buckets filled with mysterious liquids. It looked liked something you'd find in a class at Hogwarts, never mind at her humble community centre.

'These are your glazes. You can dip your coil pots in them, you can paint them on, pour them on – you can use any combination of colour. You have white, blue, brown, and clear.'

Becky watched as Jameela and Sheila smiled nervously at each other, Louise was more serious, chewing a thumb nail, lost in thought. Jack just seemed to be watching Pearl.

'As well as glazing your pots, you can decorate them by using these oxides to paint on a small pattern . . . this is cobalt carbonate.' Sasha held aloft a pot of pale pink powder. 'Mix this with clear glaze to paint onto your surfaces – as you can see it is tinged pink, but,' he looked around at the class, 'the firing miraculously turns it the most exquisite cobalt blue.'

Everyone made a low 'oooh' sound, then laughed self-consciously at how carried away they were getting. Danny just looked worried.

'When you paint on the pale pink you'll hardly be able to see it. The difference after the firing is quite startling, so don't splash it on like you're giving the Forth Bridge a lick of paint.'

The potters looked keen as mustard to get cracking. Becky was thrilled – there was a fizzing energy in the air.

'Now you may have noticed the room is a little less fun, and if we're honest, a little quieter this week – Elliot has left us for the sun, sea, and shots of Ayia Napa, so may I suggest that you Becky,' all eyes turned to her and she felt her cheeks grow hot, 'do the honours and decorate your son's pot? It's what he would've wanted,' he added mournfully.

This wasn't really part of the plan – as manager, her role was to make sure the class ran smoothly – but Becky didn't want to be a spoilsport, so she nodded and went to grab the pot. Pearl clapped excitedly.

'Now – pressie time,' Sasha said, and he walked a circuit around the benches, handing each potter a small black notebook and a pencil. 'To be a successful potter you need to remember what you did in one glaze and then respond to that in the next. Write everything down – how many spoons of cobalt to glaze, for example, then next time you can adjust amounts to change the outcome if necessary. These little books will become your bibles, every potter has one.' Sasha smiled at Becky as he approached her. 'Even you get one,' he whispered. Becky felt nervous, as if she was about to perform a risky surgery. 'Now class,' Sasha grimaced slightly, 'at this glazing stage a great pot can be ruined and an average pot can be made fantastic. The power is in your hands.' He grinned and rubbed his palms together. 'Right, I can see you're all chomping at the bit, so come on!'

Sasha waved them all forward, and the potters edged up to the front, gazing in the buckets, chatting in low voices about what they might do, like farmers eyeing up livestock at market. Just Becky remained at her bench. She opened her book, and there, on the inside cover was written:

This could be the start of something beautiful.
Love, Sasha

24

Louise

Louise reached for the same jar as Jameela, and both women pulled their hands back in surprise and laughed. Louise noticed how beautiful Jameela's eyes were as she smiled.

'Oops sorry, after you,' Jameela said.

'Thanks,' Louise said, feeling a little shy – the other woman was so tall and held herself so well.

'Your pot is so good,' Jameela said, 'I noticed it on the board and thought it must've been yours, you looked so relaxed in the first class – have you done pottery before?'

Louise was flattered. 'No, well, a little at college a long time ago. Are you enjoying it?'

'Yeah.' Jameela seemed startled by her own reply. 'I am actually. I'm enjoying meeting new people too – it's a chance to take off my lawyer hat and be someone else for a couple of hours.'

'Yeah, I know what you mean. It's nice to wear a different hat – here I'm not meeting a deadline or being Mum, I can just be Louise.'

Jameela's smile faded slightly and she nodded. 'Well, we'd better get on with it I guess. See you for a coffee in a bit?'

'Yeah sure – good luck.'

Louise peered into the buckets at the chalky glazes, as Sasha said, 'Remember potters, the natural oils in your skin could stop the glazes attaching to your works, so hold them as lightly and as little as you can.'

Some of the potters were now jotting down notes in their little books like waiters taking dinner orders.

Louise joined the others around Sasha as he demonstrated, dipping a sample pot as if baptising it in the milky glaze. Then it was their turn.

Louise made two journeys back to her workbench with gently sloshing buckets and little pots of oxide. Some decided to dip their pots in the glaze – holding them firmly on the rim with forefinger and thumb in a crab-like pincer, trying not to cover too much of the pot with the fleshy part of their thumb so the glaze could reach as much of the pot as possible.

Louise was ready to try, and did her best to ape Sasha's movements. She snaked her arm in a figure of eight so the glaze would swirl over all the surfaces and not linger in any corners or pockets. Her heart was thumping with the concentration of it. She looked over her shoulder at Danny and suppressed a small smile as she watched him grip his pot as if he was holding the head of a tiny vicious serpent. She saw a bead of sweat trickle down the side of Danny's thick neck as he lowered the pot in to the blue glaze as if he was trying to drown it.

She picked up a paintbrush with a fine head and dipped it in the cobalt she'd already mixed. She made a first mark and could hardly see the pale pink, but held her nerve, remembering Sasha's words. She painted a series of tiny marks that looked like arrowheads in an offset ring around the hip of the pot. She clustered some together at the highest part of the ring and they almost looked like birds flying in formation, the ones at the back trailing behind. For now they were a dusky pink but once fired, the heat would transform them into blue.

'Pretty!' She looked up to see Becky peering over her shoulder.

'Thank you. How's your pot going?'

'Well, I'm doing my best, but it's nowhere near as lovely as yours. Luckily I don't think Elliot will be too worried that I've taken over his masterpiece – he'll be too busy partying.'

'Oh gawd,' laughed Louise, envisioning a packed club and almost shuddering at the thought. 'I can't think of anything worse these days, but good for him. Are you missing him?'

She saw a flicker of something in Becky's eye, anger maybe. 'No. I'm relieved he's gone.' She glanced over her shoulder towards Sheila and lowered her voice, 'His dad turned up out of the blue so I was only too glad to wave Elliot off – they've never really got on.'

'Tony?' Louise was shocked – she thought Becky was well rid. 'I didn't know he was knocking about again. I saw in *The Echo* he'd been sent down a while back?' She remembered showing Danny the page, a mugshot of Tony's scrawny face sneering at them.

'Yeah, well he's back, sadly.' Becky seemed deflated. 'But not for long – I've told him he's got to be gone in a few days.'

'Good.' Louise reached out, touched her arm gently. 'Hey, do you fancy a drink some time? What with work and Danny and the girls I never have much time for friends, it'd do me good to have some female company that doesn't perform continuous TikTok dances while we chat.'

Becky chuckled. 'Yeah, yeah I would, that'd be great. Once I'm rid of Tony we can toast his absence.'

25

Jameela

Jameela stood, hands on hips, surveying her pot. A double stripe, like minuscule train tracks, wound its way around from the base to the lip.

One of Sasha's many mantras was 'know when to stop', so she resisted adding any more decoration and instead headed off in search of refreshment.

In the kitchen she found Sheila making a brew, using a spoon to chase a teabag around the cup with such intensity that a small puddle of hot tea had formed on the worktop underneath. She didn't notice Jameela, and kept stirring.

'Sheila?' Jameela said gently. Sheila jumped and hot tea splashed onto her hand. 'Oh, ouch Sheila, be careful, come here.' She instinctively took her friend's hand and walked her to the tap, running the cold over the pink skin of her knuckles. Jameela stopped herself thinking for the hundredth time that day, as she did every day, wouldn't it be lovely to be doing this for a son or daughter? Looking after them. She turned off the tap and gently patted Sheila's hand with some kitchen roll. She mopped up the spilt tea and looked at her friend. Sheila, who was wearing another jumpsuit, this one a deep purple with a thick gold zip up the centre, looked up at Jameela as if seeing her friend for the first time. She looked a little weary. 'Are you all right Sheila?'

Sheila tried to answer but instead gulped back a sob.

'Don't be nice to me. It'll set me off – not here, I can't really talk.' Regaining her composure she exhaled slowly through pursed lips as if blowing on a spoonful of hot soup. Just then the door swung open and Becky came in clutching a pair of empty mugs in each hand. She immediately clocked Sheila's teary eyes and softened, looking guilty.

'Sheila,' she said, clattering the cups down into the sink, 'I feel awful. I knew I'd upset you earlier, I didn't mean to snap, it's just . . . it's been a long week.' She walked over to Sheila. 'I'm sorry OK?'

Sheila nodded and tried to speak, but instead a low croak came out and the tears that had been brimming in her eyes now flooded down her cheeks.

'Hey,' Jameela said, putting her arm around her shoulder. 'Come on.'

Becky looked confused. 'I really am sorry, Sheila,' she said again, trailing off, but Jameela gently waved her away.

'She'll be fine, give her a minute maybe.' She nodded her head at the door and Becky, taking the hint, slipped out, looking mortified.

Sheila blew her nose noisily on a piece of kitchen roll and dabbed at her eyes. 'Becky really must've hit a nerve?' Jameela said, wondering what on earth she'd said to Sheila to upset her so much.

'Oh that,' said Sheila, 'that was nothing. Probably my fault. If you poke a cat enough it'll eventually scratch.' She looked down sadly, picking a bit of fluff off her jumpsuit and sighing.

'Well if we can't talk now, let's get together this week. Let me know yes?' Jameela offered.

'Yes,' said Sheila, 'I will. I promise. Now I need to go back out there, 'cos if I stay in here with your kind face one second longer

I'll start skriking again.' She sniffed one last time and headed for the door, almost colliding with Sasha who was on his way in.

'Oops! Sorry Sheila! You OK?' he asked.

'Yes fine,' trilled Sheila, not stopping. 'Hayfever!'

Sasha smiled at Jameela. 'Oh hi.'

Jameela noticed not for the first time how handsome their teacher was – no wonder Becky was clearly so smitten, hanging on his every word. 'Hiya boss. Coffee?'

'Boss?' Sasha laughed. 'I could get used to that. Yes please. How did you find the glazing?'

'Good I think. How about you, are you enjoying it here?' She watched as he chewed over the question.

'Yeah, I am,' he said eventually. 'Lovely people.'

'True.' Jameela nodded. 'What brought you here?'

'Ah well,' said Sasha, 'bit of a long story, but basically I'd been teaching at a private boys' school out in the wilds beyond Edinburgh, and was ready for a change of scene.'

'Oh nice – *très* Hogwarts.'

'Yeah you're not far wrong, though sadly no wizards knocking about . . . it was an impressive place and the money was too – best thing about teaching at a boarding school out in the wilderness is you've nowhere to spend your hard-earned cash. Unless you want to blow all your wages on gobstoppers at the tuck shop.'

'So you just teach down here at the community centre?'

'For now, yeah. I saved enough to get by till I get another school position, and I make my own stuff too at home. I've got a wheel and mini kiln at home – had it for years – and I've sold to craft shops in the north-west and the Lakes for a while now, so it keeps me ticking over.'

'Really? Must be quite intense making all that at home?'

'Yeah, let's just say my Feng Shui isn't great with all my gear squeezed in along with a tiny bed as an afterthought. I don't mind though, I love it. Plus I'm definitely happy to have a break from schools, the last post got a little . . . intense.'

His smile frosted over slightly as if he regretted saying the last bit and wished he could wind his words back in. Jameela noticed of course – she had a lawyer's instinct for a juicy nugget.

'Right,' she paused, a trick she used at work, leaving a silence so the other person felt compelled to fill it, giving away more detail than they intended to.

'I never really stay in a place too long; I like new adventures.'

'Like the littlest Hobo?'

'Who?' Sasha looked confused.

'Don't you remember? The TV show where this little dog turns up and sort of helps solve problems, then just as everyone falls in love with it, it ups and leaves, on to the next place at the end of every episode.'

'Ha,' said Sasha, 'I've been called many things over the years, but never a stray dog.'

'Well he's more than a stray – he's a hero.'

'Hmm.' Sasha winced, 'I didn't really leave a hero. I was a villain – well, only to one person.'

'Ah,' Jameela's eyes lit up, 'sounds ominous.'

'Yeah, schoolboy error – I mixed business with pleasure after some staff drinks, and the pleasure – the head of the music department – wasn't best pleased the next day when I told her I thought it best if it remained a one-off. The gossip and the icy stares in the staffroom all became a bit much.'

'Oh dear.' Jameela shook her head. 'You heartbreaker. So I suppose in a way you are a bit of a dog?'

'Nooooo!' Sasha held his hands up, laughing 'absolutely not, she was a lovely girl . . . just not . . .'

Jameela waited. Sasha looked to the ceiling as if for inspiration, and then he looked back at Jameela. She saw a sudden seriousness in his eyes, like a sky that had grown darker. As he went to speak, the door swung open again; this time it was Pearl, a lilac sparrow with matching lip gloss. She looked excited. 'I'm on a mission, I need a snack for Jack; please – do we have any bourbons?'

'Sure we do,' said Sasha, looking at Jameela.

'Saved by the bell,' she said gently.

'Well, by the biscuit,' he smiled.

Jameela returned to her bench and noticed Becky and Sheila chatting by Sheila's bench – it looked like they'd made up. The potters placed their works on the drying table. Jameela was pleased with hers until she saw Louise's – the smooth oval pot made all the others look amateurish, including Jameela's. She felt a twinge of envy – her competitive streak was never far below the surface.

26

Louise

The spring sunshine continued for the next couple of days, and over on Lovelace Lane, Louise and Danny had been enjoying something of a honeymoon period. Louise felt more positive than she had in ages and had thought of little else but being creative. Pottery seeped into her dreams, where she made the twins from wet, grey clay and they came to life and danced for her.

She was drawing more. Danny would wake up after sleeping off a long drive to find her at the kitchen table with her pads and pencils.

She daydreamed about new beginnings as she drove the girls to their gymnastic and drama classes, oblivious to their giggling and squabbling in the back seat.

Danny had told her he'd enjoyed the classes too. As a couple they'd been running on empty, so it felt good to top up the tank, spend time together that was just for them.

Plus, there was the added bonus of a bag of chips at the end too.

Louise had even begun to enjoy work in the way one suddenly begins to enjoy something just before it ends. It was like the morning of a much needed appointment at the hairdressers when your hair suddenly looks magnificent – showing one more flash of its former glory before you change it.

Each morning when she arrived at work, smiling broadly at everyone tinkering at the huge machines in the workshop, she'd think about how long she'd worked there and how weird it'd be if she had something else to focus on beyond leaflets, billboards and the graphics for a pensions convention at the Holiday Inn.

She wasn't thinking she could jack in her managerial position and all the perks and steady income that came with it, but maybe she could scale it down.

Even the thought of this put a spring in her step. She allowed herself the little daydream of escaping.

The nagging feeling of needing something more was still there, but its sharpness was now softened slightly by the hope that there could be change for the better with her work.

Louise still felt uneasy when she thought too deeply about her relationship with Danny. Did she feel in a rut because of work or because of her marriage, or both? Since the pottery class, her mood had been lighter and she felt less suffocated by their routine, their groundhog days of work, kids, meals, repeat. She'd found it easier to be kinder to him, and more patient. The relief in his eyes was palpable, but Louise worried she was giving him a false sense of security when she still didn't know what she wanted.

Louise had spotted her boss June, clanking up the metal stairs that always made her think of massive cheese graters, the gaps between the steps still giving her the heebie-jeebies after all these years.

June was a woman who, even if she was just making a cup of tea, always had the panicked look of someone sprinting down a station platform about to miss the last train. Louise toyed with the idea of approaching her boss and striking up a casual conversation about her hours, her future at C&J Commercial Printing.

But she knew June would immediately panic that Louise was going to leave, abandon her.

It was a running joke amongst some of the staff about how much June clung to Louise like a shipwrecked sailor to a life raft. During Christmas drinks when lips had been loosened, a couple of the sales team had let slip that they called Louise 'Whatwould', because all June ever seemed to say to her was, 'What would I do without you?' Or to her fellow workers, 'What would have happened if Louise hadn't spotted that error?' when she'd averted a minor disaster.

June, with the beleaguered manner of the president of a small war-torn country whose fortunes she was trying to turn around, saw Louise as her vice president – steadfastly by her side as each day brought new life-or-death drama. In reality, Louise was just helping June finalise a contract for the large format window displays of a chain of local bakers.

Louise was a pragmatist and knew now was the time for change, that this new impetus was a fleeting moment that would wane if she didn't act soon.

She was determined to harness this new energy before it slipped through her fingers, taking her marriage to Danny with it.

27

Becky

The atmosphere at Becky's neat terraced house on Harrison Lane had soured quicker than a saucer of milk left in the sun.

Tony and Becky's relationship had started when they were teens, and theirs was not a story of a love surviving despite the odds. To Becky, theirs was a tale of disappointment and fear, punctuated with Tony's violent outbreaks, controlling behaviour, and drinking.

Becky would've cut all ties with him decades ago, but there was that one strand that kept them attached – Elliot. The only silver lining on this Tony-shaped cloud was that Elliot was loving his summer job in Ayia Napa – insisting he went was the best five minutes of work Becky had done.

Each morning, as she came down the stairs and into the living room she hoped that Tony wouldn't be there.

But of course he was, despite his promise to move on.

He insisted that going to his mate's house was still a possibility – there'd been a hold-up, that's all, something to do with the couple's visas that had involved a trip to the Thai embassy in London.

Relations with his mum were by all accounts slowly thawing – helped by Tony using Becky's razor to have a shave, and cadging a fiver from her to spend on petrol station flowers.

His mum had told him that she still had a recurring nightmare about the police raid in which she's dragged out of her flat in front of her neighbours in just her bra and pants, and Jean from next door fainted. One of the police officers was Welsh crooner Tom Jones.

She loved the flowers though apparently, just as much as she loved his promise that he was sorting himself out and was working with his mate on his house clearance business.

The job at least had not been a lie, though Becky only believed it when she saw the white transit van pull up with 'Hamilton House Clearance' emblazoned across it in clumsy amateur lettering.

Tony had got the gig after bumping into his old mate Howard Hamilton down the pub – he was to temporarily replace Stu, who'd come a cropper when a miscommunication led to him being pinned to a wall by an upright piano that'd skied at speed down a flight of stairs.

Early one morning, after a fitful night's sleep, Becky came downstairs to see Tony pop the last of her loaf into the toaster. She felt something give. 'Jesus Tony,' she snapped, glancing at the cluttered kitchen, 'look at the state of this place.'

He didn't react. Instead, he got the butter from the fridge, whistling as he did. He opened two drawers to look for a knife, second time lucky. 'Tony,' she said, as he continued to whistle an infuriatingly jaunty tune, 'please don't ignore me. I need you gone.' She saw his shoulders lift, a subtle tension across his back that made the fabric of his T-shirt tighten.

'I am on it, Becks,' he said, quietly and slowly, as if he was talking to a toddler.

'I don't think you are though Tony.' She turned and walked through to the lounge area. 'The only thing you're "on" is my sofa.' She drew the curtains, light spilling into the room. She opened the window, her nose crinkling at the stale smell in the room. 'This is my . . .' she lifted the crumpled duvet, which revealed underneath it, on the floor, an empty bottle of whisky and a glass, sticky with amber residue '. . . house.'

It is an amazing thing, the human brain. Later, as Becky looked back on this moment she would mull over how quickly her brain had calculated the ramping up of risk to her safety in that split second – how as her eyes saw the empty whisky bottle she added it to the smell of the room and knew in that moment he would be hungover and volatile and that she was now in danger.

As if to confirm her fears, her brain instantly replayed the sharpness of her own tone as she spoke, and she knew he would attack.

Later, as she tried to zip up her coat with shaking hands, she recollected that she was already braced, ready for him even before she heard the approach of his rapid footsteps and felt his fingers around her neck, squeezing. Firmly enough to restrict her breathing ever so slightly, but not enough to leave a mark.

It was, in a way, his signature move from the bad old days. He would run at her, his arm outstretched, wrap his fingers around the front of her neck and just keep walking, propelling her backwards towards the nearest wall or door, her legs struggling to keep in step and keep herself upright.

'I know,' he breathed, the smell of booze engulfing her, his spittle on her cheek as he spat his words, 'I know it's your house. I know that because you don't let me forget it, do you? Never stop shoving it in my face.' He knocked the back of her head gently onto the wall. 'Just how much better you are than me, how you don't need me.'

'No,' she began, but he shook her then, like a doll. She knew from experience, to stay quiet, to go limp, to submit.

'All I want is a roof over my head, just a couple of days, Becks. That's all I ask. Is it really so hard for you to do something nice for someone for a change?'

She looked down and felt his grip loosen, there was no slap

yet, but instead he shoved her sideways and she landed on the arm of the sofa. Again he was in her face, his finger an inch from the bridge of her nose. She flinched. 'Here's the deal Becks. I will go in a day or two, but if you keep on, I will give you something to complain about, understand? And don't think Elliot is safe. I know people – even people in Ayia Napa.' She whimpered then, an uncontrollable guttural noise. She wished she could grab the butter knife he'd been using a minute before and slide it between his ribs.

'What?' she whispered, confused. 'Why?'

'Why?' he shouted, again, inches from her face.

She bit down on her lip, bit down on the urge to scream, to sink her teeth into the flesh of his cheek, to hurt him – how dare he threaten Elliot?

'I'll tell you why.' He straightened. He sounded triumphant now, he knew Elliot was her Achilles heel. 'You've turned that boy against me, always have done. That's why he's . . . soft.' Even in anger he couldn't say his son was gay – she'd laugh if it weren't so tragic. 'He needs toughening up, it'd do him good. You speak to me like that again and I'll make a phone call – a good slapping could be the making of him.'

He walked back through to the kitchen and started to whistle again. In that moment Becky hated Tony, but she hated herself more – how could she have been so stupid to let him stay that first night? She was shaking now, heartbroken at her own stupidity. Furious with herself. Had the passage of time so blurred her memory of his brutality? He hadn't mellowed, he was the same old Tony, and she was stuck with him until he decided to leave – he'd made it clear he was in control now and worst of all, it was all her fault.

Two minutes later Becky jumped as she heard the front door slam. She'd already slipped from the lounge and had taken refuge in Elliot's bedroom. She watched from the window as Tony, slice of toast hanging from his lips, shrugged on his leather jacket and slid into the passenger seat of the van.

Off they went to clear the homes of the dearly departed. To rifle through the bare carcass of someone's life, the house already stripped clean of any precious belongings by circling family. Becky herself felt ransacked.

She watched the van roar off and remembered the time, many moons ago, when Tony, barely twenty years old, had left for work as a scaffolder, picked up by a brotherhood of tanned, tattooed young men in a flatbed lorry. Faded copies of *The Sun* and crumpled pop cans littering the footwell, the occasional can clattering out onto the road as Tony flung open the wagon's door. She remembered the sound of the metal poles on the back clanking as it set off, and thinking that their flaking pale pink paint looked surprisingly pretty.

Elliot couldn't have been any older than two, because that particular drama had erupted over nappies. Or the lack of them.

Despite Becky receiving benefits and Tony working on the scaffolds, they still couldn't make ends meet.

Then one day little Elliot had started to develop an angry-looking rash on his bottom because Becky had perhaps not been changing his nappy as often as she should. Not through laziness or lack of care, but because she couldn't afford to; nappies, even own-brand ones, were expensive.

She had felt awful when she saw the rash. She changed him into the last nappy from the pack, and pushed him in his buggy around to her nan's, almost running through the streets.

She borrowed ten pounds from Nan and bought two huge packs of nappies, nappy rash cream, and some other essentials – milk, bread, beans, washing powder and shampoo. She may have been a teenager still, but she had her priorities straight – other eighteen-year-olds were spending their money on make-up and going out, but not Becky.

Besides, Nan had lent her the money without hesitation despite not having much herself, and she'd folded Becky into her arms for a hug when she'd seen the grateful tears well up in her grand-daughter's tired eyes.

'I hate asking you for money Nan,' she'd whispered into the nook of her nan's neck, which always smelled of Avon face powder. 'I'll pay you back as soon as I get my income support through.'

'I know sweetheart, don't worry,' Nan had said, cupping Becky's face gently in her hands. 'Your mum would be so proud of you, I know times are tough, but you,' her own eyes had grown watery then, 'are a good mum Becky. That little boy,' she had looked at Elliot, engrossed in smearing yogurt on his face, and laughed, 'is so happy – and it's all because of you.'

'Thanks Nan. It's just so hard – Tony's trying to earn, and there's been a mix-up with the post – I'm owed two weeks' benefits now, but I've not had anything through the door apart from pizza menus.'

Becky saw her nan's eyes harden at the mention of Tony. 'You sure he's not had it?'

'Nan,' Becky shook her head, 'he wouldn't do that. Look, I'm sure it'll get sorted.'

She spoke to the benefits office three times, and each time they'd insisted the cheque had been posted out. 'Could anybody else at the residence have accidentally opened it?' The lady on the other end of the line sounded bored.

'Of course not,' Becky had replied, 'it hasn't arrived in the first place.'

The lady made a sort of 'Hmm . . . heard that one before' noise, but promised to look into it. Becky felt fobbed off and tried to suppress the panic in her throat.

Arriving home from her nan's that day, Becky had struggled through the front door, plastic bags hooked onto the buggy handles.

She remembered it as if it was yesterday – it had felt great unpacking the shopping. She'd planned to bath Elliot and smother him in nappy cream and make him a slap-up tea of beans on toast.

First though, she'd put a wash on. She emptied the washing basket and started to load in Elliot's little joggers and jamas, along with a nightie of hers and some leggings. She spotted Tony's jeans crumpled on the floor by their bed and, feeling benevolent, thought she'd wash them too. She checked the pockets for tissues like Mum had taught her, and pulled out a couple of cigarette papers from one pocket and from the other, a screwed-up brown envelope. Immediately she knew what it was. She knew because it was the sort of envelope she'd been scanning the doormat for every morning for the past two weeks. Her stomach had lurched as she straightened out the envelope. It was empty of course. Printed in black on the top left of the envelope was 'HM Revenue & Customs', and just below the now empty window, was scrawled her signature three times in blue biro. Though it wasn't her writing – it was wobbly, as if she'd signed it on a bumpy car journey.

It was a practice signature. Tony had obviously needed a couple of goes before forging her income support cheque and cashing it behind her back. Becky's breathing had become shallow. Elliot was sitting on the floor amongst the dirty laundry, happily kicking his little feet as if he was playing in a pile of autumn leaves.

She knew then that she could never trust Tony again. To steal from her was bad enough, but to deprive her baby of nappies was worse. To be too lazy to destroy the evidence only added insult to injury.

Since Elliot's arrival, their relationship had been strained. They were still kids themselves, kids playing at grown-ups. Tony hadn't changed his lifestyle at all – he still went out drinking with his mates, spending money they didn't have on speed that kept him up and made him ratty and sallow skinned. Becky knew to stay out of his way for the few days following 'a mad one'.

Over the months, Becky had just focused on Elliot and found, despite her young age, that she loved being a mum.

She knew she'd never really loved Tony, and now, on finding the envelope, she felt a new feeling – hatred – blooming like spores of damp. A fury began to hatch in her gut; how dare he treat them both like that.

She would confront him when he came home, she'd ask for her money and tell him to leave. She was sure he'd be relieved – he spent half his time around at his mum's anyway, being fed, and smoking her fags – he'd probably love to be kicked out and into her waiting arms.

Becky had scooped up the scattered socks and put on the wash. She pushed the envelope into her pocket and used the last of the bubble bath for Elliot.

As she slipped him into the warm water, his excited giggles filling the bathroom, she planned how she'd confront Tony.

She didn't know it then, as she gently washed her son's chubby legs, but a whole new horrifying chapter was about to begin. One that would last over twenty years. For the first time that evening, furious and humiliated at being caught out, Tony hit Becky.

Clouds gathered over the morning sun, blocking the light as Becky tried to block out the memory of Tony's first violent attack. The years that followed were punctuated with flashes of violence towards Becky. The shoves, the pushes, the sudden grip of his hands on her upper arms – enough to leave four sausage-shaped bruises on each side. Once, when she'd joshed him about the way he'd pronounced a word wrongly, he'd pinned her down on the living-room carpet and what started off as playful tickling ended with him biting her, nipping her all over her chest, shoulders and belly, leaving dozens of tiny marks, each the size of a penny.

When he snapped, it came suddenly and with shocking force. There was no warning sign Becky could watch for, no darkening of the skies around his mood. Though the violence didn't happen often, when it did, it was frightening, and painful enough to shock Becky and chip away at her confidence. She perfected the art of walking on eggshells, and it was exhausting.

A little shiver ran up her arms. She looked at the Polaroids pinned up around Elliot's headboard – her gorgeous son in big bear hugs with pals, in fancy dress as Sandy to a girlfriend's Danny, a drunken shot on holiday of him being held across his friends' outstretched arms like a Force's sweetheart. She smiled. Tony had brought chaos and disruption into her life, but he'd also given her the greatest gift: Elliot. It was Elliot she now had to protect at all costs; the only way to do that would be to get rid of Tony.

28

Sheila

Sheila was feeling like a teddy with half its stuffing pulled out. She'd barely slept since finding the knickers, and was desperate for a second opinion. She couldn't trust April at the food bank with her woes (she may as well hire a town crier – discretion wasn't exactly April's middle name). She'd seen Jameela at pottery, but they hadn't quite found the right moment to chat.

Sheila washed the breakfast dishes and watched Martin through the window. She felt disconnected from him, curling inwards and away from him to protect her heart, like a hedgehog rolling into a defensive ball. Martin sat on a wrought-iron garden chair, his fleece zipped up to his salt and pepper stubble. The morning was fresh, but the pale blue sky promised warmth later.

Laid before him on the table were some of the treasures he'd brought back from his latest mudlarking trip, and he was gently buffing a Victorian bottle with a cloth.

Such care he took, tenderly rubbing, almost caressing the bottle, that Sheila snorted in derision. 'Lucky bottle,' she muttered to the bubbles in the sink, wondering what, if there was a house fire, he would grab first? His wife, or the trunk of debris found at the bottom of the Thames?

Martin looked up at that point and their eyes met. He half smiled as if he only vaguely recognised her, and then gestured for her to come outside.

'Look at this my turtle dove,' he said, as she stepped out of the back door. He held up a bottle and his gold-rimmed magnifying glass. She took both from him roughly enough to make him flinch slightly.

'Martin, I can't believe we still have this in the house – you know this handle is ivory?' She looked him squarely in the eye. 'It makes me sick.' It felt good to say these words out loud to him.

Martin looked confused. 'It's antique Sheila, the one Mum got me for my fortieth. I can't help that it has an ivory handle – different times Sheila. You know what the Victorians were like – they'd shoot, stuff, or eat anything that moved.'

Sheila remembered the present very well – it had outshone the watch she'd bought Martin, and his mum knew it of course, smiling beatifically at her as he gushed over the magnifying glass.

Sheila recalled how Martin had eventually realised his reaction was irritating Sheila and had made a show of pointing out to his mum the engraving on the back of the watch – a line from one of their special songs: 'Nothing more, nothing less, love is the best, Sheila'.

Now she doubted if she could ever listen to Madness again.

'Well to be honest Martin,' she said now, turning the magnifying glass this way and that, 'if I got half a chance, I would get rid of it – it's an awful reminder of man's cruelty.' She glared at him.

His eyes widened at the threat. 'But Sheila love, you still have your mum's old fox fur in the loft.'

'That is different,' she snapped. 'Foxes are ten a penny – they're hardly endangered are they? You don't see many elephants squashed by the side of the M60 do you? That's your problem Martin, you don't understand that when something is precious you should appreciate it. You should protect it and look after it. Or,' her eyes filled with tears, 'you'll lose it.' She slammed the objects on the table with a little more force than intended, and as she did, clipped one of the bottles with the ivory handle. The bottle clattered over, rolled off the edge of the table, and landed with a crack on the decking. Martin gasped and grabbed it. The blue glass was thick and the bottle was still in one piece, but a large shard had chipped off the thick base.

'What is going on with you?' he said, staring at her, but he wasn't quick enough – Sheila had retreated indoors, slamming the door behind her.

For the rest of the morning Sheila avoided Martin. *Let him stew like a pound of prunes*, she thought. If he was having an affair and thinking of leaving her, she would need to be match fit for such trauma. Who knew – maybe one day she'd be out there dating again? The thought horrified her, but there was no harm in investing in a bit of me-time while she worked out her next move.

So when a delivery man rang the doorbell and she ripped open the packaging of the parcel, she was excited to find it was from Yogasm, a yoga and wellness brand she'd seen pop up on Facebook. Her starter kit included a mat, leggings, and ankle weights, all in lilac.

She'd treated herself to a subscription to the online classes, and by mid-afternoon was perfecting her mid-forward fold when Martin came to find her in the lounge.

He let out a wolf whistle when he came face to bottom with her ample behind. Sheila ignored him.

'Cup of tea?' he asked, crouching to see her face, which was upside down and slightly puce. He'd obviously forgiven her for earlier. *Sign of a guilty conscience if ever there was one*, thought Sheila.

'No thank you,' she answered curtly, trying to retain an aura of aloofness despite having her bottom in the air.

'Okey-dokey then,' he said, then paused. 'Sheila, what have I done love? I was paranoid I'd missed an anniversary or a special date, but I definitely haven't. You've not been yourself since I got back from London – are you annoyed I went? If I don't know what I've done, how can I make it better?'

At that moment, the landline rang, making them both jump.

Martin went out to the hall and answered it. Sheila lowered to her knees and pressed pause on the iPad. Her ears pricked up, though the thumping of her heart drowned out Martin's low voice. Surely it wouldn't be his mistress? It'd be silly even for Martin, to hand out their landline number. She stood and felt a little light-headed. Steadying herself on the back of the sofa she crept to the door just in time to hear Martin say, 'OK, thank you, see you soon.'

He turned to Sheila and his face was ghostly pale. 'It's Mum,' he said.

'Get some sweet tea please Julie,' said Mrs Blackstone as she folded her long slender frame into a chair. Mrs Blackstone had been general manager of Oakview residential home for the last twelve years and, as she once told Sheila, 'she was used to giving bad news to good people – it is a big part of the job.'

Now it was their turn for the bad news. Sheila had been doing much of the talking because Martin had fallen silent, like a shy child when the grown-ups are being serious. Sheila suspected he was in shock.

She reached out her hand to still Martin's clenched fists as he knocked his knuckles together as if tapping out a message in Morse code.

Martin's silence filled the room, making it stuffier. Oakview was always stiflingly hot, the thin skin on the residents no longer providing any insulation. Sheila smiled at Mrs Blackstone, feeling awkward. She was no good with a silence, but she was, luckily, very good at small talk. 'You've got lovely hair,' she said to Mrs Blackstone, admiring the caramel tones pushed back by a navy hairband. 'My friend April who I volunteer with at the food bank has a sister with the exact same colour. She breeds Shelties – you know, the mini versions of Lassie?' Mrs Blackstone looked confused, but nodded. 'Well, her new hairdresser could never get her colour quite right, so in the end she took her best breeding bitch to the salon and said "THIS is what I'm after Marcus".'

'Oh how funny,' said Mrs Blackstone, just as Julie, who was clearly as clumsy as she was keen, bustled back into the room sloshing drips of tea onto the pale carpet. Julie plonked the drinks onto the desk in front of them.

Sheila looked at the spilled tea but, judging by the smell of the place, she presumed the carpet, like everything at Oakview, was no stranger to strong bleach.

Sheila thought the pale green cup and matching saucer looked very formal – maybe this was the crockery reserved for bad news.

'You've had a shock Martin. It's completely understandable to feel this way. Your mum is doing what quite a few of our residents choose to do.' She smiled.

Martin shook his head and spoke at last. 'I don't understand – she was on quite good form last week. Did something happen to make her stop eating?'

Mrs Blackstone sighed and dipped her head until she made contact with Martin's eyes. Her voice was low and soothing. 'Sadly, it's quite common. She's made the decision to not eat. After years of confusion and compliance, perhaps she feels she's had enough. I need you to be prepared Martin,' she paused before pushing on very gently, 'that this may be the last decision your mum ever makes. She's taking back a bit of control of her life, and she may be trying to let us know she's had enough. She's ready to go.'

The suddenness and the volume of the sob that escaped Martin made them all jump. Sheila had seen her husband down and depressed, but had never seen him cry like this. She pulled him to her and he wept on her shoulder, silent sobs now, his body shuddering. Sheila resolved there and then that whatever was happening in their marriage now had to be filed away to be dealt with at a later date. She had to suppress the anxiety and feelings of rejection; her role now was to support the love of her life through the darkest of times. It wouldn't be easy, but she owed him that much.

Martin straightened, sniffing. 'I want to see her.'

Mrs Blackstone offered him the tissue box and as he took one with a shaking hand she nodded kindly. 'Of course.'

29

Jameela

Jameela's phone buzzed in the bowels of her expensive handbag. Already that day she'd led three client meetings back to back, each slightly duller than the one before. The team planning session that followed had hoovered up the last crumbs of her energy. It was a text from Sheila, and she was grateful for the distraction. 'Happy Friday! Looking forward to tonight. Coffee or wine, yours or mine? Ooh that rhymes! Seriously though, really appreciate your POV.' Jameela checked her watch – jeez time really did fly when you were discussing contractual law . . . she tapped out her reply: 'Absolutely! Come to mine, 7.30? Need wine after the day I've had!'

Sheila responded with a thumbs-up emoji.

Jameela smiled. She liked Sheila and she liked having a friend who lived close by. It seemed all her other friends were busy with their families, and Jameela couldn't bring herself to hang out with any little ones until the rawness of the latest miscarriage subsided.

Jameela changed into her running gear and set off for home. It was an eight-mile run. She didn't listen to music; she needed her wits about her as she nimbly negotiated not only the traffic, but the flood of people – tourists, shoppers, office workers and pub goers – that streamed through the streets of Manchester city centre.

It was the perfect distance for her to let off steam and think. She hadn't heard from Simon and, as she sped along, feet slapping lightly on the wet pavement towards the outskirts of town, she thought maybe no news was good news. Simon was right, they needed this space to breathe. She thought about the hair on the bathroom floor. Maybe it was nothing. Eventually, breathless, she arrived home to another crushed can shoved in the bush by her gatepost. Another reminder of Reju. She ached to see her little sister, to apologise for her outburst that day, but Reju was still ignoring her calls and the dozen texts pleading for forgiveness.

When the doorbell rang an hour later Jameela found Sheila standing there, bottle of rosé in hand, sporting another jumpsuit, this time black velour with thin white, pink, and green stripes on the waist, wrists and ankles. She reminded Jameela of a Licorice Allsort.

'At last,' chirped Sheila, 'I've lived round here for years and never seen inside of one of the Tull Avenue mansions.'

Jameela laughed. 'Come in! It's hardly a mansion – I didn't know a look round was on your bucket list?'

'Not quite. Though if you insist on giving me a tour I wouldn't say no.'

Jameela was happy to – she was proud of the house she'd turned into a home for her and Simon and the children they'd hoped for. Recently though, the house felt too big, as though it was waiting to be filled with laughter, chaos and love.

As they descended the stairs having had a look around, Sheila said, 'It's a beautiful home Jameela, you clearly have good taste in interiors as well as in pottery friends.'

Jameela laughed, then looked serious. 'Absolutely. I know how lucky I am to have nice things. Honestly, growing up sharing bunk beds with my sister in our two up two down, I never dreamt I'd have such a lovely home.'

'Well, you work hard, you deserve it,' Sheila replied. 'Though I have to admit I'm jealous of your bed – it's the size of Asda's car park! I need a drink to get over it.'

They made their way to the spotless kitchen and Jameela opened the wine. It was a balmy evening so they sat outside on the decking, Sheila admiring the cherry tree in full blossom at the end of the lawn.

Jameela could tell Sheila had something to tell her, she looked like a pipe about to burst, but clearly didn't know where to start. Instead, she was gabbling about the garden.

'Of course April at the food bank says she's saving to go to Japan to see the cherry blossom. You'd think she's the female Monty Don the way she talks, though she's anxious about the food – the only time she tried sushi she had to spit it out into the sleeve of her brand new designer blouse! Can you imagine? A slice of raw tuna up your best Michael Kors?' Sheila shook her head, taking a gulp of the wine.

Jameela's phone buzzed in her pocket, probably an update from the restaurant she'd ordered dinner from – hopefully it was on the way, the wine was proving moreish and they needed something to soak it up. She took out her phone and gasped audibly enough for Sheila to stop her chatter and look at Jameela. 'What is it?'

'It's from my sister, Reju. The one I told you about.' Jameela was relieved that the frost that had formed between them was finally thawing. 'Seems she at last wants to make up – though it's weird . . .' Jameela murmured, chewing her top lip. 'She says, "Hello sis. Miss you. I'm sorry. I love you and I'm sorry".'

'I don't understand,' said Sheila. 'Why is it weird?'

'I dunno – it's me who is in the wrong, I've been apologising, so why is she saying sorry?'

'It's obvious,' said Sheila, rolling her eyes comically. 'She's sorry for making you jump through hoops, for not returning your calls.'

'Do you think? I mean, to be fair, it is pretty typical of Reju to think of others first.' Jameela felt warmed by the text, it was a sign – like changing the colour of the flag at the beach to show it's safe to enter the water again.

'See,' said Sheila, 'exactly.'

Jameela put her phone away. 'Anyway. Enough about me and my drama,' she said gently, 'what about you Sheila?' She paused, 'I presume you didn't want to come round tonight just for a guided tour?'

Sheila sighed sadly and studied her coral-painted nails for a moment, and when she looked up, she focused on the cherry blossom to try to stop the tears that had filled her eyes.

'Hey,' said Jameela, 'come on, it can't be that bad? What's going on?'

Sheila took a deep breath and the whole sorry tale tumbled out. Jameela was a good listener – Reju always told her that – and she listened now, as Sheila told her about her tough day at the food bank, Martin's loud music, the Michael Ball CD, and finally, the ladies' underwear.

'And to top it all off, Martin's mum is now gravely ill – she is basically on her way out. So whatever is going on with Martin, I can't confront it even if I wanted to, not while my mother-in-law is on her last legs.'

'Sheila I feel awful for you,' said Jameela. 'It seems so far-fetched though – I've only met Martin twice, admittedly I was squiffy on wine the first time, but when he dropped the cross trainer round we chatted a bit, and he just seems, well, nice. Not the sort to cheat.'

Sheila sniffed. 'Whoever is "the sort" though Jameela? Ordinary people have affairs all the time – they're not a type. They don't have gold medallions nestling in their chest hair and give out business cards with "philanderer" written on them.'

'True.' Would she, a year ago, ever have dreamt that solid, kind, hard-working Simon could be unfaithful?

'I'm just so scared, and it's not like me,' said Sheila.

Jameela topped up her wine glass. 'Right,' she said, 'let's think this through.'

The doorbell rang – Sheila looked startled as if talking about Martin had conjured him up at the door.

'That'll be dinner,' Jameela said. 'I'll be right back.'

Over bowls of green curry and sticky rice the two women talked.

'Are you absolutely sure Martin doesn't know you know?' Jameela asked.

Sheila snapped a prawn cracker in half. 'Well, he knows I'm not right, that I'm upset with him, but he definitely doesn't know why.'

'I'm surprised Sheila, I thought you wouldn't be able to keep it to yourself?'

'I can't say anything until the situation with his mum is . . . resolved.' She lowered her voice to a respectful whisper. 'When she dies, I will be able to sort it out. But I'm worried that if I start to talk to him about it I won't be able to stop – I will lose control. If it weren't for his mum I feel I could murder him with my bare hands.' Sheila, ashamed, shook her head slightly. 'Also,' she said in a small voice, 'we've been together so long, we've always been a team, or so I thought, and if I say the words out loud – if I ask if he's in love with someone else, there's no going back, it'll be real, and we'll have to deal with it.' She sniffed and sipped her wine. 'And I don't know what I'd do without him, I guess,' she said, now meeting Jameela's eye, looking childlike and vulnerable. 'If I don't say it out loud, it isn't happening.'

It grew dark, and Jameela switched on the garden lights and gave Sheila a throw for her legs.

Jameela, with her lawyer brain fired up by two large glasses of rosé, went through the facts.

'We need to discount all the possible ways the pants could've ended up on the floor of the wardrobe.' Sheila hiccupped and nodded. 'They weren't a gift for you from Martin?'

'No – too small, no label,' Sheila shot back.

'And you don't use a laundry service that could've made an error?'

Sheila looked horrified. 'Having my smalls washed with a load of strangers'? No thank you very much,' she huffed.

'It can't be a weird prank that went wrong can it?'

Sheila shook her head. 'Absolutely not. Just not Martin's style – he's never been frivolous . . . and besides, he would've revealed all by now, wouldn't he?' Sheila was delicately nibbling the strands of chicken satay from a wooden skewer.

'Hmm . . .' Jameela was running out of options. 'You've said there's no way they could belong to your son's girlfriend, but what about your neighbours? Any way they could've have got mixed in with a neighbour's laundry off the line?'

'Impossible.' Sheila popped the skewer into the empty takeaway bag and reached for a napkin, dabbing the corners of her mouth. 'For numerous reasons, the main one being that we're an end of terrace, so our only neighbour is Mr Potts, and he is at least a size 20 and uses a mobility scooter.'

Jameela grabbed her laptop from her rucksack. 'Come here so you can see.'

Sheila budged up her chair so they were side by side, the light from the screen illuminating both their faces. 'Right,' Jameela said, clicking on Safari, 'what's the name of the knicker brand?'

'Oh now you're asking, hang on I know it . . . it's something like "Red roses" . . . but not that,' Sheila looked up at the starry sky as if the answer was written there, 'in fact try "Rosey reds".'

Jameela typed it in and read the results. 'Nope not an underwear brand, but a type of minnow, and also something to do with Cincinnati's baseball team.'

Despite the stress of the situation they laughed.

'"Ruby Red's"!' Sheila shouted. 'That's it – definitely. Ruby Red's, Soho.' And there it was.

'Bingo,' said Jameela, 'Ruby Red's. Here's the blurb – "established in 1984 – bespoke ladies' underwear for special occasions that makes you feel good, inside and out".' Jameela grimaced.

Her phone buzzed loudly, making them both jump then laugh at their reaction. Jameela's smile faded as she saw Simon's name flash up. After a deafening silence from him, he now saw fit to furnish her with four words: 'We need to talk.'

That phrase never preceded good news: 'We need to talk – you've got the job!/marry me!/we found the treasure!' – it just wasn't a thing. The dreaded phrase that – like running upstairs in a horror film – never had a happy ending.

'Is it Reju again?' Sheila asked.

'No, it's Simon,' replied Jameela briskly.

'And?' Sheila's eyes twinkled optimistically in the gloom.

'It just says "we need to talk",' Jameela said.

'Well ten out of ten for originality there,' tutted Sheila. 'Where did he get that? *The Little Book of Love Clichés*?'

Despite herself, Jameela laughed. 'Perhaps by talk he means he wants to tell me I was right all along, he loves Belle.'

Her throat tightened at the thought as her mind galloped ahead: maybe they're setting up home and . . . it was important she heard it from him, Belle is pregnant.

As if reading her mind Sheila said, 'Hey. Come on. Pointless winding yourself up like this. You need to go and see him.'

'You're right,' smiled Jameela, papering over the cracks of her panic, for now. Tonight was supposed to be about helping Sheila. She tossed her phone onto the table and turned back to the laptop.

'Right. Where were we? OK, so it looks like the knickers aren't available to buy online, they're only available in the shop.'

'Right,' said Sheila. 'So she bought them there, or he did, or they shopped there together . . .'

'Don't think about it,' said Jameela quickly. 'Look – "Our hand-stitched under garments are loved by our clients from the world of Burlesque, theatre and fashion."'

Sheila sighed. 'Seems almost unfair on the pants that they're now living such a boring life in the pocket of my padded jacket.'

Jameela snapped shut her laptop, pleased with her investigation and drained the last of her wine.

Sheila looked at her suspiciously. 'What?'

'Well,' Jameela said, 'Martin goes to London when he goes mudlarking. Maybe he bought them while he was on one of his trips.'

'It seems it's not only treasure hunting he gets up to in London – maybe it's all just a cover for him to visit her.'

Jameela's eyes widened. Jesus, maybe she was right. Sheila looked as if she might cry. 'Well,' said Jameela, 'if you really don't want to ask him, there is another way we could find out what's going on. Next time he heads off to the big city, we could too! Undercover of course . . . Fancy a girls' weekend in London?'

30

Louise

Louise had been trying all day to get hold of Danny, who was on a long haul trip up to Carlisle in his wagon. She'd had some exciting news she wanted to share. She'd just found out she'd been given a weekend volunteering role at the Manchester Art Gallery after applying the week before. It was only a few hours, but she was thrilled, and as with any news, wanted to tell Danny first. She couldn't though, as he'd gone AWOL, which was not like him at all. As his phone clicked to voicemail for the fifth time she felt a creeping unease. His phone was hooked up to his cab via Bluetooth, so even if he was moving he'd always answer. If he was chatting to the lads at the depot, he'd usually return her missed call within minutes. Her heart thumped as she imagined a motorway pile-up, twisted metal, blue lights. She felt guilty – why had she been pushing him away all these weeks? What if something awful had happened? She made a small deal with God – bring him home safe and I'll be nice to him. Just return him to me so I get the chance.

Louise had always catastrophised – fretting about disasters around every corner. Even as a young girl she'd worried about car crashes, earthquakes, war. Could she blame this trait on her habit of 'settling' – with her career, her marriage? Not brave enough to take a risk.

It was Monday lunchtime, and she was on a half day. She was

attempting to sketch, but was distracted by Danny's absence. Each time her pencil touched the page she had flashes of his face, bloodied, by a roadside. Maybe some fresh air would help. She headed out with the dog. Olaf seemed thrilled with the impromptu trip and, as he trotted along next to her with his light lurcher gait, she felt her brow relax. She tried Danny's phone again – straight to voicemail. The girls' recorded message played again, their squeaky four-year-old voices sucking Louise backwards through time, 'Daddy is busy please leave a message' recited in unison in matching sing-song voices. As she approached the community centre she saw Jack and Sasha standing next to what appeared to be an open fridge. Olaf suddenly lunged towards the group, taking Louise with him.

'Oh hi,' said Sasha, first to the dog and then to Louise. Olaf had made a beeline for Sasha and immediately buckled against his legs, folding around his shins, awaiting attention.

Jack laughed. 'Hiya Louise! Seems your dog is a fan of Scotsmen.'

Olaf was now on his back, tongue lolling, and Sasha had leaned down to tickle his tummy.

'Seems that way. How are you guys? I'm looking forward to tomorrow.' She gently tugged at Olaf's lead, but he was in too much bliss to notice.

'Yeah us too. Wait till you see your pot. I've only peeked into the kiln, but it looks like the glaze has worked beautifully Louise – I think you'll be pleased.'

Louise's heart leapt. 'Really?' She grinned. 'God that's so cool, I can't wait. How's Danny's?'

'Err . . .' Sasha straightened up, patting a few strands of dog hair from his hands. 'From what I could see, it's definitely unique.' He smiled.

Louise nodded – she only hoped Danny would be back in time for the class. 'Nice fridge,' she said, taking in the yellowing interior and sticky-looking shelves.

'Don't you start,' he warned. 'Becky has already been taking the Mickey out of me – I was so excited when I found it in the shed. I stand by my excitement though, Louise, because an unplugged fridge,' he tapped the top, 'is basically a giant Tupperware container – any unfinished pieces will retain their moisture in this beauty. It means we can start a piece one week, and finesse it and decorate it the next. We'll get much more done.'

'Ah cool!' said Louise. 'Do you need a hand getting it indoors?'

'Well, this strapping young lad Jack can help carry it in, but if you got the door that'd be helpful.'

Once inside they deposited the fridge in the stockroom.

Jack's stomach rumbled loudly. 'Right, that's the lunch bell,' he chortled. 'Can I tempt you two with one of Sprinkles Café's finest sandwiches? Pearl usually pops in there for a mint tea about this time, so I'm hoping our paths may cross.'

'Go on then,' said Sasha, 'whatever you recommend Jack. Louise?'

She'd been so stressed all morning trying to track down Danny she'd neglected to eat, and she suddenly felt starving, but didn't want to intrude. 'No, you don't need me getting under your feet, I'll make something at home.'

'Nonsense,' said Sasha. 'You can help me set up for tomorrow if you like, think Becky's out on an errand so I'd would appreciate a hand unloading the kiln. Jack claims to have been quite the fielder in cricket back in the day, but I'm not sure I trust him not to drop those priceless pots.'

Louise laughed.

'Oi, I'll drop you in a minute,' growled Jack. 'Sound good?'

Louise nodded, and Olaf wagged his tail in agreement.

'Even the dog thinks it's a good idea. Right,' said Jack, 'I'll leave you to it, by the time you've finished I'll be back with refreshments.'

*

Twenty minutes later, Sasha and Louise had emptied the kiln, carefully transporting all the pots onto the display table at the back of the hall. Meanwhile Olaf had found a warm spot where the sun shone a golden patch on the floorboards, and he was curled up, snoozing. Sasha's phone buzzed and he looked at the screen. 'Oh it's Becky – "There in two mins",' he read out, '"sorry, mad day".'

Louise noticed a lightness in his voice when he saw the text was from Becky, his eyes brightening. They stood and admired the pots. Louise was indeed thrilled – the heat of the kiln had worked its magic, and the pink oxide markings had transformed into a trail of tiny pale blue birds that swooped around her pot. Louise thought that Jameela's pot was definitely up there with hers, if not better; the deep blue tracks on the white glaze looked like a winding road cutting through a snow-covered landscape.

Two minutes later they both heard the front doors bang open. Olaf lifted his head.

Sasha put his fingers to his lips and crouched down behind one of the workbenches, signalling to Louise to do the same at the opposite bench where she was standing.

She felt awkward. She didn't want to play a prank on Becky, but also didn't want to be a spoilsport.

She could hear Becky's footsteps coming down the hallway, and then the door swing slowly open. Olaf let out a low growl, but didn't get up. Louise couldn't see Becky from her position on the floor but she could hear her soft footsteps walking slowly down the centre of the hall towards them.

Louise was sure Becky would be able to hear her heart hammering in her chest, it sounded so loud in her own ears. She looked across to Sasha, who had his hand over his mouth to stifle his laughter.

Sasha waited until he saw Becky come level with the bench, and Louise, on seeing the feet instantly knew the scuffed black trainers didn't belong to a woman. Neither did the ankle tag. Before she could recalculate and warn Sasha, he had sprung up from his prone position, lunged towards his victim, and shouted '*Rarrrr*' at the top of his voice.

The stranger screamed in response and leapt back, knocking over a stool and nearly falling backwards over the pottery wheel by the bench. Sasha let out a small shriek of surprise too, his hands still making claw shapes up by his face. Louise thought he looked like a camp T-Rex. He slowly lowered his arms, while Louise stood up.

'What the fuck?' said the man, in a nasal Mancunian accent. He gave a short, hollow laugh, but was clearly shaken. He gripped the workbench with bloodless boney hands.

'Oh God I'm so sorry. I was expecting someone else,' said Sasha. The guy saw Sasha clock the tag around his ankle and quickly moved his jean leg to cover it again.

'Fuck's sake you're not kidding,' said the man, any humour now drained from his voice.

'How can I help you?' Sasha asked.

Louise knew who it was – the greasy hair, the weasel face, chipped tooth – older now, as if he'd withered a bit. 'Tony?' said Louise.

He spun to face her, noticing her for the first time.

He moved closer. 'Fuck me! You're Emma's little sister aren't you?' He still breathed heavily from the shock, and smelt of stale fags and fresh booze even though it was barely midday.

'Yeah, Louise. Long time no see. What are you after?' She tried to sound relaxed because Tony had always been volatile, but her voice sounded forced.

'I came to find Becky – my son's mum.' He directed this at Sasha. 'We had a bit of a row, and I just wanted to make sure she was OK. Think she's avoiding me.'

Sasha bristled. 'A row?'

Tony paused, slowly looking Sasha up and down. 'Yeah. A row. All old couples have them. Sure you and your boyfriend do some-times.' He swayed slightly, then turned to Louise. 'And you know what you women are like – going on and on . . .' he trailed off.

Louise didn't rise to the insult, she just wanted to get him out of there – he was drunk and spoiling for a fight. 'She's not here Tony, but we'll tell her you popped by.'

'I can see she's not here Louise,' he smirked, 'well done anyway. You were always the brighter one, compared to your sister, though that don't take much. Though we always had fun, me and your Emma.' He leered, eyes dead. Louise felt anger rise, but swallowed it down. Saliva glistened on his teeth.

'Seeing as she's not here, I might as well have a quick look round – see what all the fuss is with this pottery shite she's been banging on about,' he sneered.

'Righty-ho,' said Sasha, his accent sounding less jocular than usual. Louise noticed Sasha pull himself up to his full height, which was considerably taller than the man in front of him. 'Well, like you say mate – she's not here, and we've got a lot to be cracking on with, sorting out all this "pottery shite",' Sasha grinned a hard grin, and Louise marvelled at how a smile could so clearly say, 'Fuck off immediately'.

Tony studied Sasha for a moment, his bloodshot eyes stumbling blearily over Sasha's features. 'You're a Jock eh? I knew a few smelly socks inside . . . bunch of twats most of them.' He looked around the room as he spoke, as if they were acquaintances making small talk at an art gallery opening. 'You the bloke with the girl's name? Susan? Sally? Summat like that.' He was slurring now, but Louise saw his eyes became sharper – maybe the adrenaline from trying to push Sasha's buttons was putting a bit of fire in his belly. 'Yeah Becky has mentioned you a few times . . . I believe, knowing her as well as I do,' Tony winked as he said it, 'you might be in with a chance with her. She's a good-looking woman still . . . though of course she's not as pretty or young as she used to be.' Sasha bit his lip. 'You know what they say, women are like dog shit – the older they are the easier they are to pick up.'

Louise felt rooted to the spot – Sasha looked down at his knuckles as if deciding which fist to punch Tony with first.

'Look Tony, Becky's told me all about you,' at this he looked Tony up and down, 'about what a hard man you are, as long as it's women half your size you're hitting. I don't want a fight, but if I have to, if I really have to, I'll happily kick your scrawny wee arse all around that car park for the whole estate to see. From what I hear about you, I imagine there'd be a few people who'd enjoy it.'

Tony looked shocked and drew his bony head in. He hiccupped.

Louise could see him taking in Sasha's build and height not to mention how fit he looked; a quick calculation and Tony seemed to work out it was probably best he didn't push it further. He took a step back away from Sasha, but Sasha stepped towards him at the same time so they were now toe to toe.

'I'll maybe mention to Becky you popped by, but in the mean-time, I think it's probably best if you . . .' Sasha leaned in close and whispered hard, 'fuck off.'

Tony took another step back. He looked affronted, wrinkled his nose as though Sasha had just farted on a first date.

As he stepped back he swept his arms upwards as if being held up by a gunman. His left hand caught a jar of oxide and sent it spinning across the top of the bench. It rolled off the edge and shattered on the floor, a mini mushroom cloud of pink powder rising up. He stumbled slightly and leaned backwards with one elbow onto the display table behind him, knocking off one of the pots. Louise knew immediately it was Jameela's. She gasped.

Tony smiled. 'Oops,' he said, acting all casual, but Louise could tell he was shaken.

Suddenly the doors swung open and banged on the walls behind, making both men jump and breaking the stand-off.

'Everything OK here lads?' It was Jack, looking stern. He addressed both the men, but was glaring at Tony. He held a baguette in his hand like a sword. Next to him stood Becky, looking absolutely mortified. Her eyes were wide as they travelled over the broken pot, the spilled pink powder, and lastly, they landed on Tony.

'Becks!' He dropped his hands to his sides, brushing off the specks of pink powder that had dusted onto his jeans on impact.

He wiped his nose with the back of his hand and sniffed. 'I've been meeting your lovely mate Samantha here,' he gestured to Sasha.

Becky looked as if she might burst into tears. Her skin had gone grey. 'You're drunk Tony,' she said quietly. 'What are you doing here? Embarrassing me in front of my friends like this? At my place of work?'

He smiled menacingly, and Louise watched as he casually strolled towards the pair. 'Well, I've not seen you for days, you're clearly avoiding me, so when I finished a job nice and early I thought I'd come find you – and this is the welcome I get?'

'Just go Tony – get out,' she whispered.

'Getting a bit of a habit this Becks – you telling me to "Get out". You wanna be careful with that mouth of yours, you know what happened last time.'

Louise saw Becks lift a hand to her neck momentarily, the subtlest of moves, but it spoke volumes. She stepped aside as Tony approached, Jack only moving just enough to let Tony squeeze through the door.

'I'll see you at home Becks,' Tony shouted from the corridor.

Becky covered her face with her hands, reminding Louise of the girls when they were little, as if by blocking their vision they became invisible. Louise went to her and gently put an arm around her shoulder. 'He's not changed has he?' she murmured to Becky. 'He was a waster then and he's a waster now.'

Sasha approached them. 'Hey,' he spoke softly, 'are you OK?'

'Not really,' said Becky, giving a brave smile and shaking her head. 'I'm mortified. I'm so sorry Sasha – you shouldn't be dealing with idiots like Tony, he's dangerous.'

Sasha smiled. 'Don't worry about me, I've dealt with people bigger and uglier than him.' He paused. 'Well, definitely bigger than him.'

Becky smiled, though tears still welled in her eyes.

Despite the stressful situation there was an undeniable frisson between Sasha and Becky. Louise would've felt like a gooseberry, but luckily Jack was there too, and now he spoke: 'Right, we'll get this mess sorted out, but first – grub's up.'

Louise went to make tea and, as she did, Becky appeared. Louise was sure there were marks on her neck, but didn't want to stare.

'Look, I don't want to talk out of turn here Becky,' she said gently, 'but are you safe at home with Tony? I'm worried you're in danger, and if you are, there are places you can seek refuge you know, that can help.'

'I know there are, I just feel like I need to bide my time, and if I keep my head down he'll leave. He's on a promise to stay at a mate's place or, if not, he'll crawl back to his mum's. My main worry is Elliot, but he's away thank God, so as long as he's safe . . . Besides, I don't want to leave, it's my home and I've worked hard to get it just how I like it. Why should I be the one to run from him?'

Becky got the milk from the fridge and passed it to Louise, who sighed heavily. 'It's so messed up though, makes me so angry, he's vile.'

'I know, I'm actually embarrassed I was ever with such a despicable human being.' Becky laughed grimly, then tears caught at the back of her throat. She took a deep breath and rubbed her face; she looked knackered. 'Thank you for being so lovely, Louise,' she said, 'and for not judging.'

Louise shook her head. 'Judging who, you? You need to realise Becky, people round here have huge respect for you, everyone knows you've not had it easy, yet you've survived. If anything, people just feel bad for you having Tony to deal with whenever he's out.'

Louise was looking for teaspoons, and Becky pointed to the cutlery drawer. 'That's almost worse, I bet people think I'm a real mug for taking him back.'

'No they don't. Look,' Louise stopped stirring the tea and turned to Becky, 'nobody's life is perfect Becky. Every relationship is complicated. Take me and Danny. I love him, but we're struggling a bit at the moment.'

On cue, Louise's phone rang in her pocket, she rolled her eyes. 'Speak of the devil . . .' She got out her phone and, sure enough, it was him. She'd been worried all day, and any dread about his safety was now swallowed up by a mixture of relief and irritation.

'Danny, where have you been, I've been calling all day?'

The voice that replied wasn't Danny, it was a woman: 'Louise? It's Rania from Whittaker and Son – I've just been in Danny's car to collect some paperwork and realised he's left his phone. I knew you'd be worried.'

Louise felt a flutter of panic in her chest on hearing the familiar singsong voice of Rania. 'Thanks so much – what a nightmare. He's up to Carlisle for three drops, and on to Dundee, he's going to be stuck without a phone – it's got all the numbers on there for the depots, plus his sat nav apps —'

Rania cut her off, 'No Louise, you've got it wrong love. He's only on a local run today, Oldham, then across to Leeds. He should be back in the next hour, but as soon as I saw his phone I thought I'd best ring you anyway.'

'Oh,' said Louise, her heart racing. Becky was watching her now. 'My mistake. Thanks Rania, bye.'

'Everything OK?' asked Becky.

Louise felt sick, her stomach churned. 'Fine – diary mix-up.' She grinned, but it felt like she merely bared her teeth, like an animal in pain.

Danny had lied to her – he definitely said he'd be back late and not to wait up. If he wasn't in Scotland, then where the hell was he, and why had he lied?

31

Becky

The morning after the terrible scene with Tony at the community centre, Becky felt hungover despite not drinking a drop.

The rush of adrenaline and cortisol mixed with the hot embarrassment caused by her ex's behaviour had drained her, a cocktail of shame making her feel hollowed out. She hadn't slept, eventually giving up on the escape of slumber, padding downstairs in the empty house at 4 a.m. to make tea.

She was still reeling from Tony's violent attack under her own roof. Her feelings of despair had developed as vividly as the bruise on her neck where Tony had grabbed her. Despite the chain being on the front door and the back door being bolted, she didn't feel safe at home any more. Ironically she'd sought refuge at the community centre, hoping the humdrum routine of work in the company of Jack and Sasha would provide distraction and solace, but Tony had showed he could ruin that too by turning up and causing trouble. No part of her life was beyond his poisonous reach. Would she ever feel safe anywhere again?

Despite his heavy promise that she'd 'see him at home', Becky hadn't seen Tony since he'd staggered away from the community centre. His detritus still littered the sofa – empty cider cans and a twisted knot of duvet, but no Tony. She had half expected that – he had form for going underground after bad behaviour, like a dangerous dog lurking in its kennel after biting someone. Nevertheless her heart had been thumping as she'd turned the corner into her street and relief had flooded through her when she'd found the house empty. She'd checked every room, her legs feeling liquid, shallow breaths coming too quickly, before locking herself in.

Becky hoped that by some minor miracle his mother had taken pity on him and maybe this would be the beginning of the end of his residency at her house, stinking up her sofa.

Despite feeling delicate and worn that morning, Becky looked in the bathroom mirror and, even as she dabbed concealer on her neck, she promised herself that the day would be a good one. She could see the old Becky cowering in the shadows behind her eyes, the bruised one who flinched at life, but Becky didn't want her to re-emerge, even though Tony's violent outburst had been a stark reminder of how it felt to be at his mercy. She'd managed to shake off that feeling of dread during the time he'd been in prison; not all at once, but as the days turned into weeks then into months, she had shed the fear scale by scale, like a snake shedding its skin.

No, she promised herself, today would be a good day. She didn't feel too convinced.

Luckily the morning flew by in a flurry of emails, and around midday there came a gentle knock at her office door. Sasha, in white T-shirt and dark jeans, peered around the door.

'Hey,' he said, with a small smile. Becky felt her tummy flip; he was cute when he was his usual Tigger-like self – bouncing about with bags of enthusiasm – but this calm and quiet Sasha was even cuter.

Becky smiled. 'Hello. Thank you for your texts.'

Sasha shook his head sadly. 'I was worried, hated the thought of you being anywhere near him when he was in a state like that,

I didn't really sleep thinking about it.' Now Becky looked closer, his face did look a little crumpled.

'I was fine,' she said. 'Thank you though – I knew he'd most likely slink off somewhere.' She didn't mention how sick with fear she felt when she'd set off for home.

'Do you know where? Or when he'll be back?'

Becky shook her head. 'To be honest, I'm trying not to think about him today.' She widened her eyes dramatically. 'I'm trying to keep him shoved in a cupboard at the back of my mind!' She hoped her jolly demeanour was concealing the desperation she felt.

'Understood . . . understood.' Sasha shuddered slightly as if to shake himself from his sombre mood. He rubbed his hands together and grinned. 'Well, OK, in that case, I'm gonna do my best to make sure you have a lovely afternoon – stand by for our next project, slab building, it should be fun!'

A little before 7 p.m. the potters started to arrive, and Becky and Sasha intercepted Jameela at the front door asking her to come for a quick word in Becky's office. She had arrived with Sheila, who was interrupted mid-sentence and was left in the corridor with her mouth still moving but no words coming out, like a goldfish in plum-coloured lipstick.

'I'm so sorry Jameela, we had a little trouble here yesterday, and your pot was damaged,' Sasha explained.

Becky studied the floor, embarrassed.

'Oh no, that's a shame. It's OK though – accidents happen. I wondered what was happening then,' Jameela gave a relieved laugh, 'you both seemed terribly serious!'

'I'm sorry,' Becky said, 'you might as well know, it was my ex partner Tony who smashed it, he came in drunk, waving his arms about, and . . .'

'Hey,' Jameela said firmly, 'Becky, it doesn't matter, honestly.

I've got bigger things to worry about at the moment, and by the sounds of it you have too. Can it be glued?'

'Already done,' said Sasha, 'though it's nowhere near its former glory sadly. You'd done a great job too – the glaze had turned out beautifully. Louise said yours was the best one.'

'Louise?' said Jameela.

'Yes, she was here when it happened,' explained Becky. She thought she saw a tiny spark of irritation flash in Jameela's eyes, but then it was gone. 'Oh well, like I say, these things happen.'

On rejoining the class, Sheila was all over Jameela, a puppy sniffing a sibling returned to the litter.

Becky watched as Jameela filled Sheila in, paranoid both women would look her way when the name Tony was revealed, but instead they looked towards Louise, Sheila's eyes narrowing slightly as she murmured something to Jameela, who laughed and shook her head.

Sasha had insisted that Becky join in with the class again, and she had to admit she was loving it. Once everyone had collected their finished coil pots from the table to a chorus of *oohs* and *aahs* – Jameela playing down the damage to hers – they began slab building. This entailed rolling out the clay and cutting it into small rectangular and square slabs that could then be 'glued' together at the edges.

'Slip,' Sasha said, holding up a pot of murky red liquid, 'is a mixture of clay and water, it will bind together your crosshatched edges.'

The potters gathered around as he demonstrated. 'When you crosshatch you simply slice lots of small lines in the clay, creating ridged areas that, when used with slip, will stick to each other, the indentations can hold onto each other much better than two smooth sections ever could.'

The potters got to work and the room fell largely silent. Becky felt herself again be seduced by the clay – slicing it with a sharp tool was incredibly satisfying, like drawing a knife across the top of a block of fridge cold butter. She was immersed in the sensation, and was taken back to memories of rolling out gingerbread dough with her mum in their small kitchen. She could almost smell the spices and feel her mum next to her. What was it with clay that seemed to focus you so much that it could block out the present and slide you sideways or backwards into your own thoughts?

Sasha was suddenly at her elbow. 'Very nice,' he whispered so as not to break her concentration. Too late, though she didn't mind snapping out of her daydream for him; her skin tingled as he stood close to her. 'What are you planning?' he asked, looking at the small sketch she'd made in her notebook.

'A trinket box I think,' she said, suddenly conscious of her breath as he stood so close. Heat bloomed up her neck.

'Ah, for the family jewels?' He smiled.

'Something like that,' she said. 'Obviously amongst all the conker-sized diamonds and priceless gems I have a favourite – my mum's ring, used to be my nan's. It'd be nice to have something lovely to keep it in, or failing that, a lumpen, crooked box made of clay to keep it in. Either will do.'

Sasha chuckled, and again Becky marvelled at how making him laugh felt like winning a prize.

Happy with her trinket box, Becky thought she'd better do her actual job, so went to put the kettle on and slide some biscuits out onto a large dinner plate.

Louise came in. 'We must stop meeting like this,' she laughed. 'Seems we're always hanging out in this kitchen.' She found a glass and let the tap run cold.

'I know,' Becky said, 'I think you're secretly drawn to the glamour – the stained Formica, the cracked lino . . .'

Louise looked a little careworn to Becky, and she suddenly had an idea.

'We ought to go for a little potters' outing, some drinks or something.'

Louise brightened. 'Definitely.'

Becky started to wrestle open the biscuit packet. 'So, you tracked down Danny OK in the end?'

'Yeah,' Louise said. 'He insisted he'd told me the job had changed, said he'd mentioned it in the morning, but . . . well, the girls are like a whirlwind getting ready for school, so maybe I missed it.'

Becky nodded, though she knew this scenario only too well – being deceived, gaslighted, undermined. Though Danny seemed nothing like Tony.

'Thing is,' said Louise, 'we've been having a bit of a bumpy time, mainly because of me. I felt I just needed a bit of space, and now,' she tipped the remainder of the water into the sink, 'I'm worried I've pushed him away.' She looked teary. 'Who knows? Maybe I'm imagining it, I'm just paranoid, or maybe,' she sighed, 'it's a case of "be careful what you wish for" – I only wanted space, not to be apart from him. I've no proof he's lying, but if I'm honest, I know he is, and it's . . . awful – it's completely out of character.'

Becky hugged her. 'Come on,' she said. 'I'm sure there's a reason, maybe he needed some time to himself and he's too embarrassed to say. Or maybe he's giving you a taste of your own medicine – you asked for space and he gave it you. Either way, you'll work it out I'm sure. He's mad about you!'

Just then Sheila came in, her oversized turquoise shirt cinched at the waist, making her look as if she'd been playing dress-up with the grown-ups' clothes. 'Just in time for a biscuit I see?' she said. 'I'll take one for Jameela – poor thing, she's very sad about the pot smashing incident.'

Becky noticed she said the last bit to Louise. 'I know, it's awful. Her pot was so good too.'

'Yes,' said Sheila, 'both yours and hers were the best, such a shame hers was damaged. Did you see what happened Louise?'

'To be fair Sheila,' cut in Becky, 'it was Tony who smashed it, and we were all horrified when it happened, particularly Louise. When we spoke to Jameela she was absolutely fine about it.'

'Course!' gushed Sheila, as if to suggest otherwise was ridiculous, even though she'd just done exactly that.

Becky knew she had Sheila on the back foot – she wasn't about to let her upset Louise when she was already stressed enough.

'It was a complete accident,' Sheila continued, 'she knows that. It's just a shame that out of the two best pots only one remains undamaged.' She smiled sweetly and took the plate of biscuits from Becky. 'I'll hand these round shall I?'

She left, and Louise turned to Becky. 'Hang on, was she just implying I'd sabotaged Jameela's pot?' She laughed incredulously.

'Oh God, take no notice,' said Becky. 'As my nan would say, she could start an argument in an empty room.'

At the end of the class, the slab-built boxes were placed on a table in the storeroom to dry, and the potters washed their tools and hung up their aprons for another week. Becky loved how with each class, they became more familiar, chatting as they shrugged on their coats. Jack helping Pearl into her cardigan as she talked with Louise about her girls, Danny chatting to Sheila about her jewellery box, Sasha asking Jameela how she'd enjoyed the class. As the echoes of the last good wishes and goodbyes fell silent, Sasha and Becky headed off to The Apollo at his suggestion. There they ate souvlaki, and again tried but failed to resist the extra carafe of wine brought over by Apollo's wife Zoe.

'I think we should make this our weekly date,' Sasha said as they weaved through the streets afterwards. Becky had tried to resist his charms, fooling herself that she could keep her growing affection for him on ice until Tony had gone, but it was a struggle to hide how taken she was by him.

'Date?' She'd laughed, then instantly regretted it when he looked a little bashful.

'Well, not date. OK, a regular, post-class work appointment.'

'A debrief,' she added and, despite the wine, resisted making an inappropriate quip about briefs. It wasn't necessary anyway – Sasha's eyes twinkled as he agreed.

'Aye. A full debrief.'

Once through the front door Becky paused and listened to the house, silence. It felt calm. Tony was still gone.

32

Sheila

The days following the news of his mum's refusal to eat were some of the hardest of Martin's life. Sheila could almost see the grief on him. It hung from him throughout the day. During the nights she was roused by his whimpering in the darkness as he dreamed about his mum: 'We were on the beach in Wales, Sheila,' he whispered sadly, 'I couldn't find her, but I could hear her calling my name.'

The day at Oakview when they'd been given the news, Sheila had gone to help with some paperwork in the office before going to find Martin sitting with his mum as she slept. The window was open and the gentlest of breezes played with the floor-length net curtain. Sheila tried hard not to imagine how many lives had slipped away in that very room, it freaked her out a little. How many sons or daughters had held the hands of a parent in their last days and hours.

Sheila had studied her mother-in-law's face as she slept; this once formidable woman with a brain as sharp as her tongue now looked almost translucent, her thin skin stretched too tightly over her features.

Her closed eyelids had looked bruised, as though she was wearing a dab of lilac eyeshadow ready for a night on the tiles.

Martin had spoken suddenly, making Sheila jump. 'I feel like I'm at the top of a slide I don't want to go down. Like this, right now is the beginning of the end, and I'm powerless . . . and at the bottom of the slide she won't be there to catch me like she has all my life.'

Sheila had gently stroked his hair. 'I'll catch you Martin.' He'd smiled as though he appreciated the gesture, but she wasn't what he wanted. Sheila bit her lip and tried not to take it personally.

They'd both sat there for a while, but eventually Sheila's bottom had started to go numb. 'Sweetheart, do you want to come for a leg stretch, some fresh air?' But Martin shook his head. He reminded Sheila of the collie dogs who wouldn't leave their master's grave.

Sheila did a couple of laps of the gardens and called Ollie to tell him the news about his grandma's decline; his girlfriend Charlotte answered – Sheila was sure she heard her hair swish as she shouted for Ollie. Her son took the news harder than Sheila was expecting, and she wished she could've been there to hold him; instead his voice became muffled as Charlotte comforted him with a hug. He rang off tearfully. Sheila felt bruised at the thought of another woman comforting her boy.

The sky had started to darken by the time Sheila got back indoors. She found Martin asleep, his head rested on the covers next to his mum's hip, a patch of dribble already formed on the soft waffle blanket.

A small tray with a cup of tea and some juice had been left on the bedside table, and Sheila felt embarrassed for him – a middle-aged man, vulnerable and childlike, snoozing on his mummy.

As they walked home that night, Martin glanced around constantly, as if startled that the world was carrying on around him as usual.

Sheila tut-tutted at a bunch of kids on the precinct shoving each other about on the bench and shrieking.

'It feels all wrong,' Martin said. 'Like everything is changing for me, yet no one knows, and normal life is just rumbling on. No one realises I'm about to lose the woman who means the most to me in the world, who's always loved me despite everything . . .'

Again, Sheila bit her lip.

Martin walked each morning and evening to Oakview to sit by his mother's bed. Sheila went every few days – she had her volunteering to think of, plus, her mother-in-law, who was always well turned out, would probably insist that Sheila mustn't let herself go, and her hair, nail and facial appointments must be honoured – it's what Margaret would want, Sheila was sure of that.

When Sheila accompanied Martin, she preferred it if Margaret was sleeping as opposed to lying glaring at them both, her eyes rolling as she strained to think who this couple was, as if they'd met at a party once but out of context she couldn't quite place them.

One morning, Sheila arrived at Margaret's room first, as Martin was chatting to the manager Mrs Blackstone.

Sheila tried to hide her dismay that her mother-in-law was awake, not that Margaret would notice – she was staring out of her window at the grey sky.

Sheila tidied the room, to make herself useful. Long abandoned novels and sudoku books gathered dust on a shelf. She was just changing the water in a vase of carnations, when Sheila heard a croaking sound. Sheila's head whipped around, hoping someone else had slipped into the room, but no, it was just the two of them, and Margaret was trying to speak.

Sheila filled a plastic beaker with water and, using a sponge like she'd seen Martin do, dabbed Margaret's lips, a drop of water breaking loose and running down her neck onto the collar of her nightie. The moisture disappeared into the cracked skin of her lips.

Margaret's eyes were no longer glazed, in fact they looked sharp and focused.

Able to speak now the water had loosened her lips, she whispered something, but Sheila couldn't catch what. Glancing around the room, she leaned in closer to the old lady's mouth: 'Look after him,' Margaret whispered, 'and Anne-Marie.' A faint smile crossed her lips.

Then she closed her eyes.

'Margaret,' Sheila gently shook her mother-in-law's shoulder, but she was now fast asleep. *Who is Anne-Marie?* thought Sheila, her imagination going into overdrive. Was Margaret just delirious, or was it a secret daughter given up for adoption? If Sheila didn't know who Anne-Marie was, how was she supposed to look after her? Then the thought flitted across her mind, casting a quick shadow – what if Anne-Marie was the owner of the mystery pants? The very idea made Sheila's heart flutter in her chest like a trapped bird. She felt a heat travel up her neck. Margaret had always been an upstanding member of the community, surely her mum-in-law – a trustee of a cat charity – wouldn't condone Martin's affair? *That's ridiculous*, thought Sheila, *the notion that I'd have to look after Martin and his mistress? No, this must be the dementia talking.*

A moment later Martin reappeared, carrying a vase of flowers. 'From the birth centre.' He smiled. It was quite common for the new parents in the birth centre next door to donate their numerous bouquets to the home as they left clutching their newborns; a gift from those entering the world to those about to depart it.

'Lovely. Darling your mum just spoke.'

Martin froze on the spot. 'Really?'

Sheila nodded. 'Yes, I don't suppose you know who Anne-Marie is?'

At that moment the vase slipped from his grip and landed with an almighty crash on the tiles. The water sluiced shards of glass all over the floor, and the flowers lay in a soggy pile on top. Sheila and Martin both looked at Margaret, who was still sound asleep.

Julie, Margaret's favourite nurse, popped her head in and spotting the glass, she shouted, 'Nobody move!' as though it was a bank heist.

'Julie,' said Sheila calmly, 'be a love and fetch me a brush and dustpan please, I can clear it up.' The woman did as she was told.

'Sorry,' said Martin. 'It was just a shock hearing that Mum had spoken and I'd missed it. The only Anne-Marie I know of is our cleaner when I was a lad, maybe it was the drugs talking.'

'Yes,' said Sheila, 'I thought as much myself.'

Later on as they were leaving, Mrs Blackstone called them in for a quick chat. Sheila sensed she was drip-feeding Martin information, no doubt knowing from experience that some relatives couldn't cope with a single wave of information for fear of drowning in grief and panic.

Martin nodded and Sheila took notes on her phone as Mrs Blackstone skilfully peppered facts through her small talk about the possibility of Margaret eventually 'forgetting how to or becoming unable to' swallow. She mentioned 'malnutrition', and 'dehydration', and talked of 'making her comfortable', and 'blood pressure checks'.

Sheila was glad her head was bowed as she made notes – the words blurred as her eyes swam with tears.

It was the following Tuesday when Sheila was at pottery that her phone rang. She's just finished glazing her trinket box and was a little annoyed to feel her phone vibrating deep in her dungaree pocket. It was Martin. 'Mrs Blackstone has just called, she said we need to go now.'

They arrived at Oakview ten minutes later.

*

Sheila didn't know what to expect when they burst into her room; maybe a scene like something from a hospital drama – doctors and nurses working on Martin's mum, shouting instructions at each other. But her living will clearly stated a 'do not resuscitate order'. Margaret had made it years ago, getting organised after her husband had died, knowing that Martin, if it came to it, would move heaven and earth to keep her alive even if it was her time to go.

The room was empty and quiet, apart from his mum and Julie the nurse, who, on seeing the couple, stood up from the chair by the bed, and whispered, 'Sleep tight Mrs Harris.'

She slipped out, touching Martin lightly on his shoulder as she passed him.

They both sat down on the chairs next to his mum's bed. Her breathing was laboured, the gap between each breath becoming longer. Martin held his mum's hand and told her how much he loved her.

She looked so frail, yet peaceful. The lamp was on its lowest setting and cast the faintest of golden glows across her face, illuminating the map of pink veins on her cheeks. The tiniest of smiles played across her lips as if she was having a lovely dream. Martin sat talking softly to her, not daring to move from her side. He told stories Sheila had heard dozens of times that had gone down in family legend. The time his dad put too much brandy on the Christmas pudding and the flames were so big he had to run and throw the pudding onto the snowy back lawn, where it lay, blackened and sizzling like a meteorite. Martin talked about how she and Dad used to always jive at family parties, and about how her scrambled egg was the only thing he'd eat when he was poorly. It seemed as if he was rifling through five decades worth of memories – his memories – pulling out good times, funny times, poignant times, and laying them out before her.

Sheila rummaged in her bag for another tissue as Martin said, 'Dad will be waiting for you Mum. If you see Dad, go to him, he'll look after you. And tell him I love him too will you?' A little later he said, 'Just relax Mum, I'm here. Just imagine we're back in Spain, sitting in the sunshine with Dad. The sun on your skin, the sound of the waves. Dad will be along soon. When he comes, you go to him. I'll be OK, you go to Dad.'

It was as though he was finally giving her permission to die.

A while later Sheila came back with coffee for the two of them.

As she sat by Martin they watched as Margaret's shoulders slackened and the gap between her breaths lengthened. Her fingers very gently squeezed his hand. She took another deep breath, exhaled, and then, silence. She was gone, they knew it. Sheila put an arm around Martin as he sobbed like a child into the bedclothes and gripped his mum's hand.

33

Becky

At the community centre, Becky was working on a new class schedule that she planned to print out and pin up in the reception area. Sheila, who was on the estate committee, had suggested she also place it in the estate's bi-weekly newsletter. 'Reach a broader audience,' she'd said to Becky over three Bourbon biscuits during a break at one of the pottery lessons.

An unexpected side effect of the pottery classes was a subtle upward trajectory in the centre's fortunes, and Becky thought she may as well embrace it. The place was still a touch tatty, but more classes meant more money to neaten up the place. An article in the *Lennington Echo* the week before had prompted even more enquiries about hiring the centre.

Sheila knew the assistant editor at the paper from when they did a charity piece to support the food bank, (featuring April and Sheila holding tins of soup as if ready to lob them at a coconut shy). The assistant editor – a skeletal woman called Sue with bifocals clanging on a pearl chain across her bony chest – had complimented Sheila on her new plum denim dungarees, and Sheila in turn had sent her the link to buy them, so they'd kept in touch.

Sheila said the pottery class was an upbeat local interest story, and Sue agreed. The short piece featured on page 5, and under the headline 'Have a nice clay!' was a shot of the whole group gathered around Sasha at the wheel, all of them wearing aprons and grinning, holding up their coil pots.

Since then enquiries had been coming in about using the centre for everything from life drawing and chess masterclasses, to 'confidence in the workplace' coaching. Becky reckoned with the deposits alone she could buy supplies and maybe chat Jack up to give the small hall a lick of paint.

As usual he'd been enthusiastic about the upturn in business. 'Your mum would be dead proud Becky,' he'd said. 'I reckon I'll join the new pilates group, get a six-pack to impress Pearl.'

The main priority for Becky though, was the pottery classes and, more to the point, the teacher Sasha. Over the weeks, Becky had found herself falling for Sasha. Whatever mood she was in when she arrived at the community centre, she would leave in a brighter one thanks to Sasha. He was, of course, very handsome, but his kind soul and natural warmth only served to make his good looks shine through even more. Their regular Tuesday evening dates felt just like that, a date – sharing souvlaki, warm pitta and wine. There'd be moments where she felt like there was absolutely no alternative but to kiss him, but then would chicken out at the last second, swallowing the temptation with a gulp, the adrenaline ringing in her ears as the moment passed. She started to make more of an effort – treating herself to some new mascara and a new top.

As the pair manoeuvred sacks of clay together, lugged buckets of water, arranged new shelving units, they talked. He made her roar with laughter about his scrapes as a kid growing up in Leith, playing knock-a-door-run. He'd talk of his work and his travels.

She'd tell funny stories about her mum, and he didn't make her feel silly when she told him her ambitions for the community, and her dreams of being in the police.

Becky sometimes felt as though Sasha spent extra time at the centre that wasn't exactly crucial. She allowed herself to wonder if maybe he was doing it to be close to her, but then scoffed at herself.

She couldn't deny that there was something there between them, but she was paranoid she was mistaking a simple friendship for something more. There would be moments when their arms would brush against each other as they shifted some equipment, and she was sure he felt it too – like static electricity. A fizzing feeling on the skin that spread like a heat to her loins. Occasionally he'd pass her an apron or a bottle of glaze and, being mischievous, wouldn't let go for a split second too long, and a brief tug of war would ensue. They would maintain eye contact in these moments, him raising an eyebrow in challenge, a wind-up, but somehow it was a sexy one. 'Thank you very much,' she'd say as he eventually relented and relaxed his grip, allowing her to snatch away her hand. 'Buffoon,' she'd mutter with a tut, though butterflies danced in her stomach.

Surely for there to be this stomach-churning heat and electricity, it had to come from the two of them, like a circuit.

Becky was feeling better than she had in weeks. Tony still cast a cloud over her life, but she rarely saw him as they both made the effort to ensure their paths never crossed. She would leave for work early while he still snored on the sofa, and in the evenings he would head straight to the pub after he'd finished with the house clearance crew, returning after last orders when Becky was asleep. It was easier that way, and Becky found she was good at pretending Tony didn't exist, for now anyway.

On Monday afternoon, the day before lesson number four, Sasha came to find Becky. She was trying to get the yoga mats into some kind of neater order.

'Can I steal you away please?' he said.

'Please do,' she replied, wiping her brow with the back of her hand. The day was warm and the stockroom was stuffy.

'Follow me,' he said.

In the large hall he'd set up his wheel – there was a cabbage-sized ball of clay and a bowl of water on a table by its side. 'Tomorrow,' he said, eyes glinting, 'is the first lesson where we'll be throwing something on the wheel.'

'Really?' said Becky. 'This is exciting news!'

'Yes,' nodded Sasha, 'wheely exciting!' Becky groaned. 'And,' he continued, 'no doubt the potters will get in a spin.'

'OK, enough now,' said Becky. She adjusted the strap of her white vest top – it was a cheap one that kept slipping down, and all morning she'd been flashing the edge of her pink bra. Sasha seemed to be trying his best to keep his gaze firmly on the clay.

'So,' he said, 'I thought I could give you a little demo then you can have a go if you like?'

Becky squealed. 'Oh my God – no. I couldn't – I mean, I'd love to, obviously, but . . .'

'Then you will. Look it's easy.'

Becky watched as Sasha put on an apron to protect his clothes – how was it even possible for an apron to look hot? It was like the Midas touch, but everything he touched turned not gold but slightly sexy.

'Come closer,' he said, sitting down at the wheel. She did as he asked.

She quickly scooped her blonde hair up into a bun to keep her neck cool, and stood over him, hands on hips, watching.

He grabbed the glistening ball and as he did, he pressed the foot pedal, making the wheel spin smoothly. Sasha threw the ball with some force onto the spinning surface and wet his fingers, dragging large drops of water with him and onto the clay as it spun.

'Woah,' said Becky under her breath; she was completely entranced, watching the wet, spinning clay be manipulated by his cupped hands and his fingers.

She loved how he harnessed the power of the wheel's motion, the clay yielding to his touch, firm one moment, feather light the next. 'It's as if it's under your spell,' she said. He beamed. It was like a performance, a dance – though there was a purity to it. His concentration was so intense, yet natural – he wasn't showboating. It was as if the clay became an extension of him.

She watched, mesmerised and almost a little dizzy, as the undulating lump of wet clay morphed within a few moments into a beautiful and recognisable shape – a simple bowl. The wheel slowly came to a standstill. He looked up at her.

'Wow,' she said. 'I mean, I hate to say it Sasha, but you're brilliant at that. It's like you're creating life!'

He laughed. 'Why thank ye kindly pretty lady.'

'I could watch you do that all day.' She knew she was swooning all over him, but couldn't help herself, she was genuinely impressed.

'No time sadly – 'cos it's your turn.'

Becky tied on one of the aprons and sat down. She felt a trickle of sweat make its way down her back, along her spine. Ringlets of hair had escaped her scrunchie and were now stuck to the moisture on the back of her neck. The cause of the heat was the late afternoon sun coming through the windows in the hall, but also the close proximity of Sasha.

He was behind her, and she was suddenly self-conscious about how she looked from that angle, all sweaty and hot, her bra cutting into the flesh under her armpits.

'Relax,' he said. He leaned over her and was so close she could feel his breath on the bare patch of skin just behind her left ear.

'Right Ms Becky, here we go.' With one swift motion he threw a fist-sized lump of clay onto the wheel with a thump. 'Slowly now,' he said, and he gently reached around and pushed her left knee down, so her left foot pressed gently on the pedal that controlled the speed of the wheel. The pedal reminded her of the one on her mum's old electric sewing machine.

He moved his hand from her knee, but remained hovering above her shoulders as she gently cupped the reddish-brown clay in her hands as it spun. Her hands quivered with the energy from the clay – she must've looked like a shivering victim of a near-drowning holding a mug of hot tea.

The more she pressed on the pedal, the faster the wheel spun and the faster the clay whizzed around, as if it had come alive and was trying to break free from her grasp.

If she let go now it would surely fling itself from the wheel and hurtle through the air. She felt a little out of control and giddy. 'Oh God!' she shouted, as the clay spun faster and faster and she pushed harder and harder on the pedal like a novice rider panicking and pulling on the throttle to slow a motorbike.

'Woah . . . slow down, ease up on the pedal,' laughed Sasha. He grabbed her knee and the feeling of his hand on her kneecap snapped her out of her trance. 'Steady . . . jeez Becky you're a wild one. Right, just feel the pulse of the clay, tune into the rhythm between your foot on the wheel, the clay and your body . . . don't be afraid to be firm.' Sasha craned his head around to look at her and, seeing her pink cheeks, smiled. 'And remember to breathe.'

He was right – Becky let out a long breath and laughed, realising she'd been holding her breath the whole time. 'OK, God, sorry, I went a bit mad there,' she said. She worked on breathing steadily, sucking on her lower lip like she always did when she concentrated, and within a few moments had found a steady pace. The clay seemed suddenly to settle, like a startled horse coming under control, relaxing its twitching withers.

'OK, good,' said Sasha. He occasionally dipped his fingers into a pot of water and scooped small amounts onto the clay as it spun to keep it moist and keen.

'Right, when you're ready, you're going to keep the heels of your hands together, still cradling the clay, and then firmly push your right thumb into the top of the clay to create a hole, so we can open it up into a bowl.'

The clay succumbed and gave way like a sink hole, allowing Becky to push down into it and stretch it.

She slowly started to push her thumb into the wetness, feeling the clay yield to the pressure. Sasha was silent and so was she, the only noise in the room was the wheel and the gentle slap of the clay against her hands. It was as if the whole room was holding its breath at this make or break moment.

Her left thumb joined the right and, by pulling the two slowly apart, the small hole began to stretch. Sasha sprinkled on a few more drops of water as the clay started to transform miraculously into a bowl. A lumpy, slightly lopsided bowl, but still, a bowl. Sasha guided her hands, leaning over her so she could feel his firm chest against her back. She pushed thoughts of Patrick Swayze from her mind. Together they gently squeezed the clay in their hands so it had nowhere to go but upwards, forming the walls of the bowl, Sasha dripping more water on, their hands working together, fingers slipping over the pulsating clay.

'Right, that's pretty good,' Sasha said. 'Easy does it, Becky, slowly release the pressure on the pedal.'

The wheel gradually stopped and they both froze. She could still feel Sasha as he crouched, leaning close to her as they both stared at the pot. Becky felt a thrilling surge in her stomach – a mixture of pride and exhilaration. She looked over her shoulder at Sasha and he met her eyes. She felt breathless. Before she could stop herself, she planted a kiss on his lips. His eyes widened with shock but he didn't pull away. Instead he slowly spun the stool around so she was facing him, and he crouched down and kissed her, slowly and gently. The tip of his tongue traced hers. They stopped, and he cupped her face in his hands. As he did, they both realised he had dark red wet clay on his palms, which was now smeared along Becky's jawline. She had no choice but to return the favour, so she lifted her wet slippy hands and took hold of his face. They burst out laughing at the painted-on beards they now both sported.

A loud bang caused them both to spring apart as Jack came bumping backwards through the double doors, carrying a large box.

Jack swung around on his heels and spotted them. 'Paper towels,' he announced, as Becky and Sasha scrubbed at their faces with their aprons.

'Thank you very much Jack, great work,' said Becky, still wiping her face.

Jack did a small bow. 'You're welcome – right, coffee anyone? I'm gasping,' and off he went.

Becky turned to Sasha, who was now busying himself wiping down the wheel.

She felt suddenly shy. 'That was nice,' she said, and Sasha looked up from his position on the floor.

'Aye, it was,' he replied, almost wistfully.

Oh God, she thought, *he regrets it already – we got caught up in a moment and now he wishes it hadn't happened.*

As if reading her mind he cleared his throat. 'Look, Becky, I like you, I really like you – you're a good mate . . .' her heart sank, here came the 'we're better as friends' speech, '. . . but I just can't, I mean . . . I shouldn't — '

She cut him off to spare them both the humiliation. 'Sasha. Stop. It's fine. Look, it was a silly kiss in the heat of the moment. I mean – look at that pot,' they both glanced at the wonky bowl, 'no wonder it got us all excited.' She smiled.

He chuckled grimly and went to speak, but she cut him off again – she didn't want to hear any lame excuses, she was embarrassed enough already. 'Come on,' she said, 'let's get cleaned up.' And she walked away as casually as she could muster, the door to the ladies loo banging shut just as the first tear fell.

An hour later Becky texted Sasha to say she had a migraine brewing and was off home. The first part was a slight exaggeration, and the second was delayed by the sight of Louise and her dog as she was leaving the community centre.

'Oh hello,' Louise said, 'perfect timing. I was just walking Olaf and thinking to myself, it's a beautiful day – perfect for a beer garden . . . can I tempt you with a quick drink?'

'Oh, I'm not sure.' Becky grimaced.

'Come on,' said Louise, 'it's too tragic if I only have a lurcher with a wind problem for a drinking partner.'

Becky looked at her watch – 4 p.m. – Tony would be arriving home to her house any minute. 'Go on then.' She smiled. 'Why not?'

The Queen Anne was a beautiful Victorian building with a very pretty beer garden to the rear. The two women sat amongst the hanging baskets in silence for a minute or two, sipping their wine and enjoying the calm, watching the bees dance around the flowers.

'This is just what I needed Louise, thank you.' Becky sipped her wine and sighed.

'No, thank you. I needed some female company – Olaf isn't much of a conversationalist, and as for Danny, I still don't know what's going on with him.'

Becky watched Louise gently rotate her wine glass on the table, lost in thought. 'What is going on with him?'

Louise smiled limply. 'Nothing. That's the problem; he's acting like everything is hunky-dory and normal, when it isn't. I know when he's lying, and I know that he wasn't on errands that afternoon when he told me he was on a job up in Cumbria. But I can't prove anything. I'm not sleeping – it's churning round in my head the whole night.'

Becky shook her head. 'Have you seen the way Danny looks at you Louise? He almost has cartoon hearts as pupils. Whatever he's up to – if anything – maybe it's something good?'

Louise nodded and said quietly, 'Yup, maybe.' Though she didn't sound convinced. 'How are you? Have you still got a lodger?'

Becky felt her jaw tense, picturing Tony's face, and said softly, 'Yeah, he's still there, I'm desperate for him to go, but if I'm honest Louise I'm too scared to kick him out.' She felt as if she might cry, remembering the way he'd slammed her against the wall. 'He's cruel, and I'm frightened of what he'll do if I push it, so I'm biding my time, hoping he leaves soon.'

'I feel awful for you Becky. I hate the thought of him having this power over you.'

Becky sipped the last of her wine; it was certainly helping. 'I messed up letting him stay that one night, 'cos now he thinks he's got his feet under the table.'

Louise lifted the dripping bottle from the ice bucket and topped up their glasses, looking deep in thought. 'I wish I had a gang of big tough brothers I could send round to boot him out . . . but I don't. Danny's a big softie – in fact the girls are probably tougher than him. Maybe I should send them round – they could TikTok

Tony to death, drive him slowly mad with their constant dancing and twitching.'

Becky smiled sadly. 'I'd try anything at the moment.'

'At least there's one silver lining on this Tony-shaped cloud – a handsome Scottish lining at that.' Louise waggled her eyebrows.

'What? Sasha?' said Becky, but she could feel her cheeks blooming pink. 'There's nothing going on there.'

Louise nudged her. 'Come on . . . you can tell he fancies you like mad.'

Becky shook her head. 'Nope. He doesn't.'

Louise laughed. 'Are you actually joking? All the potters have noticed how you look at each other. You two are so cute together.'

Becky could feel the wine unknotting her shoulders, loosening her thoughts. What the hell – she needed someone to talk to.

'We kissed,' she whispered, 'earlier today.'

Louise squealed. 'I knew it! I'm buying a hat.'

'Hang on,' Becky said, 'don't waste your money. We kissed, it was lovely, but then he pushed me away – he instantly regretted it. And now I'm mortified.'

Unbidden, the moment replayed again in her mind – he'd returned the kiss with gusto, so what was the problem? He was giving more mixed signals than a broken traffic light.

'Why though?' Louise looked confounded. 'Does he have a girl-friend? Or,' her eyes widened, 'a boyfriend?'

'Not that he's said.' Becky studied her wine.

Maybe he just didn't fancy her after all, and all those moments, the stomach-flipping glances, the smiles that made her insides quiver, had all been innocent. Perhaps he was fond of her in a purely platonic way?

'It doesn't make sense,' said Louise, 'his eyes aren't painted on – you're gorgeous and he clearly fancies you; more than that, the way he is around you, you can tell he just really likes you.' She shook her head as if to reorder her thoughts. 'When Tony was there that day, you should've seen the fury in Sasha's eyes when Tony spoke about you. I thought he was going to wipe the floor with him.'

Despite herself, Becky felt a glimmer of hope, and slightly giddy at the thought of Sasha defending her honour. Maybe it was the wine.

34

Becky

Becky closed her front door on the shrieks of a clutch of kids playing out in the street – one last hoorah before they were called in for tea.

The house was quiet. No television blaring, neither Tony's trainers nor work boots were in their usual pile by the door – he couldn't wear both pairs at once, so maybe, just maybe, he'd packed up and left as he'd said he would.

Sweet baby Jesus she prayed. If Tony is gone I promise to never be bad again – I will fundraise for the poor, rescue old ladies' cats from up trees, and never eat a Burger King meal deal in bed ever again, if, dear Lord, you have rid me of this bastard. She kicked off her shoes and headed to the lounge. Bracing herself for disappointment, telling herself his work boots might well be in the lounge, she swung open the door and gasped.

She couldn't hear the telly, not because it was switched off, but because it wasn't there. Neither was the Sky box, or the Bluetooth speaker she'd treated herself to in the sales.

What was there, was a tangle of wires where the telly used to be. And no sign of Tony.

She didn't know whether to laugh or cry. Or scream. Or all three in quick succession.

Despite the fact he'd robbed her, she was thrilled he was gone. Not only that, he'd now so thoroughly burnt his final bridge with her that there was surely no coming back from this. He'd broken the law, and therefore the terms of his early release. She was rid of him, and she'd come through it unscathed, almost anyway.

As soon as she reported the theft, the police would be able to trace him and his ankle tag and chuck his scrawny arse back in jail.

Before calling the police, she thought she had better check what else he'd nicked. In the kitchen, the microwave was gone, as was the smoothie maker she'd bought herself for her birthday. The fancy coffee machine she'd got for Elliot in the Boxing Day sales was missing too. She noticed her baking cupboard was open, and that her food mixer and electric whisk were also absent. Jesus – was he stealing to order for Mary Berry?

All his kitchen quarry lumped together would barely scrape in a hundred quid down the pub. He was obviously desperate.

The kitchen unit looked weirdly bare – just an empty photo frame of crumbs where the toaster had been.

She ran up the stairs two at a time to Elliot's room and could've cried on seeing the space on his neat shelf where his pride and joy once sat – his pair of Technics decks and mixer. Elliot had saved up for two years until he could afford them; he didn't fancy himself as a club DJ – he just loved music, and loved to play his records at family parties or for friends as they chilled in his room after a big night. The neat rows of vinyl next to the empty shelf looked redundant and lost.

'The bastard,' she said.

On Elliot's chest of drawers was his small collection of designer body sprays – Tom Ford Ombré, Dior Sauvage, Aesop, all arrayed neatly as if on a counter in Selfridges. Next to that was a framed picture of Elliot as a pink-cheeked toddler in blue stripy dungarees sitting on his great-nan's lap. Becky remembered taking this picture, them both laughing into the camera as she tickled him. Becky's smiled faded as she spotted, next to the photo, Elliot's Colman's mustard tin where he kept his spare cash: it was empty. She hoped he'd put the contents in his pocket before heading off to Ayia Napa.

How low could Tony go? Stealing from his own son.

At least she didn't have much worth taking – all her jewellery was Topshop and Primark. There was Nan's ring, which had been in the family for years, but that was safely hidden. Wasn't it?

She didn't know it was possible for a person to feel the colour drain from their cheeks, but in that moment that's exactly what she felt. She walked as if in a bad dream to her room. It was turned upside down. Every drawer had been emptied, make-up was scattered across the bed, tights, scarves, handbags, jumpers, bras – all thrown around the room. She thought she might throw up when she saw, amongst the piles, the red socks.

Seems she hadn't been so smart, keeping Nan's ring in a balled-up pair of socks in with all the others – she'd chosen the red socks because they stood out among the dozen or so pairs of navy, grey, and white ones. She felt like an idiot – she didn't have a safe or a loose floorboard like in the movies, so thought that instead of in a jewellery box – which would be the first place thieves would look – she would hide her most precious item in plain sight, in boring old socks. Even Elliot had thought it was quite clever. Some of the grey socks were un-balled, but from the look of it some criminal instinct had made the red catch Tony's eye. Sure enough, Nan's small sapphire engagement ring was gone.

She sat down on the edge of the bed and the tears came. She allowed herself to topple softly sideways and lay like that for a moment, her head resting on a glittery Christmas jumper; the pressure of her head on the raised fluffy nose of Rudolph activated its 'hidden surprise', and the tinny sound of 'Rudolph the Red Nose Reindeer' played from the tiny hidden speaker.

It was so ludicrous she let out a brittle laugh as she lay amongst her worldly goods, when the only worldly good that really mattered was her nan's ring.

Wiping her tears away with the back of her hands, smoothing down her hair, Becky sat up. She needed to get her head together – no use lying here wailing whilst that pig flogged her possessions to the highest bidder.

Her only hope was that the police would find him before he had the chance to sell on her stuff. She pulled her phone from her back pocket to call them and, as she did, the doorbell trilled, making her jump.

She opened the door to two police officers, and it dawned on her immediately why they were there. They'd only know to come around if his tag had been tampered with. The older of the two was a buxom woman with frizzy blonde hair wrestled under her hat, and the ruddy-cheeked smile of a comely farmer's wife. She introduced herself as Sergeant Garvey. Her colleague, who stood as if weighed down by a huge invisible backpack, was petite, with dark hair swept back tightly in a ponytail, and large brown eyes that darted from side to side. She politely asked after the where-abouts of Tony, as if expecting him any minute at a drinks party.

Becky, relieved to be able to offload, told them everything in one long stream of babble, peppered with occasional swear words, apologising after each one.

'Why don't you put the kettle on,' said the senior officer with a calm smile, 'and while Constable Glover here takes an initial statement from you, I'll have a quick look round if that's OK?' Becky felt comforted by the woman's kind face – every motherly dinner lady she'd ever met rolled into one. The handcuffs and taser suggesting it was a particularly rough infants school she patrolled.

A couple of minutes later it was actually Becky who found what they were after. She opened the food bin to chuck in the used teabags and there, shoved inside amongst the eggshells and potato peelings was the mangled grey ankle tag.

'Excellent detective work, you should join the force!' said Garvey.

Becky smiled limply at the irony.

35

Jameela

Jameela was distracted. After getting Simon's text, she'd called him twice on his mobile, but it'd gone straight to voicemail, and then his dentist practice a couple of times. The third time, the young receptionist sounded flustered as she insisted to Jameela she'd passed on her earlier messages, but Simon was super busy that afternoon with a double wisdom tooth extraction.

'You're right at the top of the list for call-backs I promise,' she said.

Jameela, despite her irritation, felt sorry for the woman – it really wasn't part of her contract to fob off an angry wife and cover for her coward of a boss.

Simon leaving had hurt her, but not as much as the lack of contact since – despite the fact the miscarriage had left her body traumatised and her mind wretched, he hadn't called once to check on her. She found it ironic that a health professional could be so callous with the woman he had supposedly loved. Even if their marriage was ending, surely he would have the common decency to check she was OK? Clearly not.

Jameela liked to be pragmatic even when dealing with her marriage breakdown – it was the lawyer in her. She didn't want to analyse her feelings too much – she was aware that along that route lay desperation: sobbing, surrounded by snotty tissues, glugging wine on her sofa. No thank you. No pity party for one would be happening here. Much better to shove down her feelings and concentrate on the next stage.

Of course, she wasn't stupid, she was self aware enough to know that in the long run this wasn't the best way to deal with feelings of abandonment and rejection, but after the past few years with Simon and the failure, *her* failure, to conceive, she just didn't have the strength to confront her feelings head-on. Not yet, anyway.

She was throwing herself into work, and clearly so had Simon. *Perhaps he was throwing himself into his assistant Belle too*, she thought drily.

She felt eerily calm about the thought of Belle replacing her. That would merely be the final cut in her marriage. As her marriage to Simon bled out, she felt weirdly in control, standing over its cooling corpse.

Still, Simon ignoring her calls was making it impossible for Jameela to concentrate. A particularly fractious disagreement surrounding a contract for the building of a new out-of-town shopping centre should've been her focus, instead all she could think about was how irritated she was by Simon's inability to respond to her texts and calls after all she'd been through. *They'd* been through.

She decided she needed to see him.

Being distracted at work was unacceptable, plus she wanted to call Reju later – she intended to concentrate on her real family now.

How stupid she'd been – she'd pushed away the one person who throughout her life had been her support, her friend, and her partner in crime. From first kisses and Saturday shopping trips, through Jameela's years at uni, when Reju had visited regularly to help quash her homesickness, her little sister had been there for her.

If Simon and the state of her marriage was the darkness and the shadow at the moment, the ray of sunshine was Reju and the chance to salvage their relationship. Reju had texted her, after all, so was finally ready to make up.

Jameela left work and drove to Simon's dental practice. She parked over the road from The Smile Co, but for some reason she didn't feel quite as brave as she had on the way there.

The afternoon traffic was building and the road was busy. She watched the cars at a standstill – people on their way home for tea, to people they loved, partners, family, flatmates. She envied them. Here she was, spying on her husband, braced for the worst.

Maybe she was scared of what she'd find after all?

She suddenly wished Sheila was with her for moral support; she'd know exactly how Jameela was feeling right now, but she couldn't even call her – they were burying her mum-in-law today.

The plan they'd hatched to go on a sleuthing weekend, following Martin and catching him with his mystery women, had been put on hold when Martin's mum had died. But Jameela quite fancied the idea of them as some kind of modern day Cagney and Lacey, solving crimes of the heart.

At that moment, the door to the dental surgery opened. Jameela wriggled down in her car seat, sinking low so whoever was coming out didn't spot her. Her heart was racing. It was Simon and Belle. Despite her suspicions, she wasn't sure how much she had truly believed they could actually be having an affair, so seeing them now looking so cosy was a jolt.

Were they leaving work to stroll back to their love nest? Jameela thought she might vomit over the dashboard.

The happy couple chatted on the doorstep as Simon locked up, pulling down the shutters with both hands. Belle was laughing, throwing her head back – her big square teeth glinting in the late afternoon sunlight. Whatever Simon had just said was clearly hilarious, the way she was guffawing. She was pretty sure Simon had never made her laugh like that.

They continued chatting, Simon casually spinning the ring of keys around on his index finger. Peeping over the bottom of the car window, Jameela saw Belle look at her phone as if a text had pinged and, as she did, Simon smiled and gesticulated over Belle's shoulder, pointing at a young pretty woman walking up the street. She was skinny with coltish legs that protruded from cut-off denim shorts, her peroxide hair in two plaits resting on a baggy blue jumper. Belle turned towards the young woman as she reached them and grinned. The two women kissed. Not a kiss on each cheek, not a peck reserved for best friends or a sister. It was a full-on hot smooch – enough to make Jameela's eyes widen like saucers from her spying position, and enough to make Simon squirm on the spot, wave an awkward goodbye at the two snogging girls, and turn on his heel and stride off.

Jameela laughed. A full-on proper laugh. She felt giddy with . . . was it relief? For months, her brain addled with grief and hormones and medication, she'd been suspicious and jealous of Simon and Belle's relationship, and all for nothing.

She felt thrilled, kind of excited. Maybe Simon wanted to talk about fixing their marriage after all.

She didn't know, in that moment, what she felt about that. What did she want? To fight for her marriage or take flight from this whole mess, even if Belle was no longer part of the picture?

Either way, she had to have it out with Simon. She needed to know where she stood. She suddenly felt more in control.

She leapt from the car and weaved through the rush-hour traffic and around the corner to Simon's flat. The street was suddenly busy – laughing schoolkids jostled past eating fried chicken, two mums chatted over the top of their babies' buggies, a street cleaner wheeled his cart through. The wind picked up, whipping her hair around her face. All this both slowed her and obscured her view of Simon. He was just opening the door to his flat and she could now see he was with someone; whoever it was must've been waiting for him on the doorstep. The door to the flat swung open and they went in, but not before Jameela caught sight of the light blue trench coat and the long wavy brown hair she'd know anywhere. It was her sister Reju.

Jameela felt her legs go weak, but swerved and pushed on past Simon's street, then crossed the road, cars beeping at her. She zigzagged through the moving traffic, doubled back on herself, and collapsed into her car, slamming the door shut.

The heavens suddenly opened and she was grateful that the rain on the car windows obscured her from passers-by as she sat, in shock. Her ally. Her best friend. Her sister was calling in on her estranged husband. The same husband who'd turned his back on her during the toughest weeks of her life. She felt the betrayal slice through her. Was Reju helping Simon, or were they supporting each other through the trauma of having to live with a woman as flawed as Jameela? Were they each other's counsel and coach? The weight of her sister's disloyalty sat like a stone on Jameela's chest.

36

Sheila

Across town at St Mathews, Margaret's funeral was going as well as could be expected, despite the service being delayed a couple of weeks by family arriving from Australia and Canada. Sheila had asked Louise, who worked at a printers, to help out with the order of service, and between them they had done a lovely job, everybody said so.

Despite Sheila and her mum-in-law not being particularly close, she of course wanted to do her proud. It was silly to hold onto minor resentments now.

The two women did have one thing in common – their love for Martin, and that had been enough to allow a small fondness to grow between them as the years went by.

Sheila had dug out some old photographs and arranged them throughout the pamphlet amongst the readings and hymns.

The first couple of photos showed Mrs Margaret Ann Harrison née Bakewell in sepia tones – sitting up in her pram in a frilly bonnet, and then posing in her school uniform, straight-backed and beaming. Then colour crept in, pale at first, with Martin and his dad Frank smiling out from behind ice-cream cones on a wind-swept Welsh beach, a shot of her with her pupils eating cake and laughing on her last day as a teacher, and one of her building a snowman with a six-year-old Oliver, the two of them in matching red bobble hats.

The last one was taken just a few years ago, and went on the back of the pamphlet. Curled up in an armchair by the large window, looking out onto her old back garden. She was reading (of course), and had paused to look up for the photograph. She wasn't quite smiling, but looked serene and calm, her eyes seemed to reassure that everything would be OK. A whole lifetime summed up by a handful of snapshots.

Oliver looked like a little boy again as he shuffled up in his work suit to read his and his grandma's favourite poem from his childhood by Dr Seuss, 'How did it get so late so soon?'. Sheila wept softly at the sight.

Julie and Mrs Blackstone – 'please, call me Stella' – had arrived to pay their respects, as had some of Margaret's old colleagues from work.

Former pupils, now in their thirties and forties, wept, and told Martin afterwards how she was the kindest most brilliant teacher, and that they'd never forget her.

At the wake at the cricket club, the few friends Margaret had left squeezed Martin's arm with one hand, the other holding a paper plate of sausage rolls and quiche, and told him his reading was lovely and she'd be so proud.

Once home, Martin fell exhausted into bed even though it was barely 7 p.m. Sheila tucked him in like a child and gently stroked his hair till sleep took him. As she did so, she considered her next move. With Margaret now laid to rest, she'd completed her duty as supportive wife. She now needed to know if she and Martin had a future.

37

Louise

On the way home from the pub Louise took the long way round, Olaf trotting happily by her side. As she walked, she rang Danny, telling herself she was just saying hi, but really, from the queasy feeling in her stomach, knowing she was checking up on him. He was at home and asked what time she'd be back.

'Why?' she asked, suspicious.

'No reason, just wondering babe.' He sounded fake, like a regional TV reporter pretending to be relaxed whilst holding a bird of prey for a news item.

As she opened the front door she heard some urgent shushing coming from inside, and Jodie hiss, 'Shut up, she's here.'

Louise was confused – it wasn't her birthday or even any anniversary, so why were her family making the sorts of noises you only heard just before everyone jumped out at a surprise party?

She took off her shoes in the small hallway, unclipped Olaf's lead, and he followed her into the lounge. She noticed Olaf's dogbed had been squished between the sofa and an armchair. The dog stopped halfway to the bed and looked up at her. If a dog could shrug, he would've done.

She pushed open the door to the dining room, to find Jodie and Jemma standing behind the dining table and in front of the window, each holding one end of a bed sheet. It was pulled taut to create a screen to cover whatever was behind it. Possibilities raced through her head – they'd better not have got another dog. Or any kind of pet for that matter. Was it a person? She didn't think she had any long lost relatives or friends she was desperate to see.

Danny stood to the side. He looked pleased as punch.

'At last! You're here!' He beamed. 'Right girls, get ready to reveal all! Louise,' he said, and his face softened with emotion, 'I love you so much, all I want is for you to be happy and follow your dream,' Louise heard the girls groan softly at the soppiness, 'so, introducing . . .' he nodded to the girls, who dropped the sheet as he shouted '. . . your very own art space!'

Louise gasped, her hands automatically coming up to her face. She couldn't believe it. The whole area had been cleared, including, she noticed with satisfaction, the box of CDs she'd been campaigning to be moved for weeks. The old desk, usually just a dumping ground for clutter, had gone, and in its place was a gleaming brand new architect's desk with two elevated work areas and a smart stool. On top of the desk sat a brand new sketch pad, and on the right-hand side three smooth, white pots, the first one containing a few pencils.

The sun was just starting to fade in the sky, casting a calm, golden light through the window and onto the desk.

She looked at the girls, who had the palms of their hands together in prayer position and were clapping gleefully just with the tips of their fingers, caught up in the moment with her. 'It was all Dad – he's been sorting it out all day,' beamed Jodie.

'Yeah,' chimed in Jemma. 'We came home and helped with the last bits – the styling. Otherwise it was all Dad – he even hoovered!'

She turned to Danny. 'Wow!' was all she could say, before bursting into tears.

Danny went to her and gathered her up in his arms as she

sobbed, whilst apologising for sobbing and somehow at the same time laughing.

The girls took this as their cue to leave, and bundled out of the door taking the sheet with them.

Louise was so touched – it was such a thoughtful thing to do. For now she pushed away any thoughts that it was going to be a struggle for all four of them to eat tea around the dining table in its new position. She was just so thrilled that Danny had used his initiative like this. That not only had he bought the desk and set it up, but he'd chosen so well. She was genuinely thrilled with her new area.

'Go on – have a go,' Danny said gently, nudging her towards the desk. She obeyed and sat down gingerly on the stool, gently swivelling into position. It was fantastic. She couldn't believe the extra raised platform – like Tom Hanks' architect's desk in *Sleepless in Seattle*, her favourite film.

'It's brilliant Danny. Thank you.' She felt tears spring to her eyes again and sniffed them away, reaching for a pencil. 'When did you do all this?'

He grinned bashfully. 'Well, I set it up today, but I had to go collect the table from Blackpool the other day, that's why I fibbed about working late, sorry if I stressed you out.'

She noticed the little drawers in the desk and slid them open, they glided out and in smoothly, then closed with a satisfying click.

'It's fine.' She glanced up at him sheepishly. 'I knew there was something going on, but I couldn't work out what. I thought I'd pushed you away too much.'

'Nah, it'd take more than that to be rid of me! And don't worry about me ever lying again – I hated it!' He laughed. 'The only upside is I probably lost half a stone with the stress of it all.' He took a breath. 'I love you Louise, I just want you to be happy. I know I'm a bit useless, but I'm trying, I want you to make whatever changes you need to be happy – as long as those changes don't involve swapping me for someone else.'

'Course not.' She squeezed his hand. 'I just need to maybe think about another job . . . I'm going stir crazy stuck at the printers.' She placed the palm of her hand on her forehead, as if she were checking for a temperature.

He nodded firmly as if it was decided. 'We'll manage, whatever you decide, we're a team.'

She thought she might cry again. From relief? Happiness?

'I can't wait to sit here and draw, Danny,' she said, looking at him properly for the first time and noticing the dark rings under his eyes. 'You look shattered; after tea why don't you get to bed, while I work on a masterpiece at my new desk? Let me get the oven on.'

'No need,' said Danny, 'I've bribed the girls, and they're going to run to the chippy for tea – think we deserve a little celebration to launch your new creative space.'

Louise smiled. 'Wow, I mean can tonight get any more perfect?'

'Oh aye,' said Danny, coming up behind her and wrapping her in a bear hug. 'Maybe I'll show you my own masterpiece later if you're lucky.'

38

Sheila

On Harrison Lane, Sheila and Martin were dining in the back garden, having an early dinner as it was a Tuesday – pottery day – and Sheila was keen to get going.

Despite her worries, which she carried everywhere with her like an organ donation card or brolly, Sheila felt fabulous in her outfit – a bright floral sundress.

'Wow, you look like Kew Gardens!' Martin exclaimed when she'd floated outside.

They'd laid out a selection of tapas, bought on a whim from Waitrose by Martin, who was clearly on a high after finding his first treasure using his new metal detector. Well, new to him, he'd bought it second-hand on eBay from a nice lady in Wigan whose recently deceased husband had, according to Martin, enjoyed many hobbies over the years. As Shelia ate the last of the chorizo, Martin continued his story: 'She tried her best to sell me a dart board, a bread maker, two canoes and a set of golf clubs too.'

Sheila smiled. It was genuinely nice to see a spark back in Martin's eyes in the weeks since his mum had passed. As his spirit returned, though, she felt hers slowly weaken. Burying her feelings had become exhausting.

Sheila was very much biding her time with regards to the pants – she could never really find the right moment to confront Martin, and the shock of the discovery had faded slightly, a death in the family can do that. Put things into perspective. Nevertheless she still felt sad, and intended to fulfil her promise to Jameela to go to London. Even if the appeal of playing sleuth had waned, Sheila was very much up for a girls' weekend. If they caught Martin being unfaithful, she'd cross that horror bridge when she got to it.

Maybe she was in denial, and, not for the first time in her marriage, treading water – trying to support Martin, keeping him from slipping under the surface at the cost of moving life forward.

A lump of chorizo had lodged in a molar, making her wince. Martin was watching her.

'You OK my love? Enjoying a taste of Spain?'

These days Sheila noticed Martin was less reticent about mentioning Spain, as if he sensed she'd fallen out with the idea. Before now, he'd almost been too scared to mention the S word, as if it was a spell and would zap them in a puff of smoke to Playa Flamenca.

'Yes, lovely thanks.' She worked the lump of chorizo free with her tongue and swallowed. The truth was she didn't know how she felt about Spain – she was enjoying the friendships forged at pottery, and maybe in part the whole thing had subconsciously been about escaping Margaret. Now she was gone, what was there to escape from? On top of that, Sheila's anxiety about her marriage made her think now probably wasn't the right time for upheaval. Perhaps she'd feel better after the trip to London.

Hopefully they'd discover Martin's treasure-hunting trips were just that, not seedy encounters with a woman in sexy designer knickers. Sheila took a swig of sparkling water; she was desperate to escape to pottery and see Jameela.

Martin was talking again. 'It's a lovely place, the farm over Howlesden you know. I got the bus straight there with my new bit of kit. I wasn't expecting the bloke to be so willing to let me on with my detector – he was quite scary, with his massive hands and ruddy cheeks,' laughed Martin, sipping his sangria, 'but he was nice – he just boomed "as long as we can split any fortune you find", then he was off with his collie. Quite a successful début methinks.'

Martin gestured at the bumbag on the table, next to it his finds: a small toy racing car, a bottle with a metal cap, a ring pull from a can of Cherry Coke, and a 1901 Victorian farthing. Sheila strained a smile.

'Pass me the *patatas bravas* please,' she said. As he reached over, his phone buzzed loudly on the table, emitting a clown horn sound that irritated Sheila beyond measure.

'Who's that?' Sheila asked, and was surprised at how her stomach had instantly churned.

'Mike,' said Martin, reading the text out loud. 'He says: "Hi mate. Do you fancy a trip, maybe Friday? New exhibition at the Tate Modern: 'Rivers and their secrets', about treasure found in the world's rivers over the last 500 years . . . sounds brilliant. You up for it?"' Martin looked up, eyes wide with excitement.

'Sounds great,' Sheila said briskly, starting to clear the plates. 'You should go, it'll do you good.'

39

Jameela

As Jameela walked towards Sheila she could feel a fizzing energy coming from her friend – she was shifting from espadrille to espadrille as if doing some kind of jig. Jameela was braced for drama as Sheila had fired a warning shot, texting, 'Let's meet early, I have news'. She welcomed the distraction from her own thoughts.

Since spotting her sister sneaking into her husband Simon's flat, she'd felt deflated and sad. (Was Reju sneaking? That's how it looked to her, the thousands of times Jameela had replayed the scene in her head, from the moment she woke up.)

At work she was her usual professional self, but that facade used up so much energy she'd lost her vim and vigour for everything else. She was still running of course, it felt as if it was the only thing keeping her sane, but her eyes blurred with tears as she ran, thinking everything through. It was on her runs that she came to realise the betrayal that stung the most was her sister's. That Reju had taken Simon's side in all this, had become his confidante, devastated Jameela.

She was yet to confront either Simon or Reju. Those few moments outside Simon's flat had left her feeling as though she was standing in the centre of a creaking, frozen pond, small cracks slowly appearing around her feet. If she moved to confront either of them about their new friendship, she was sure the surface would give way and plunge her into oblivion.

She was grateful for the pottery class.

She could lose herself in the clay. It yielded to her push, it was forgiving and full of grace when she was heavy-handed, releasing frustration through her palms.

'At last!' Sheila said, fanning herself with both hands. 'I've been standing here getting sunstroke for fifteen minutes.' She set off in the direction of the community centre, looking back over her shoulder at Jameela as if they were running a relay at the Olympics.

Jameela quickened her step to catch up. 'Go on then – what's going on? You look like you might implode.'

'That'll be the heat,' said Sheila. 'Right. Martin is going to London on Friday, and I think we should too.'

'Okaay,' said Jameela, squinting in the evening sun at her retreating friend. Sheila stopped and turned to face her. 'This was your idea Jameela, and, like all your ideas, it is brilliant because you are brilliant and smart, and besides,' she raised her eyebrows, 'whatever happens with Martin, we could have fun – dinner and cocktails in Soho, some time away from here.' Sheila marched off again.

Put like that, Jameela thought, *it actually sounds quite nice*. She could do with escaping for a few days – away from her house, which echoed with loss, away from the park that was home to the band-stand where Simon had proposed, away from the fertility clinic near work, which had hosted some of their hardest moments and held all their doom-laden test results.

'OK, you had me at cocktails,' she called out to the pink velvet scrunchie that was holding up Sheila's ponytail, which bobbed in response.

'Great!' shouted Sheila, a triumphant smile in her voice.

They arrived at the community centre and greeted the other potters, who were tying apron strings and rolling up sleeves. Some studied their little notebooks, which over the weeks had become worn and were all the better for it. Smudges of glaze on the pages, clay thumb-prints, and pencil sketches gave them a magical quality, as if they were books of spells – and that's what they kind of were to the potters.

Jameela reached for two aprons, handing one to Sheila, who was engrossed in trying to earwig a conversation currently happening between Sasha, Jack, and Pearl. Last week the two septuagenarians had come out as boyfriend and girlfriend, to no one's surprise but everyone's joy. Now they looked like a matching pair, made to be together, like salt and pepper shakers.

Sasha slowly nodded in agreement at something Jack had said, and replied, 'Aye, it's a bad do. Poor Becky – seems like he's long gone.'

More drama, thought Jameela. She looked around for Becky, but couldn't see her. Sheila's eyebrows were working overtime as she tried to figure out what had happened with Becky, making Jameela laugh. Sheila didn't only hear things on the grapevine, normally she *was* the grapevine.

Sasha finished his conflab with Jack and Pearl, who then walked arm in arm down the centre of the hall as if just married – the workbenches the pews. They went their separate ways at the end, adjusting their aprons.

Jameela breathed in through her nose and slowly exhaled; this was *her* time, she needed to focus on one thing only – clay.

The practice of pottery was at once anaesthesia, numbing the day's irritations, and a stimulator – awakening her senses and drawing her in.

The chatter in the room died down as Sasha stood at the front and smiled. Jameela thought he looked a little weary.

'Potters,' he said, 'your trinket boxes fired beautifully, and we will get around to glazing them, however,' he looked around at his audience, 'I thought it'd be fun to do some throwing today.' The group looked confused. 'That is the term we use for making something on the wheel.' He grinned.

'I was thrown there for a moment myself!' said Sheila.

The potters laughed and shared excited glances; Jameela noticed Louise do a little fist pump at Danny. Pearl looked as if she might burst.

Sasha gathered the group around in a semicircle as he threw a small bowl, followed by a simple cylinder.

Jameela was completely spellbound, and couldn't wait to have a go.

'OK,' said Sasha, 'three bowls – have a go, good luck.'

Each potter had a small pile of clay spheres stacked like cannon balls by their wheels. There were some disasters – Jack's first two bowls folded in on themselves, the momentum of the speeding wheel making it impossible for him to keep the wet clay under his control.

'Hey speedy Gonzales,' chuckled Pearl. 'Take it down a gear, you boy racer.'

Jameela's bowls improved with each attempt, the walls of the bowls getting slightly thinner and less lumpy.

She glanced at Louise's attempts – they looked annoyingly good. Just then Sheila appeared at Jameela's bench. 'Get you Emma Bridgewater!' she almost shouted, looking pointedly at Louise, who glanced up confused. Jameela knew her friend was praising her to wind Louise up. 'Will you still speak to the likes of me when you've got your own range in John Lewis?'

'Probably not,' Jameela replied, deadpan.

'Cheeky. So,' Sheila leaned in conspiratorially, 'I managed to corner Jack by the loos – turns out Becky's ex, Tony, has vanished.'

'Well, from what I gather that's good isn't it?' Jameela knew all about the day Tony had made a drunken idiot of himself at the community centre, smashing her coil pot in the process.

'Yes, that bit is good, the bit that isn't good is that when he left he helped himself to anything he'd be able to sell for a few quid. Including Becky's nan's ring.'

'No!' Jameela gasped. 'The one she was making the trinket box for?'

Sheila nodded grimly. Jameela felt awful – poor Becky.

'How does Jack know all this?'

'He was still here last night, about to lock up, when Becky came back to the centre with two police officers in tow looking for Tony.'

'Right,' Sasha said from the front, 'quick break – please put your practice bowls on the drying tables.'

It was a pleasantly warm evening, so the two women grabbed their water bottles and sat on the grass outside the centre.

'I've got to confess I'm weirdly excited about the weekend,' said Sheila.

'Good. You're right, it'll be good to get away,' said Jameela. She watched as a plane cut slowly across the sky. They sat in silence for a few seconds. At last, Jameela said quietly, 'I saw Simon. With my sister, Reju. Going into his flat.'

Sheila looked confused. 'Eh? I don't get you, what were they doing?'

'I don't know.' Jameela pulled at a tuft of grass. 'They've never been close – I imagine their hatred of me pushed them together.'

Sheila's eyes widened. 'What? Not in that way?'

Jameela shook her head 'Noooo. Definitely not,' she laughed. Then she stopped abruptly. 'I hadn't really thought of that – it's impossible. No. Ridiculous.' Reju was madly in love with Tarik – plus surely neither of them would stoop so low? Reju would never do that to her sister, and Simon had proved himself to be callous and cold, but a betrayal on that scale wasn't his style. Was it?

Sheila was still talking '. . . so that's probably it – Reju is trying to help save your marriage by chatting to Simon about you.'

The two women stood up, straightened their clothes, and headed inside.

'Right potters,' said Sasha, 'I need all of you to bring me your second-best bowl please. Up to the front.'

The potters did as they were told and stood around the table. Sasha held up a wire with small wooden handles at each end. He moved towards Jack's bowl and, holding the wire taut, slid it underneath the bowl before carefully pulling it up through the centre, slicing it clean in two from bottom to top. The potters all gasped – Jack just chuckled.

'Ouch!' said Sheila.

'Ouch indeed,' said Sasha, 'only by dissecting a pot like this can you look at the cross section and see the true thickness of the walls and the bottom.' He pointed to the slaughtered pot. 'The thickness of the clay is crucial – too thin, it'll be too delicate and might not survive a firing, too thick, it could hide bubbles and be lumpy, like here,' he pointed at the base. The potters leaned in, students observing a post-mortem. 'Now Jack,' said Sacha, holding up one half of the pot, 'you lost control of your rim here . . .' he paused for the inevitable giggles, 'we don't want sloppy or jagged rims, we want smooth, strong rims.' Jack nodded solemnly.

Sasha sliced each of the potters' pots in turn, and each time the potters gasped as he garrotted their work, the wire sliding through the wet clay like a hot knife through butter. 'Out of all of them,' he said, 'Louise, your bowl was very consistent and neat.'

She did a small curtsey and looked very chuffed. Danny gently nudged her, looking proud as punch.

Jameela felt a little deflated, she hated not winning.

'However,' continued Sasha, 'yours Louise was just pipped by Jameela's.' All eyes turned to Jameela. She tried to look modest. 'Beautiful work Jameela – lovely smooth sides, the bottom was a consistent thickness all across, topped off with a near perfect rim.'

'I've had worse compliments,' she quipped, then felt immediately embarrassed. Luckily no one noticed, they were too busy clapping. Louise looked genuinely pleased, but Jameela clocked the smug grin on Sheila's face as she clapped a little longer and louder than the others, all whilst staring at Louise.

'Probably best it's already damaged,' Sheila whispered to Jameela, 'at least it can't be sabotaged now.'

'Right,' said Sasha, 'lob your sliced bowls into the waste bucket please. I need you to throw another two bowls, and then choose your overall favourite to decorate once they've been fired.

'One last thing,' Sasha said, suddenly a little louder than before, prompting all eager faces to lift, 'I have a nice surprise. In a couple of weeks, for our final class,' there were disappointed groans and sad looks exchanged, 'before we break for a month, we will go out with a bang, though hopefully not literally . . . We will be doing a pit firing.'

The potters glanced around warily at each other; this was a first.

Sheila raised her hand. 'Does it involve Brad Pitt?' she asked.

Sasha laughed. 'Alas no,' he said, 'but it does involve an overnight stay – we will dig our own pits in the ground, and fire our pieces in them; you will be on duty, tending and nurturing your pits through til dawn.'

The group grinned excitedly at each other.

'You'll throw three pieces – vases, bowls, whatever you want to try — next week, then the following Saturday afternoon, we will meet here with warm clothes, sleeping bags, and maybe even a couple of bottles of red – just to keep us warm of course.' The group let off a couple of small whoops and chatted animatedly,

Sasha now almost shouting over the hubbub, 'You may want to create a pattern or mark on the surface of your pieces by wrapping mementos around them – fabric, wire, wool . . . I've emailed you and printed out some suggestions, and also the full list of what you'll need to bring, so pick up a copy on the way out. It's going to be a lot of fun.' The potters all gave an impromptu round of applause.

Jameela was excited – she liked the idea of a night under the stars stoking a fire, drinking wine in the glow of the flames.

She was also starting to look forward to her trip to London this weekend with Sheila – she smiled over at her friend, who gave her an eager thumbs-up.

Jameela's sadness about her marriage coated her like a grime she couldn't wash off, but in moments like this, here in this slightly shabby hall with a group of random people who'd started to become her friends, she almost forgot her woes and felt something akin to contentment.

Louise caught up with Jameela as she walked back to her bench. 'Hey,' she smiled. 'Well done – your bowl was near enough perfect. Well, it was until Sasha murdered it!' She grimaced.

Jameela smiled back. 'Thanks.'

Louise grinned. 'You didn't want to grab the wire yourself and avenge your coil pot being smashed did you? Think Sheila thinks I made Tony smash it as part of my evil plan.'

Jameela laughed. 'No. Don't worry, I know it was nothing to do with you – Sheila's just got a wild imagination. Though if you must know, I was a teeny bit jealous for a moment there, you're so infuriatingly talented.'

'Thanks, not that it ever got me anywhere, being OK at art – I'm just a mum with a boring job. Look at you, top lawyer with a dazzling career AND an artistic streak.'

Jameela reached out and touched Louise's arm. 'There's no such thing in my books as "just a mum" – I'd give everything up to be one.'

Louise looked embarrassed. 'I'm sorry – I didn't mean to . . .'

'Don't apologise! I guess I'm just saying you've kinda got it all – you're a mum, and you're super talented – you should believe in yourself more.'

Jameela's phone buzzed then. It was a text from Reju.

'I'll leave you to it,' Louise said.

Jameela read the text: 'We need to talk, Sis. Come round tonight. Tarik is at his mum's with the kids, so I have the house to myself. I miss you Jam. Please say you'll come.'

Jameela sighed. This stalemate couldn't go on for ever. Her heart thumped as she replied. 'OK, be round just after 9.' Then she shoved her phone in her bag and hung it on the coat hooks – no more distractions. *At least*, she thought to herself, *whatever happens tonight, I've got a weekend away to drown my sorrows.*

40

Becky

Becky rolled over and blinked at her phone in the darkness. It was midday, but she had the curtains drawn and was spending most of her days in bed, nursing the tail end of a cold, cocooned against the world by a wall of duvet and reruns of *Friends* and *Frasier*.

There was still no news from the police about Tony's disappearance, along with half the kitchen, her son's decks and her nan's ring.

She thought of Elliot – he was due home from Ayia Napa soon.

'I need to recharge my brain and my liver,' he'd messaged, and she believed him, judging from the photos he'd sent – Elliot brown as a berry, pouting behind sunglasses on a jet-ski, sipping luminous cocktails with his new gang of friends. Of course he'd proved to be a hit with the other holiday reps – he was naturally charming and easily sweet-talked the young crowds into joining him in the bar for free shots and drinks deals, promising the most banging tunes, the fittest lads, the hottest girls.

Becky hadn't told Elliot about the burglary – why burst the bubble for him? He was having the time of his life, he'd know soon enough. *Hopefully by then*, Becky thought, *Tony will've been caught and flung back into jail where he belongs.*

Where was he, and where was her nan's ring? First rule of

scumbag club is 'sell on dodgy goods asap'. *Nan's ring will be long gone*, she thought, tears welling up again. Whose finger would it be on? The pudgy pinky of some gangster's wife? Maybe a birthday gift to a mum from her wayward son – she'd be showing it off to her friends, choosing to believe her boy's tall tale that he bought it from an antique dealer pal.

Just then the doorbell rang. Becky dragged herself from her prone position to answer the door.

Sergeant Garvey was on the doorstep.

'Oh, I thought it was my pizza,' said Becky.

'Nearly – police,' smiled Garvey, unnecessarily pointing to herself. 'Get dressed, we've got to go shopping.'

Once in the squad car, Sergeant 'call me Joan' Garvey explained they needed to visit a couple of pawn shops on the off chance Tony had already passed on the ring.

First they visited Swift Sale and viewed a depressing hotchpotch of people's worldly goods – a games console cashed in to placate a landlord; a cordless drill or acoustic guitar swapped for a few quid to feed a family or a habit.

Becky didn't see any of her stuff there.

En route to the next stop, Joan asked about the ring. 'How did such an exquisite sapphire end up in your family?'

Becky smiled. 'It's quite a story.'

'Well,' sighed Joan, 'looking at this traffic I think we have time.'

'OK,' said Becky, who loved telling the story now as much as she had loved hearing her nana tell it when she was little. 'My great-grandma Elizabeth was three years old when her dad Edward went to fight in World War One as part of the British expeditionary force, east of Paris. Thankfully he returned from the front, but with one less leg.'

'Right,' said Joan, inching forward through the traffic.

"Edward fought in the first battle of the Marne and showed incredible bravery fighting off half a dozen German soldiers during an ambush, saving the life of his 2nd Lieutenant.

He was awarded the Military Medal. The sapphire ring was a gift from his superior's mother, a wealthy lady who gave it as a token of her gratitude for the safe return of her son. Since then it's been handed down through the generations.'

Becky smiled proudly, but then her face crumpled at the realisation that maybe it would never be handed down again. She looked out of the window at the dishwater sky.

'Quite a story,' said Joan softly. 'We'll find it you know, I can feel it.'

'I hope so,' Becky whispered at the window. Rain started to fall. 'My son Elliot will be devastated when I tell him. I used to let him hold the ring as he lay in bed – he'd study the jewel and his eyes would shine as I told him for the millionth time the story of Steady Eddie.'

'Pardon?' said Joan, confused.

'That was my great-great grandad Edward's nickname – according to family legend he could play darts and even badminton balancing on his one leg.'

Joan laughed.

Becky's mum had worn the ring on special occasions, but when she died, Becky's nan had kept it safe until her twenty-first birthday.

'Here we are.' Joan parked up, and Becky looked through the rain at a small shopfront squatting behind grimy security grills. Philip Carver and Sons was a single cramped room filled with hundreds of trinkets, watches, and jewellery displayed behind locked glass shutters.

Philip himself was a thin, crooked man with a habit of panting between sentences like a trapped animal.

Sadly, the ring wasn't there. 'Promise me Phil, if anything with even a hint of a sapphire turns up let me know and in return I promise not to look too closely at the altered reg on that BMW outside – the PH1 is fine, but you've clearly nudged up the L from the other side . . . and if I WAS to notice, you could be fined.' Phil panted a promise to keep a close eye out.

Joan was actually great company, and back in the car she regaled Becky with the various scrapes she'd gotten into as she worked her way up through the ranks of the police. 'I've been spat at, slapped, managed to duck just in time when a scaffolding pole was swung at me.' She grinned. 'I joined the force as a thirty-fifth birthday present to myself, and it really is the gift that keeps on giving.'

'You love it though?' asked Becky.

'Yes. Yes I do. There are moments when you can really help – I've returned many a lost grandma who's gone walkabout from her care home, and the look on the family's face when I bring their loved one back in one piece makes all the bad stuff worthwhile.'

'Bad stuff?' Becky was rapt.

'Well, I made the front page of the *Lennington Echo* after being commended for tackling a knifeman who was running from the post office after a robbery . . . but it earned me this,' she pulled up her sleeve, revealing a deep purple scar along her arm. 'Missed an artery by millimetres. Still got the bastard on the ground though. Turns out,' she smiled, 'being captain of the girls' rugby team at uni came in handy after all.'

Becky was only seven years older than Joan had been when she'd joined the force. Maybe she hadn't missed the boat? She shared her long-held ambition with the sergeant.

'It's the greatest decision you'll ever make Becky. You should go for it, I can totally see you in the police. The money's not great, the hours stink, there's mountains of pointless paperwork, and politics and you may occasionally get punched, but . . . it's the best job in the world.'

Becky had found the whole trip exciting, and secretly imagined she was already a cop, out on an investigation. She knew it was a bit silly, but the fantasy was a distraction from the devastation she felt about the robbery. Once Joan had dropped her back at home she almost skipped up the path, still high from the buzz of playing police. Her pizza was even waiting for her, stashed behind the bin.

Dreaming of a new career was the only thing likely to put a bit of fire in her belly at the moment – especially since the doomed smooch with Sasha had dampened any hopes of something more serious.

She still got that awful feeling in her stomach when she thought of that kiss. Sasha had texted to say he needed to talk to her afterwards, but Becky wasn't in any frame of mind to be let down gently – some speech about it's not you it's me . . . What hurt the most though was that Sasha had seemed so genuine. She felt cross for allowing herself to get drawn in.

She could hardly avoid Sasha when he was at the community centre so much, so had texted Jack to let him know she would be off for a couple more days. She'd use her time to lick her wounds, trace stolen goods, and fret about Elliot's reaction when he came home from Cyprus next week to hear that his own dad had stolen not only his prized possessions, but also his future inheritance.

41

Louise

Louise sat in the window of Pret opposite Dawber's art gallery on Princess Street in the centre of town. A lot of time and weeks of effort had led to this moment.

Every evening after she'd got home from work she'd spent hours scouring the arts and heritage section of *Guardian* jobs, browsing the Arts Council England website, and sending off her CV.

While she'd cooked tea or sat on the bus to work or walked to the precinct when they'd run out of milk (because it seemed she'd missed the family meeting where it was decided she and only she was responsible for noticing when the milk was running low) she'd listened to art podcasts.

Tuesdays were still a highlight of the week, and she counted down the hours until the pottery class began. Her confidence with clay grew each week and for those two hours she felt her soul soar.

To relax, she drew and sketched at the desk Danny had set up, her noise-cancelling headphones playing Bon Iver to drown out her teenage daughters' many dramas and indignations.

At the weekends she left the girls to entertain themselves, whilst she volunteered at the Manchester Art Gallery. She shone at whatever she turned her hand to, and quickly became a favourite with the staff, who offered to write glowing references 'for her next move'. Louise loved how this tripped so naturally off their tongues, as if it was a given that her volunteering was just a stopgap en route to her new career in the art world. She just needed to convince herself it really could happen. She worked behind the scenes, cataloguing artworks, helping to lay out exhibitions, and assisting with archiving. Time flew. Rejection letters from private galleries and museums arrived with gut-wrenching regularity, but she refused to let these knock-backs dim her determination.

She couldn't carry on with her career as it was. Time dragged at C&J Commercial Printing. Sometimes she was so bored she thought she could feel her own eyebrows growing.

Clutching the stiff cream envelope in her hand that contained her invite to come in for an 'informal chat regarding the position of gallery assistant', she made her way across the road.

Louise pressed the buzzer by the large glass door and quickly straightened her blazer and smoothed her dark hair. A lady's face peeped around a doorway inside. She had a honey-coloured bob and large square black glasses that made her darkly kohled eyes look huge.

After her head followed her body, clad in a black polo neck, skinny white jeans, and black ankle boots. She strode towards the glass door and unlatched it, ushering Louise in and locking it behind her. Around the lady's neck hung a long string of pearls, and Louise noted that between every dozen pearls or so there was a small diamond-encrusted 'CC' for Chanel.

She looked to be maybe in her sixties, but it was hard to tell thanks to either good genes or a good surgeon. She moved very elegantly, almost catlike – Louise wondered if maybe she'd been a dancer in a former life.

She introduced herself as Carys, offered Louise a seat by a huge walnut desk, and said, 'Just need to locate the big boss,' before disappearing off back through the door from where she'd appeared.

Louise looked down at the shiny grey marble floor and tried to steady her breathing, willing her palms to de-clam.

There were three paintings on display – she recognised the first and felt her chest loosen a little with relief. It was a large oil and enamel painting of a large red heart on a patchwork of multi-coloured squares. It was from a series by Jim Dine from the early 1980s. If need be she could wax lyrical about American pop art and the artist's roots in abstract expressionism – given she'd studied this as part of her degree. Strong start – this gallery was pretty serious if it had a Jim Dine.

The second piece she'd need to bluff. She stood up and walked over to get a better look; it was a collage of sorts in dull browns and greens showing paperwork and a wine bottle – with its harsh straight lines she could definitely talk about its cubist leanings. Early twentieth century she reckoned. A small tab on the wall next to it confirmed she was right – 1913, the artist Juan Gris. Of course! She inwardly scolded herself – she should've known it.

The last picture made her head spin, this place was serious: Jim Dine, Juan Gris, and now this – she couldn't quite believe she was standing in front of an original Bridget Riley, signed by the artist.

The unmistakable undulating parallel lines, dozens of them in red, blue and grey, made you feel dizzy – drawing you in and dashing you back out again like being tossed about in a small boat in a storm.

She leaned into the lines, then rocked back on her heels, smiling in wonder at the optical illusion.

'You like her?' a voice asked. Louise spun around and was face to face with Carys again. Although she'd changed – she was wearing the same glasses, but now sported a royal blue silk jumpsuit, cinched in at the waist with a wide black belt. 'Karima,' she said, holding out a manicured hand laden with bright rings, each jewel the size of a sprout.

'Hi . . . I'm Louise, what an amazing collection you have here,' Louise stuttered, smiling broadly in the hope of ironing flat the confused expression that had gripped her features.

'Thank you, we like it.' She smiled. 'Carys is my younger sister, by eleven minutes – we run the gallery together, though I'm here every day, so it'll be me you deal with most.' She spoke in a calm but quick whisper, like a movie spy passing on a code word.

Louise nodded, marvelling at how amazing she still found identical twins, especially when they reached a more mature age. 'So, Bridget?' she said, and for a moment Louise thought she'd got her name wrong.

'Oh yes, Bridget Riley – one of my absolute favourites,' started Louise. 'I saw an exhibition of hers in 1995 at a gallery in Exeter during my degree, and was immediately hooked. I love the power her paintings can have over you. I think she's just incredibly talented – I love that she was being lauded as this cool cat in the sixties in New York, but she didn't play up to that, she didn't care – she just wanted to create art. All the other students in my halls at uni had *Baywatch* calendars or Athena prints up in their rooms, but I had my framed poster of *Shadow Play* pride of place.' She grinned and realised she was waffling.

'Well,' said Karima, who seemed either charmed or amused by Louise's enthusiasm, it was hard to tell, 'if you love Bridget so much, I think you and I will get on just fine. Come with me.'

Louise followed Karima through the side door, down some steep wooden stairs, and into a long white room. Dozens of paintings were mounted on a clever rack system, so each painting could be slid along a rail and viewed, like clothes hung on hangers. Carys came in with a tray of coffee cups, a small jug of cream, and a full cafetière, and then disappeared again.

Karima sat at a long wooden table, opened up a laptop, and pointed to three shots of famous paintings. 'I imagine you can identify these artists please Louise?'

She could – they were very well known; she rattled through each – Robert Delaunay, Peter Blake and Mark Rothko – and then spoke a little about each until Karima smiled and held her hand up to signal her to stop.

They chatted a while about where her love of art had come from, about Louise's family, her degree, her pottery, volunteering, and finally why, Karima asked, after all these years, she had decided to follow her dream.

'It's not really a choice I've made, it's felt more like an urge, an instinct. I feel I've had an awakening, and there's no going back, like I'm being pulled by a current.' She could feel her cheeks become pink and knew her eyes were becoming moist. She cleared her throat. 'When I'm looking at art, talking about art, thinking about art, I feel . . . something lift in my heart, I feel like a missing piece of the puzzle has at last been found.'

There was silence. Karima nodded and smiled cryptically. 'Well done Louise. We'll be in touch.'

42

Jameela

Jameela pulled up outside her sister's house. It was only just dusk, so the curtains on the neat semi were still open and Jameela could see Reju in the front room. She had her long dark hair twisted up in a high bun and her specs on. She was holding a wine glass in one hand, phone in the other. *Maybe she is texting Simon,* Jameela thought, her lips pressed together; perhaps Reju was warning her new best friend that his wife – her sister – was due any second. Maybe this whole thing was an ambush and Simon was there too, hidden out of sight in the kitchen.

Jameela felt like a trapped animal. She felt like jumping out of the car and running till her lungs burned and burst, as far away as she could get from this whole mess. At that moment Reju looked up from her phone and spotted Jameela. The two sisters waved weakly and Jameela got out of the car and made her way up the path.

Reju's eyes looked red raw, and Jameela noticed as they stood in her small kitchen that she'd lost weight. Reju's hand trembled as she poured some wine.

'Cheers,' Reju said, not meeting her sister's eye.

They clinked their glasses, and Jameela felt a surge of fury start to well up. She loved her sister, but this pathetic display was making her feel sick. Jameela knew her sister better than anyone, and she knew from Reju's face she was ashamed about something. Jameela started to wonder if Sheila was right, maybe there was something more than mere friendship with Simon that Reju had to admit to?

Whenever Reju was struggling to get her point across, her eyes would dart around, as if the words she was searching for could be written on the skirting board, the ceiling, or the fridge door – she'd done it since they were tiny, and she was doing it now. Jameela could feel her glare harden as she searched her sister's face, trying to read what was coming next.

After taking an unsteady sip of her wine, Reju spoke. 'I've missed you so much – I know you're angry, and I'm sorry, but I love you and I can't go on like this, I need you.' Tears welled up in her eyes, and Jameela tried to stop her gaze instinctively soften on seeing her little sis looking so bereft. Jameela inwardly chided herself, *Don't give in, she should've thought about this when she was siding with my husband.*

Reju studied the contents of her glass. 'I know you, I know how much you're hurting, and to think I've made it worse kills me, but it takes two to tango,' she said. Such an old-fashioned statement sounded ridiculous tripping off her tongue.

'Is that the best you can do?' Jameela laughed incredulously. 'Two to tango? What the hell does that mean?' she spat. Wow – Sheila was right after all. Jameela felt dizzy. 'Let me stop you there Reju. I know who your dance partner is in this delightful tango – but more to the point, has it gone beyond friendship?'

Reju's head snapped up 'What?'

Jameela could feel her heart hammering against her chest. She leaned forward, close to Reju's face, looked her in the eye, and whispered, 'I know.'

Jameela straightened up and searched her sister's face, in a perverse way ready to savour the moment when Reju realised the game was up.

Reju's feelings were always written all over her face, and now, Jameela noted, Reju's definitely looked . . . confused.

'What do you mean? You know? What are you on about?' Reju sounded more than just baffled now, she sounded cross too.

'I know about you and Simon. I saw you together, at his flat – it all looked very cosy,' Jameela said, hating that her voice cracked with emotion as she played her ace.

It took Reju a second, and there it was again, the darting eyes thing. This time she couldn't come up with the right words. So she laughed. A dry horrible laugh that sounded alien to Jameela. Then she burst into tears.

'Jesus Jam. Is that really what you think of me? Yes you saw me, you saw me going into Simon's flat,' she shouted through the tears, 'and yes, we've been talking, but there's been no affair, not with me and him.'

Now it was Jameela's turn to be confused. 'What do you mean?' she asked.

Reju sniffed. 'Tarik. It's Tarik who's been unfaithful.'

Jameela felt as if she was falling backwards, her head swirled, and she leaned on the fridge for support. The adrenaline from the confrontation was seeping away and was being replaced with so many emotions – relief that Sheila was wrong, shame at accusing her sister of something so horrible, and devastation for Reju that her husband, soul mate and dad to her kids, had broken her heart like this.

'Oh my God,' Jameela said. 'How do you know?'

'I found texts and photos on his work phone a few weeks ago. I tried getting hold of you, I tried to say sorry so we could heal our rift, but you ignored my text. I couldn't talk to Mum because she'd go nuclear.' She drank some more wine. 'I needed advice, that's why I ended up talking to Simon. I know we've never been close, but that's exactly why he was perfect – I didn't realise it, but I needed an opinion from someone who knew us, but was . . . removed.' She sniffed sadly. 'Sounds mad, but it was helpful to get a man's opinion. I obviously couldn't ask Dad or any cousin – they'd either batter Tarik, or gossip about it, or both.'

Jameela was horrified – sweet, affable Tarik. On the rogue chart more Care Bear than gigolo. Oh God. At that moment it dawned on her that the 'two to tango' was her and Reju. Her poor sister thought Jameela was still furious about the maternity top incident.

'Oh Reju, I'm sorry, I'm so sorry.' Now it was Jameela's turn to well up. 'I should've been here for you.'

'Yeah, well. Tarik's been staying at his mum's, so no doubt the rumour mill will start churning out titbits soon. I just need to decide what I want.'

Jameela pulled her sister towards her and hugged her close. She noticed there was a lot less to hug – she was ashamed that by shunning Reju she might have caused some of the sleepless nights and diminished appetite.

'Reju,' Jameela said quietly, 'did you come to our house ever?'

'Yes, I called round to talk to you about it all, but you were at work. That's when I ended up first telling Simon about it, he could tell I was upset.'

'Weird question I know, but did you use our bathroom?'

'Probably, yes – what's this about Jam?'

'Nothing.' Jameela smiled into her sister's long brown hair that'd always been a couple of shades lighter than hers. Another mystery solved. She held her little sis tighter.

'While we're at it,' Reju said, voice muffled by Jameela's hug, 'you need to sort stuff out with Simon. He thinks you've moved on without him and he's devastated. I think the only reason he was nice to me and listened to my sobbing and wailing was to get in your good books. He loves you so much you know.'

SARA COX | 246

'Really?' said Jameela. 'He's got a weird way of showing it. I've heard nothing from him.'

'He says he's texted. He admits he's useless at communicating – but he thinks the world of you. Ring him, whatever you're thinking, please?'

'Yeah,' said Jameela, hugging her sister even tighter, 'I will.'

'For what it's worth,' said Reju, 'I think you and Simon, what you have, is worth fighting for.'

Jameela shrugged slightly. 'Maybe.'

43

Sheila

On Saturday morning the clear blue skies over Lennington irritated Sheila. Today was a day of deceit and discovery – couldn't the skies at least respect that and be their usual grey of a faded bruise?

As arranged, Jameela was waiting for her on the platform at Piccadilly station, ready to board the 10.30 a.m. to London Euston. She was laden down with a fat pile of weekend papers, atop of which were balanced two large coffees and some pastries.

Martin had left for London the day before, Sheila waving him off, slightly paranoid that guilt was stuck all over her face like glitter.

'See you my little dragonfly,' he'd said at the front door, stroking her cheek tenderly and planting a kiss on her lips.

Not if I see you first, she thought, but out loud said, 'Have fun my love.'

She prayed they'd discover that the knickers were the result of an hilarious mix-up, and all she'd find Martin up to was strolling around an exhibition, and treasure hunting down by the Thames.

Sheila felt exhausted, and once in their seats Jameela obviously noticed. 'Did you get any sleep?'

Sheila sighed. 'Not really. My thoughts are piled up like Jenga pieces. Hopefully all this sneaking about will be worth it if we get to the bottom of the pants.'

The journey passed quickly and, as the train edged into Euston, Sheila produced from her bag a large floppy hat in navy and cream stripes and some huge sunglasses.

'You off to the beach?'

'Can't be too careful,' Sheila whispered shiftily. 'It's my disguise – what if Martin is lurking around? Don't want him to spot me.' She peered through the train windows into the gloom of the graffitied sidings.

'To be honest Sheila, in that hat he'd see you from space.'

While Jameela checked in, Sheila admired the squidgy sofas, velvet cushions and drapes in the cosy reception area of the Covent Garden Hotel (all booked by Jameela, so nothing showed on Sheila's bank records).

She wondered for a moment if the bearded young man with the tight trousers and tattoos peeping out from the collar of his white shirtsleeves would think she and Jameela, booking into a double room, were lovers. The thought titillated Sheila slightly. *Less than an hour in London and already I'm more metropolitan*, she thought, smiling to herself.

After unpacking, the two women stepped out from the hushed calm of the hotel foyer and into the sunshine. They walked along the smart streets, past the perfumers and independent shops of Covent Garden, towards Soho.

Jameela had done work experience in the city many moons ago as part of her degree, so she knew London quite well. She strode with all the confidence of a local through the idling traffic, dodging cycle couriers, tourists, bin wagons and the occasional homeless person shuffling along wearing their grimy sleeping bag like a sad superhero cape.

Sheila followed in her friend's wake, her stomach churning with nerves and hunger. As if reading her mind, Jameela stopped, spun on her heel to face Sheila, and said, 'Lunch. Let's have a quick bite and a nice glass of wine for Dutch courage.' She smiled, then added softly, 'You need to keep your energy up today.'

Sheila nodded her agreement – she was usually the one in charge, but she was rather enjoying being led for a change.

She felt slightly lightheaded – negotiating the narrow pavements cluttered with people all seemingly in a rush to get somewhere, coupled with the noisy traffic and the odd shout from lunchtime drinkers standing outside the pubs, was quite an attack on the senses.

It didn't help that every third person looked just like Martin. Sheila was so paranoid that they'd bump into him that her panicked mind was seeing him everywhere – passers-by in leather jackets, yoga gear, hijabs all took the form of Martin, before morphing back into their original forms as they approached. *Good grief*, thought Sheila, *I'm hallucinating now. I need that drink.*

Just at that moment Jameela disappeared through a small opening in a huge windowless wooden door, like something from a Tolkien story. Once on the other side, Sheila found herself in a large whitewashed dining room with high ceilings and an open kitchen running the whole length of one side, the chefs clattering around in the clouds of steam. Diners chatted animatedly around simple black metal tables and, after a quick word with a young clipboard-wielding woman, the friends were seated at a table for two in a corner of the room.

Steak, salad, frites and a bottle of wine ordered, they started to relax. If it weren't for the fact they were on a fact-finding mission that could potentially implode Sheila's marriage, she'd be having a lovely time. Jameela filled her in on the lastest details around the drama with her sister Reju, and when Jameela nipped off to the ladies Sheila sat quite happily people-watching, or 'being nosey', as Martin called it. A few tables away were a couple, similar in age to her and Martin. Both were dressed in expensive-looking greys, all cashmere and designer jeans. They were sharing a bottle of wine and oysters over the weekend papers. She watched them chatting intimately, leaning over to catch what the other said, reading out bits of the magazine, laughing over private jokes. At one point the man leaned over and gently stroked an eyelash from his wife's cheekbone with his thumb. Such a tender moment made Sheila well up, and she had to look away and study the bare filament bulbs dangling on wires from the white brickwork opposite. What was she going to do if she did catch Martin with another woman? She'd felt rather gung-ho about it until now, but her courage was slowly starting to seep away.

She didn't want to be alone, she wanted Martin. She loved him and his quirks. After losing his job and during his crisis of confidence, she'd felt her love for him grow even stronger. In a way she felt she'd helped to rebuild him after his mini breakdown. She was proud of the way he had his passions and his hobbies – she just hoped that his main passion wasn't the sort that wore size 10 pants.

They paid the bill and, after downing the last bit of wine, headed back out into the street.

Three minutes later they were standing by a small boutique on a narrow street. Its frontage was painted a glossy black, which contrasted with the swirly scarlet lettering of the sign: 'Ruby Red's'.

The old-fashioned bell rang loudly as Sheila and Jameela went in. The whole shop was a veritable Aladdin's cave of goodies – if Aladdin was into diamanté nipple tassels.

Pants and babydoll nighties in every hue, pale pink to mint to red, clamoured for space amongst peephole bras and suspenders. It seemed every inch – except the door and the thick black carpet – was either lace, leather or silk. The friends were drawn to a glass display cabinet.

'Ooh nice, jewellery, I might treat myself,' Sheila joked. On closer inspection she realised that the luxurious gold and silver goods were sex toys. 'Oh, on second thoughts,' she said, leaning closer. 'Good Lord!' She eyed the glistening vibrators. 'They're actually quite beautiful.' She pointed to a rose gold egg. 'That'd look lovely on my mantelpiece, it'd match my diffuser. Though I've no idea where you'd put that little one,' her finger pressed on the glass at a smaller object that looked like an expensive lipstick.

'I'm sure you could hazard a guess,' murmured Jameela, stepping away towards the lingerie section.

It was all rather intoxicating. Sheila, in a daydream, stepped backwards and on to the toe of someone standing behind her. 'Oops sorry!' She spun around to come face to face with a mannequin in a leather bodice and mask – a zip where the mouth should be. Sheila nearly screamed. She steadied the mannequin and, recovering her composure, joined Jameela.

'Bingo!' Jameela was holding an identical pair of pants to the one Sheila had found in her spare room all those weeks ago.

Examining the price tag, Sheila exclaimed, 'I've stayed in a B&B for less!'

'Yes, not cheap.'

'If they were a gift from Martin, he obviously thinks she's worth the expense, because Martin is tight.' Sheila looked around. 'In fact, he's tighter than some of these latex bras.'

'Buy one pair get the second half price on those,' said a voice. The shop's owner was hidden behind the huge black vintage cash register at the counter. She was perched on a stool looking down at her phone, but had remained so still neither woman had noticed her. She was very petite, and wore a shiny black bodice.

'I didn't see you there,' Sheila said, trying to peer through the woman's heavy peroxide fringe, which stopped at the bridge of her nose, obscuring her eyes completely. The woman smiled, some of her black lipstick had smudged onto her teeth making it look as though she'd licked some charcoal.

'Sorry, didn't mean to make you jump. Do you need any help?' She had the squeaky voice of a child, but it was hard to tell how old she was as Sheila couldn't see past the wall of fringe.

As Jameela continued to browse, Sheila got out her phone and said, 'Yes – I am hoping you can help me, actually.'

On the train down, Jameela and Sheila had come up with a plan on how to find out if Martin was a regular in the shop. They knew they could show a photo of Martin, but they had to come up with a plausible explanation for their search.

Jameela said honesty was the best policy – there was no way they could lie and say he was a missing person, or insinuate he was in any danger.

'Jameela, I know you've got your lawyer brain on speed dial, but we still need to come up with a reason why we're looking for him.'

Sheila was quite excited at the prospect of brushing off her am dram skills. Jameela seemed less convinced however, and after poo-pooing the idea that Martin was a long lost brother or they were from the National Lottery and were trying to track him down, they settled on Sheila's third and perhaps, if not exactly plausible, at least most harmless story.

Sheila scrolled through the photos on her phone till she arrived at the one she'd decided to use. It was of Martin, on holiday in Majorca two years before. It was one of her favourites – he was sun-kissed and, even with a peeling nose, he looked handsome.

'I'm looking for this man,' she said. The lady at the till reached out her hand for the phone casually as if she did this daily, as if her shop was the go-to place in the search for a missing person.

Sheila noticed the lady's hand was tiny and bony, like a sparrow's foot. Even behind the fringe, Sheila was sure she saw a fleeting twitch of recognition from the woman's mouth.

'His name is Martin and we met in February in Tenerife.' Sheila pointed at the photo. 'Funny story. On the way home at the end of the week we were all sitting next to each other on the plane – and Martin and I had very similar bags as carry-on,' she trilled. 'Well, we didn't want the partying to end – we were quite a wild bunch – so we had a few G&Ts on the flight to round off the holiday. We were all rather squiffy by the time we waved goodbye at arrivals, and it was only when I got home,' Sheila paused for dramatic effect, 'that I realised Martin and I had accidentally swapped bags! I had his bag! Unbelievable!' She had become louder and louder with nerves, and shouted the last word in the lady's face. The fringe parted momentarily with the blast from Sheila's breath.

'Yes, unbelievable,' agreed the woman, a small smile cracking her black lipstick.

'So,' said Sheila, who was sure she could feel Jameela tensing up behind her, 'I tried Facebook, Twitter . . . but with no surname it was impossible. The bag had a John Lewis sweater, a book, some toiletries, but the only unique,' she paused to let the compliment sink in, 'and therefore traceable item in the bag were these!' At this, she whipped out the Ruby Red's pants from her pocket and rattled on. 'As my friend and I are in London on a little trip to celebrate her . . . fiftieth,' Jameela looked around at this and Sheila noted her friend's smile didn't quite reach her eyes, 'I thought, why not pop in to the shop and see if we can get Martin's belongings back to him?'

Finished with her tale at last, Sheila bared the palms of her hands with a flourish like a magician showing the dove she'd been holding had in fact disappeared.

The woman looked at Sheila, then at the picture of Martin, and lastly down at the pants, which were now on the counter.

'So, amongst the jumper and the books he had a pair of women's pants in there?' she asked.

Sheila was sure she detected a bit of mischief in the woman's tone. 'Yes . . .' said Sheila. She faltered. It did seem rather strange, she hadn't really factored in anyone querying the details of the story.

At this point, Jameela joined Sheila at the counter, her voice low and relaxed. She sighed. 'Sounds completely mad to me,' she said, looking at Sheila, who in turn looked at her friend as if she were the mad one. 'However,' Jameela confirmed, 'having heard all about Martin and his fruity antics by the pool with his much younger, quite . . . open-minded wife, I wouldn't be at all surprised if they'd joined the mile high club on that plane home and then she'd shoved the knickers in his bag, after drunkenly forgetting to put them back on.' All three women looked down at the crumpled pants and grimaced. 'To be honest Sheila, I don't know why you hung out with them at all – they sound a nightmare. And while we're on the subject,' she added petulantly, 'I don't know why you're obsessed with tracking him down on MY birthday weekend.'

God, thought Sheila, *she's good*. The woman behind the till seemed drawn in, and instantly sided with Jameela, nodding in empathy. 'The only good thing about this whole drama,' said Jameela, 'is I found my perfect peephole bra – I'll take this please,' and she held out a lacy bra to the shop lady.

The woman seemed to soften behind the fringe – she clearly didn't want this poor woman's birthday to be derailed any more than it already had been. Sheila clocked the price tag on the bra; no wonder she was smiling – £79.99 for a bra, and one that didn't even keep your nipples warm at that!

'Lovely choice,' said the woman, expertly folding the bra in black tissue paper. 'I have seen him a few times. He comes in every month or so, though I've not seen him for a while. And, never with a wife, always alone. There you go.' She handed Jameela a stiff black bag with red ribbon handles.

'OK, well feels like we're one step closer,' said Sheila cheerfully. 'I don't suppose you know where he stays down here? I don't fancy traipsing back on the train with TWO large holdalls,' she said, rolling her eyes dramatically.

'Well,' the woman replied, 'I've bumped into him at the bar in Mimi's Hotel on Frith Street a couple of times, you could try there.' She smiled. 'Quite the sleuths you two – and all to return a bag. Good luck ladies.'

The two women exited the shop and trotted down the street, mouths clamped shut, trying to hold it together. Once they'd turned the corner they collapsed into a fit of laughter. She could unpack the hurt she felt at discovering Martin's secret shopping trips later. For now, in the heat of the moment it was, weirdly, quite a buzz.

'You were amazing,' shrieked Sheila 'Your acting was fantastic – I was even starting to feel guilty for ruining your birthday trip!'

Jameela smiled 'Oh yeah, especially with it being my FIFTIETH?'

Sheila cringed. 'Yes . . . Sorry about that, I panicked. If Martin really is at the exhibition at the Tate Modern, he'll not be back till later. So may I suggest a bottle of champagne to toast our success and your half century?'

'Very funny. OK, you're on.' And with that they headed back to their hotel in Covent Garden arm in arm, Sheila's smile only occasionally faltering when she replayed what the woman had told them about Martin's regular visits. Just wait and see, she told herself, just wait and see.

All the adrenaline and the champagne called for a little siesta before the two women got ready to head out on the town. They first called into the bar of their hotel, where espresso martinis did the job of waking them up and giving them Dutch courage. They were going to need it, after all; it was a Saturday night in Soho, and the streets were throbbing with young, beautiful, shouty things. They were swallowed up by a sea of bare midriffs, ripped fishnets and muscular men in vests tops. Cigarette smoke and music drifted along the pavement as they walked past the bars, and through people spilling onto the streets with their beers, perching on the kerb, leaning on railings.

Sheila's stomach churned with nerves. The laughter and excitable squawking was in sharp contrast to how she was feeling inside. She was potentially only minutes away from making a discovery that would cause her whole world to crumble.

If she did find Martin with another woman, if she came face to face with the wearer of the pants, then what? In her mind various scenes played out, but each one morphed into a horrible sequence like something from a closing scene of *EastEnders*: Sheila slapping the woman *duff-duff-duff* – Sheila screaming and attacking Martin accidentally killing him *duff-duff-duff* – Sheila discovering Martin with not one woman but two, twins possibly *duff-duff-duff-duff – duff-du-du-duff*.

As the two women approached Martin's hotel, Sheila felt vastly unprepared, and slowed her walk, wishing she could rewind the entire journey.

'Hey,' Jameela said, 'you've come this far, you've been so brave. Whatever we discover in there you'll be OK.'

Sheila nodded and tried to swallow, but couldn't. 'Gosh Jameela, I'm so scared. My mouth's drier than Jesus' flip flop.'

'Deep breaths,' Jameela said. 'Boobs out, belly in, let's do this.' And they walked up the steps into Mimi's Hotel.

Mimi's bar was packed, and the R&B loud enough for the bass to be felt through Jameela and Sheila's shoes.

From the relative brightness of the summer's evening outside, it took a couple of minutes for their eyes to adjust.

Slinky-hipped cool types mingled with some more grizzled-looking drinkers – who looked like remnants from the seedier, artier Soho of the past.

There was a bloke who was easily seventy, with spindly tanned arms dangling from a white vest, multiple faded leather bracelets, and shaggy hair. Sheila thought he looked like a missing Rolling Stone. His mate wore a velvet plum fedora and a thin black moustache, and was chatting to a woman who sported a huge platinum beehive and khaki mechanic's overalls.

In the darker corners of the bar only silhouettes could be made out. 'I need the loo,' Jameela shouted over the music to Sheila, who nodded and gave a thumbs-up.

Sheila started to work her way through the crowd. She couldn't help but feel exhilarated – she could be anyone here in the semi-darkness, the music pulsating through her feet, up towards her thighs. Maybe she was a little drunk. For all anyone in that bar knew, she could be a dancer, a sculptor, an undercover police officer. She smiled to herself, swaying a little. She could be an explorer back from Peru or a recovered opium addict, instead of just a housewife and food bank volunteer from Lennington. She felt a rush of adrenaline at the adventure they'd found themselves on. As she nudged her way through the wall of hot bodies, she scanned the shadows – no sign of Martin.

She was dazzled by the blue-white light behind all the optics. 'Two vodka tonics please,' she shouted above the din, and tried not to let the shock register on her face as the skinny girl with a copper Afro and aqua eyeshadow shouted back, 'Twenty-four pounds please.'

Sheila sipped her drink and felt her shoulders relax. She even recognised the song that'd just come on, Beyoncé's 'Crazy in Love'. She moved around towards the edge of the bar and peered into the darkness. No Martin. For a moment she felt relief flood over her. The alcohol was taking the edge off her nerves, and she'd rather just let her hair down and not confront the state of her marriage. As she put their drinks down at a small table and went to sit down, something caught her eye.

There was a familiarity in the movement. A hand gesture, coupled with a laugh. She saw a flash of teeth, a smile, eyes crinkled at the corners. It was all at once, in that split second, so familiar yet completely alien. Her head spun. It was Martin, but at the same time it wasn't. She recognised all the separate parts, but they were assembled in the wrong order.

Sheila drank in the details, her brain failing to compute; the dark red lipstick, the hair – bleached blonde, tousled, shoulder-length – the light bouncing off the synthetic strands. The dark eyes heavy with fake lashes, and lastly, the turquoise dress, tight and ruched and actually rather lovely. If it hadn't been her husband wearing it. Sheila turned away quickly so Martin wouldn't spot her. She blinked a few times, like someone in a cheesy sitcom when they couldn't believe their eyes. She peeked around again, sure she'd been mistaken, but the concrete already hardening in her stomach and the thumping of her heart told her otherwise. It was Martin.

There was no chance he'd spot her through the gloom – he was chatting animatedly, half facing away from her, his three friends – equally glamorous strangers with their hairpieces and lipstick – laughing at whatever he was saying. Sheila couldn't see Martin's 'Treasure fiend' friend Mike anywhere – did he even exist?

She suddenly felt light-headed; she needed to get out of there. Where was Jameela? She left the drinks on the table, pushed through the crowd, elbows knocking into her. The music was now deafening, the roar of the chat, the cackling, shouting and whooping all a thick fog of noise and sweat – then suddenly she was out in the foyer by the loos, and there was her friend Jameela. Thank God.

'Are you OK? You look like you've seen a ghost.'

'Let's go,' said Sheila.

'What?' Jameela said. 'Why?'

Sheila clamped her lips closed momentarily, trapping the words inside – she couldn't tell her what she'd just seen.

'Because he's not here, that's why. I even asked at reception if he's staying here – he's not.'

Jameela looked confused. 'He might turn up though, we might as well have a drink, c'mon.' She grabbed Sheila's hand as if to lead her back into the bar, but Sheila snatched it back with such force Jameela stopped, shocked.

Sheila felt as if she might cry. 'I would just like to go. Now. This whole idea was stupid, running around London like a couple of Columbos. I will talk to Martin about the pants when he's home – it's what I should've done in the first place. Sorry – it's been such a fun weekend so far, but he's not here, and now I just feel stupid and suddenly very, very tired.' Sheila turned on her heel and headed for the door, almost at a run, head bowed.

'Sheila, wait!' Jameela caught up with Sheila on the pavement and gently held her by the shoulders. 'Hey, I'm sorry OK? It'll be OK, come on.'

Even though she'd done nothing wrong, Sheila felt ashamed and embarrassed. Her husband was a secret transvestite? The mystery pants were his too? She could almost laugh.

How, after all these years together, had she not known? Their sex life was completely adequate, on holidays even very good. Was he gay? They weren't the sort of people whose stories were splashed over the weekly magazines at the hair salon: 'My cross-dressing husband shock!' She was on the committee of the Neighbourhood Watch for God's sake. They were mortgage free, and she was learning Spanish. She'd been in the same room as Princess Anne at a food-bank fundraiser.

All these thoughts rattled through her mind as they headed back to Covent Garden. She tried not to stumble, to act normal. Back at the hotel she said, 'I think I'll have a nice bath,' and vomited as silently as possible, running the bath taps to cover any noise.

Later, as she lay awake in the kingsize bed listening to Jameela's soft breathing, she felt a huge sadness wash over her. She felt sad for Martin – that he had to hide this part of himself, and she felt sad for herself.

44

Jameela

At Tuesday's class, Jameela watched Sasha expertly throw a huge vase – the sort you'd see beside the door of a restaurant to hold wet umbrellas. He peered out from behind it as the pottery wheel slowed to a standstill.

'Right,' he said, 'so it's up to you. You can try something like this – a big and bold vase shape. Or you can use your bowls from last week. With pit firing, we really are combining earth, water and fire in its purest most basic form – out under the skies, with less control over temperature, we're at the mercy of the weather and the materials you choose to burn around your pots.'

Sheila had arrived late and seemed very quiet to Jameela – she looked deep in thought as she filled her little dish at the sink.

'Penny for them,' Jameela said, making Sheila jump.

'Jameela! I was a million miles away . . . Ah I was just thinking . . . well, nothing really. Never mind me – you worn your new bra yet?'

'Oh sure yeah,' replied Jameela, even with a kirby grip clamped in her lips, she could make her voice drip with sarcasm. 'Had a meeting with town planners this morning about a new supermarket's loading bay, and my lacy peephole number really helped me make a great impression.' She twisted up her long ponytail and pinned it in place. 'I only bought it to distract that strange half-doll half-fringe woman – don't think I'm going to need it for the foreseeable.'

Sheila smiled. 'You never know – could be the perfect welcome home gift for Simon.'

'Hmm, we'll see.' Jameela had promised herself that after the weekend she'd finally speak with her estranged husband.

Jameela got to work. She slammed the clay onto the wheel and started to cup the spinning lump. She enjoyed the physicality of it as her whole body seemed to curve like the wall of a turret, strong, solid, all the energy flowing towards the clay in her hands. She felt in those moments a million miles from her usual world of contracts, clauses and small print.

As she threw her vase she remained deep in thought. According to Reju, Simon was desperate to reunite. Jameela had some serious thinking to do.

45

Becky

The doorbell rang not once but twice. Who was ringing on a Friday night with such urgency? Becky peeped an eye out from under her duvet and squinted at the clock. 8.15 p.m. She'd hoped it was later. The sort of hour you could shoo someone away with a 'What time do you call this?' The bell rang again. It was now 8.16 p.m., but that made no difference. It wasn't even dark outside. Becky considered pulling the duvet back over her head and sinking back into the abyss she'd created for herself by eating three-quarters of a Domino's margarita having not left the house for a few days. She felt safe here. Sure there was a slight whiff of garlic from the dipping sauce, and a ripeness coming from her armpit area, but that was to be expected – she hadn't been able to face showering for a couple of days. Tony stealing her nana's ring, coupled with the disastrous kiss with Sasha had knocked her spirit sideways. Thank you very much world, but I'd like to get off for a bit if that's OK with you?

She'd granted herself the past few weeks to lick her wounds before Elliot returned from Ayia Napa the next day.

The thought of the stolen ring forced her to throw back the duvet and head reluctantly for the door. What if it'd been found, and Sergeant Joan Garvey was standing on her doorstep now, desperate to give her the good news, the ring and box in an evidence bag in her pocket?

In her sudden rush, Becky leapt towards her bedroom door, clearing the small pile of discarded clothes by the bed, and landing on the thankfully closed pizza box. She skated on the box for a few inches, regained her balance, and knotted the belt to her crumb-encrusted towelling robe as she ran down the stairs. She took the chain off the front door and swung it open.

There stood, not a police officer, but a potter. A Scottish one at that, called Sasha.

Thirty minutes later Becky was sitting drinking a cup of tea, wearing jeans, a jumper, and with her wet hair wrapped up in a towel. The jeans felt tight – a few days of carbs and little movement can do that to you, she mused. She looked over at Sasha. He was scrolling through his phone, scanning eBay for Technics decks and a mixer like the ones Tony had taken. Even if they couldn't find Elliot's original ones, maybe they could replace them – 'A wee scrap of comfort to offer him?' as Sasha had said.

On seeing the state of Becky – 'What? It's "slept in a skip chic",' she'd said defensively – Sasha insisted she got in the shower.

Becky was pleased to see him and relieved they were still friends – the many hours they'd chatted and hung out together at the community centre was what mattered, not an awkward kiss. They were buddies, and she'd missed his company.

She didn't even feel embarrassed that Sasha had seen her in such a state – it showed they were friends no matter what.

When Becky had emerged from her shower, pink-cheeked, well-scrubbed, and feeling much better, she found Sasha loading the dishwasher. He'd located the bin bags and had filled one already with take-away cartons and pizza boxes. He'd put the recycling out, and the kettle was on.

'Wow! You some sort of Scottish fairy godmother?' she asked.

'Yes – and you shall go to the ball Cinders. Or at least to The Apollo for a quick drink?'

The walk to their favourite place was a pleasant one. It was a warm summer's evening, and kids were still playing out. Sasha passed back a stray football to a bunch of lads who were having a kick-about.

As they stepped through the restaurant door Apollo spotted them and boomed, 'The return of the lovebirds!' turning heads and turning Becky's cheeks scarlet. Zoe bustled over with a carafe of house red and some fat tiropita – triangles of golden filo dough filled with egg and feta.

'Sorry about him,' she said rolling her eyes. 'He's a soppy old romantic.'

Becky forced a laugh, but once Sasha had poured the wine, a silence fell over the table.

Then they both spoke at once: 'Look—' said Becky, as Sasha started, 'Funnily enough—'

Oh God, thought Becky, *this is excruciating.*

'You first,' she said.

Sasha took a deep breath. He chewed his lower lip and said, more to the tablecloth than to her, 'I've not been entirely honest.'

Becky readied herself. She was right! A fiancée or wife back home? A boyfriend? She took a gulp of wine.

Sasha continued in a small voice. 'Whenever you've asked me about relationships, I've always batted away your questions.'

Becky nodded. 'Yeah, I had noticed.'

'Well, the reason I got frightened when we . . .' he stammered, 'when we kissed, the reason I've been acting so fucking weird, is because I don't want to hurt you.'

'Right . . .' said Becky, her stomach churning, her chest tight. She sat up a little straighter, braced for impact.

'Because the last person I loved,' said Sasha, looking deep into Becky's eyes, 'well, I lost her.'

Becky was confused – the use of the word 'love' had shaken her, but she shelved it for now. 'Lost her? What do you mean Sasha?'

He looked down and fiddled with his napkin. 'She was called Agnes, and she was my first love. Since her, there have been others – flings, casual stuff – but no one I've fallen for, no one special . . . until now.' Becky felt her cheeks grow hot. Sasha continued, speaking slowly, 'I met Agnes five years ago – she was from Paisley, but we met in Israel and she was everything to me. It was a whirlwind, but we just knew we were right for each other. After a few months I moved to LA, and she joined me out there – she was a dance teacher.'

Despite the solemnity of the moment, Becky hated herself for feeling a prick of jealousy. A dance teacher, no doubt lithe and beautiful, and here was Becky, with her jeans digging into her muffin top.

'She was lovely, but also, she was a good person – smart, strong-willed, so funny – like you.'

Becky smiled, warming to the mysterious Agnes.

'Aggie got a placement at a dance studio in Long Beach about thirty minutes from our apartment. I was working flat out, helping a couple of friends set up their gallery, I was teaching too at three different schools; we were busy but we were happy. Then,' he stopped, studied his hands, 'we had an argument – over something stupid. We were tired and stressed and she slammed out the door saying she'd had enough of me, telling me in her best Glaswegian to "Get tae fuck!" I followed and shouted I was done with her too.' Sasha, his hand shaking slightly, sipped his wine. 'She looked hurt as she got to the car, her face kinda crumpled, and I thought she might come back, I wanted her to, but in that split second I was so angry. I stormed back inside, but then something – common sense? Love? – made me run back outside after her. I wanted to say sorry, I wanted to stop her and hug her and promise her we'd talk later. But she'd already gone. I could just see the back of our little car disappear round the end of our street.' Sasha stalled, wiping away a tear roughly with the inside of his wrist.

Becky looked down.

Apollo appeared with olives and a basket of warm pitta, but melted away, sensing the atmosphere.

Becky swallowed. 'Go on,' she said gently, though she felt she knew what was coming.

'I just feel like anyone I love ends up getting hurt, that I'm no good – a curse.' He shook his head. 'I couldn't get hold of Aggie all day – I thought she was making me sweat, ignoring my calls. By teatime though I was panicking. We'd had bigger rows than this, but we'd put it down to us both being "fiery Scots", and would laugh it off by lunchtime. I was calling the dance studio, her friends, even her parents back home in case she'd rung them. I tried to keep the panic from my voice, but they heard it. They told me to try the hospitals, and I did, and that's when I found out. She'd crashed that morning, on the way to work. There'd been a massive pile-up – not her fault. Two other people died that day, a dad and his teenage daughter. The inquest said it was just an accident, an awful terrible accident.'

Becky leaned across and gently took hold of his hand.

'Becky, I torture myself that maybe if she hadn't been distracted by the argument, if she wasn't so flooded with adrenaline, then maybe she would've acted differently – maybe her reflexes would've been quicker.' He took his hand from Becky's, as if he didn't deserve her sympathy. 'For certain I know that if I'd caught her before she'd left, delayed her a few minutes by begging her for forgiveness, making her laugh, making up with her, then the only way she'd have been affected by the crash was to be caught up in the traffic caused by it; sitting in the car watching the emergency vehicles scream up the hard shoulder, saying a silent prayer of thanks she wasn't involved. And I can never forgive myself for that. Ever. I could've stopped her, I could've saved her.'

Back at Becky's house they talked some more.

Becky told Sasha about her mum's cancer, about feeling helpless as she watched her slowly die in front of her. But mainly they talked about Aggie and about the crash.

By the early hours they were both exhausted and more than a little drunk. It'd been necessary though, and cathartic. Becky felt as though they'd thrashed through all of Sasha's feelings, untangling his emotions, separating his sorrow from his guilt – the former was OK to hold onto, she said, the latter he had to let go. Becky told Sasha he had no choice, he had to forgive himself. Aggie didn't sound like the sort of woman who'd want him to suffer for all these years.

Back home in Scotland, he said, they'd laid Aggie to rest on a typically blustery Paisley day, and her parents had told him through their tears that she was the happiest she'd ever been with him, and that he must find the strength to live on and to, one day, love again. 'Do it for her, son,' Aggie's dad had said.

'He's right,' Becky implored. 'Can't you see that?'

Eventually, as it rolled around to 2 a.m., Becky suggested he stay over. Sasha said he would, but insisted on the sofa. Becky wouldn't be budged. 'The last thing to sleep on that sofa robbed me and disappeared,' she said. 'If anything, it needs burning.'

They swept the clutter from Becky's bed and, too drunk or sad for seduction, fell asleep, cuddled up and still half dressed.

*

It was almost 11 a.m. by the time Becky creaked an eye open the next morning. She watched Sasha as he slept.

Sweet Jesus, she thought, *even with dried dribble on his chin he's beautiful.*

She slipped silently out of bed and brushed her teeth, scrubbing away the maroon crust at the corners of her mouth from the red wine. She made two brews and winced as she caught sight of the two empty bottles of rioja and the whisky glasses. Her head thumped, and she dug out the paracetamol and returned with her booty to bed.

As she slipped back under the covers, her phone buzzed twice. There was a text from Elliot: 'Hi mum, I've landed! It feels bloody freezing here!'

The second was from Sergeant Joan Garvey: 'Are you around? Pawn shop Phil has news about a possible lead on the ring. Can I pick you up in 10?'

Becky simply replied, 'Perfect', then quickly pulled on her jeans and a sweater. She dragged a brush through her hair, necked two paracetamol, and headed out, leaving the spare door key next to Sasha's mug of tea. Next to it she wrote on the back of an envelope: 'Had to go out, info on ring, see you later. Please lock up and post key.'

With any luck she'd be back before Elliot got home, and she might even have the ring!

'Get in,' said Sergeant Garvey. She was in her own car, a light blue Volkswagen, and was wearing jeans and a flowery shirt.

'You look nice,' Becky said.

Joan looked embarrassed. 'Thanks.' She pulled away from the kerb. 'There is a reason I'm not in uniform. Phil rang me – he was on a blind date at a pub called The Jesters a couple of nights ago, it's about half an hour from here.'

'Right,' said Becky.

'He said he goes there quite regularly to meet women – he'd

heard there was a DJ playing, and, as he put it, he's a very private person and didn't want anyone knowing he'd been using dating apps, especially not his wife.'

'Charming,' chipped in Becky, still unclear why Phil's love life would have anything to do with the missing ring.

'Anyway,' Joan indicated right and joined the steady flow of traffic on the dual carriageway towards Manchester, 'turns out the DJ is the landlord's daughter Alice, and the decks she was using were Technics – good ones. Apparently the landlord isn't averse to a bit of knock-off stuff, so Phil's interest was, as he put it "well and truly piqued".'

Becky felt the dull throb of disappointment. 'But I thought you mentioned the ring in your text?'

'I did,' said Joan. 'Get this: apparently the date is going well, the girl is "a bit thick but very pretty". I had to bite my tongue at that point,' Joan rolled her eyes, 'and so Phil went to the bar for another round of drinks. This time he's served by the landlady, and he notices on her finger . . .'

Becky gasped and covered her mouth with her hands. 'The ring?' she whispered.

Joan nodded.

'OK well – a ring. But hopefully THE ring – with a beautiful sapphire in it. "Lovely bit of jewellery you have there," Phil tells her, "family heirloom is it?"' Joan slowed down as the traffic ground to a halt. 'She says to him it was given to her by her husband after she caught him with his tongue down the barmaid's throat in the cellar. And the best thing is, he gave it to her two weeks ago . . .' Joan widened her eyes. 'Seems too big a coincidence surely? Decks and a sapphire ring?'

Becky's heart thumped and she nodded. Could she allow herself a glimmer of hope?

'So why aren't you in uniform? If it is the stolen stuff, you'll need to arrest them, and—'

'Hold your horses,' Joan said, holding up her hand. 'Normally yes, but it's complicated. Once I got back to the station and one of CID heard me and Constable Glover discussing The Jesters, I was told under no circumstances could I, a uniformed officer, go bowling into that pub. It's at the centre of an undercover operation – drugs I imagine – and I would cock up months of work and tens of thousands of pounds' worth of policing by just stepping over the threshold.' Becky felt her eyes widen. 'That's why,' continued Garvey, 'I'm dressed in my new Zara blouse, and that's why I need you.'

Becky was scared to ask, but did anyway. 'Why do you need me?' she said in a small voice.

'Well, I thought it'd be lovely, on my day off, to go for a Coca Cola and a bit of pub grub at The Jesters, and when the landlady appears with our ploughman's, you can get a good look at the ring. If it IS yours, then at least we know where it is, and we can then look into getting it returned to you. But there's no use worrying about any of that if it's not your ring.'

The two women found a table by the window and sat down with their drinks. The pub was quiet, just a couple of regulars nursing their pints on stools at the bar. Sky Sports was blaring from a large screen, and a faded St George's flag was pinned below it.

They'd been served by a grumpy young girl with a silver letter A on a chain around her neck – presumably the landlord's daughter Alice, who, judging by her scowl, had drawn the short straw and wasn't very happy with her demotion from superstar DJ to holding the fort for her parents on a Saturday lunchtime.

The DJ decks were nowhere to be seen.

Joan and Becky ordered cheese paninis and waited for the land-lady to make her grand entrance.

'I'd better let Elliot know I'm not at home – he'll be back soon.' Becky reached for her phone in her jeans back pocket. Not there. Damn – not like her at all – the adrenaline that had got her up and out of the house so quickly hadn't helped her to remember her phone. She pictured it still on her bed. She didn't know Elliot's or Sasha's number off by heart, and resigned herself to hoping Sasha would somehow stall Elliot, though she doubted he'd be able to stop him noticing the missing decks, coffee machine, and 42-inch telly – they were basically his three favourite things in the world after her.

An hour went by, and there was still no sign of the landlady. 'Can't we just ask for her?' said Becky.

'For what reason?' murmured Joan, sipping the dregs of her second Coke. 'Two strangers asking after her wouldn't make sense. No, we just have to bide our time. No one can know why we're here or who we are – if I mess up the undercover work that'll be my next promotion on the back burner, maybe forever.'

The clock behind the bar was moving torturously slowly, but by 2.45 p.m. the place started to fill up. 'The long-awaited Manchester derby kicks off at three!' grinned a tanned Gary Lineker from the telly.

Soon the bar was bustling with red or sky blue shirts, depending on their affiliation. Good-natured banter grew in volume.

The panini and Coke had at least settled Becky's stomach. The rush of excitement about being on a stakeout had long since blown over, and the drone of the footie on the telly was strangely soporific despite the hubbub in the bar. She yawned.

'Told you police work was exciting,' laughed Joan.

'Sorry.' Becky straightened up. 'Late night. This is probably the closest I'll come to being a police officer, so I should lap up every minute.'

The whistle blew and the game was underway.

'Should we call it a day? We could always come back.'

Becky shook her head. 'Let's give it another thirty,' she said.

Joan nodded. 'OK, well you certainly have the stubbornness of some of the best coppers I know.'

'I prefer to call it patience,' said Becky smugly.

Becky was invested now, and had a funny feeling they should wait it out. She'd already cursed herself a dozen times for forgetting her phone, getting the landline taken out at home, and for not knowing her own son's mobile number.

Becky was certain Elliot would be home by now, and would know about the robbery. She didn't like being out of control like this, with no idea what scene Elliot would come home to. What if he found Sasha still asleep in her bed, like some kind of Goldilocks, only with a five o'clock shadow?

Joan leaned over. 'Hey, keep meaning to ask, did you apply to be a special constable in the end? I know our station is looking to recruit.' But before Becky could answer, she added, 'Leave it with me, you should come down next week for a chat and a look round.'

The crowd grew louder as City were on the attack. Cheers and shouts erupted as they scored a goal just before the half-time whistle. That's when Becky glanced around and saw a curvy woman clad in a pink velour tracksuit appear behind the pumps. She had dark auburn hair pulled back from a kind, round face. She looked just like her daughter Alice, but time had trampled on her features. Becky and Joan looked at each other and drained their glasses. 'Fancy another?' said Joan.

'Yes,' said Becky, her eyes fixed on the bar. 'My round.'

In the six steps it took Becky to reach the bar she was already rehearsing how she'd tell Elliot the story about getting the ring back 'There it was, on her finger, your nan's ring.' The recovery of the family heirloom would join the legend of how it came into the family in the first place. Becky couldn't resist smiling as she reached the bar.

'There you go Jim.' The landlady was handing over a pint to an older gent in a flat cap and then turned and smiled at Becky. 'Yes love?' she said.

Becky smiled back. 'Two . . .' she couldn't resist, she glanced at the Landlady's hand and saw the ring. Sapphire set within four smaller diamonds, absolutely exquisite, and absolutely not her nana's ring. Becky felt the pit of her stomach give way and her smile fade.

'You OK love?' The woman said, looking concerned.

'Sorry yes, I'm fine. Just remembered something. Err . . . two lemonades,' Becky said, hope fading into bitter disappointment.

Not only had she blown her chance of a 'mum of the year' nomination by not being there when Elliot came home, now she knew for sure it was all for nothing.

As they set off on the journey home, Joan seemed lost in thought, and that suited Becky; she needed to wallow.

'I'm sorry,' said Joan at last. 'I'm sorry I dragged you on a wild goose chase.'

'No,' said Becky, failing to lift the flatness in her voice, 'it seemed such a coincidence – you did the right thing, we had to check it out.'

Just then Becky gave a start as three police vans and a dog unit hurtled past them along the narrow road in the direction of The Jesters.

Later, as they pulled up outside her house, Becky thanked Joan and climbed out of the car. She was desperate to see Elliot, but as she swung open the front door she was met by the kind of thick silence only an empty home can conjure.

She ran upstairs and grabbed her phone from the bed – a missed call from Sasha. She tried to return his call, then rang Elliot. Both went straight to voicemail. She put on a cosy jumper and got in her car. There was only one place she could think of to go; she knew Sasha would be there, and she hoped maybe Elliot would be there too – the pit firing.

46

Sheila

At 4 p.m. on the Saturday, according to the email, everyone was to meet at Roberts' Farm, up in Howlesden. The farmer, Bob Roberts had, for a small fee, given permission for a few tents to be erected and six holes dug in his back paddock – he'd even thrown in the use of the outside loo in his upper sheep sheds at no extra cost.

Sheila was excited about a night under the stars. She found it astonishing how she'd been able to act completely normally with Martin, even though the image of him in drag kept forcing its way into her thoughts.

'Blummin' heck mon petite pigeon,' said Martin as he wrestled her bags from the boot of their Peugeot, 'you've packed enough for an Arctic expedition.'

Sheila watched him struggle. 'You did offer to help Martin.'

'I know I did, I'm only joking. I couldn't let you come up here by yourself, you might've got lost – I know the land around here quite well thanks to my metal detecting.'

'Oh really?' she asked. 'I didn't realise, you only mentioned it a hundred and twelve times in the car on the way here.'

Martin looked wounded and Sheila instantly felt bad. 'Sorry – I didn't mean to snap. I'm glad you're here, you can say hi to everyone.'

Sasha was at the camp, unloading the last of the bubble-wrapped pots from a van.

'I see my contact at the Scouts came though then Sasha?' shouted Sheila, looking at the four large khaki tents.

'Absolutely Sheila, I owe you a drink,' he grinned.

'I'll hold you to that.' She watched as Martin stumbled the last few metres with her bags. She knew she had to talk to him, but when? Would there ever be the right time to have the 'So you're a secret transvestite' chat?

Martin dropped the bags with a thud. He looked slightly grey.

'Sasha, this is my husband Martin.'

Sasha gave a small wave. 'Nice to meet you Martin. Are you any good with one of these?' He handed Martin a spade. 'I've dug all the pits, but the sixth one needs finishing off, would really appreciate it if you could have a go for ten minutes?' Martin tried to rearrange his grimace into a smile. 'Size- and shape-wise, imagine you're digging a grave for a couple of dearly departed traffic bollards.'

Sasha carried a bale of straw over to the pit for Sheila to sit on. 'Here you go, so you can keep an eye on him,' he said with a wink, then he was gone.

Martin started digging.

'He's right,' said Sheila suddenly.

Martin didn't seem to hear. He kept digging.

She cleared her throat. She could feel her heart thumping. The wind was picking up – she thought maybe it would take each word as she spoke it and whip it away before it reached Martin's ears.

'Sasha is right,' she raised her voice now, 'I should perhaps keep an eye on you more.'

Martin was looking at the damp earth as he sliced through it with the sharp edge of the blade. Sheila went to speak again. She had to say it, and she had to say it now.

'I saw you.'

Sheila was taken aback as Martin took the words out of her mouth. She was stunned for a second.

'I saw you,' he repeated, this time looking up at her.

Her throat felt dry. In the distance, behind Martin, she could see a group arriving – Jack, Pearl, Danny, Louise, and Jameela. Striding towards them without a care in the world.

'What do you mean?' she said, confused. 'Saw me where?'

Martin straightened up now. 'At the bar.' As if sensing the seriousness of the situation, the wind suddenly dropped and Martin's words sounded too loud.

Sheila grasped for something to say.

Martin held her gaze. 'I spotted you just before you saw me. Well, not "me" – Anne-Marie.'

Sheila's confusion lasted a split second before it dawned on her. 'Anne-Marie – so that day at the hospice, when your mum said I should look after Anne-Marie,' the pieces clunked into place, 'your mum knew? That's what she meant? As she lay dying she was trying to tell me.'

'She always said I should tell you – she said you were strong enough to cope.' He sniffed and wiped his nose roughly on his sleeve. 'She hated me living with a lie so big.' He looked up at the bruised sky.

Sheila felt as if she was grasping for threads of a story. 'At the hospice, you said she was your cleaner? Another lie.'

Martin's head snapped towards her then. 'No. No, not a lie. She WAS our cleaner, she was impossibly glamorous though, always well turned out, and I idolised her, wanted to be her. Mum found me when I was fourteen, dressing up in her clothes, pretending to be Anne-Marie . . . She kept it from Dad, he wouldn't have understood. Mum didn't really, she just accepted it was part of me – that's how much she loved me.'

He lifted the shovel high and plunged it downwards, slicing into the damp earth.

'Martin, I—' Sheila started, but he put up a hand to stop her.

He spoke quickly. 'If you don't want to be married to me anymore, if you can't handle the shame, if you think I'm disgusting or a freak, I understand, but I—'

'Stop!' it was Sheila's turn to shout now. She strode over the grass to Martin. He was shorter than her, as he was standing in the hole, which only made him look more boyish and vulnerable. 'I'm not ashamed of you Martin, I love you,' she said softly, feeling tears well up. 'I'm a lot of things, but I'm not ashamed. I'm bloody angry – about all the lies. I'm confused. I just want to understand. We have a lot of talking to do.'

The group of potters was now getting closer.

'We have wine!' shouted Jameela, waving a bottle.

Sheila sniffed back her tears and swallowed. 'Now is not the time. But we'll get through this, if you want to too?'

'More than anything,' said Martin.

'Well then,' she bent slightly to hug him in the hole, then let him go, straightening the collar of his jacket.

To the group Sheila turned and shouted, 'Hurrah! Wine!' and made her way to greet them.

47

Jameela

Jameela stood, staring in wonder at the six pits dug parallel to each other in a line, like half a dozen eclairs in a box. The holes were separated from the tents by a crackling campfire with straw bales set around it. Carefully the potters carried their pots from Sasha's van and delicately placed them by the pits.

Jameela had a vase and two bowls to fire. She sat on one of the bales and slowly unwound the bubble wrap from her pieces.

Sasha spoke: 'OK potters, you have all brought with you stuff from home like I asked, ready to tie and tether around your pots – the more the better.'

Jameela peeped in the carrier bag between her feet.

'It could well be cathartic, strapping these items to your pots, sacrificing them to the flames.' Sasha looked around. 'Maybe you'll be celebrating the end of sadness, or a new chapter.'

Jameela dug around in the bag and pulled out a length of lace from her wedding dress to wrap around the neck of the vase, hoping the delicate pattern would leave a pretty mark on the pot's surface. It didn't mean her marriage to Simon was over, it just symbolised a new beginning – either for her alone or the two of them together; they still had to work that out. Tomorrow they were meeting for dinner at their favourite restaurant.

She also strapped the six used pregnancy sticks to the belly of the pot that for some reason she had kept in her 'miscarriage drawer' by her bed (full of hospital notes and painkillers and leaflets from various charities on how to cope). She stuck the sticks to the vase, wrapping the tape around and around. Already it felt good, as if the burning of this stuff was cleansing her soul of some of the heartache, letting go of the pain.

She smiled over at Sheila, who had joined her on the next bale. 'Where's Martin?'

'Gone,' said Sheila.

'What are you burning Sheila?'

Sheila had made a neat pile next to her pot. 'These,' she laughed, holding up a long sock. 'These are Ollie's old rugby socks. They're ribbed, so I'm hoping they'll leave a little stripe somewhere if I tie them on tight enough. I need to let go of Ollie a little I think; he's no longer my boy.'

Jameela smiled. 'Course he's your boy, Sheila.'

She watched as Sheila pulled one of the socks taut and wrapped it around her bowl, knotting it firmly. 'Maybe,' she said, 'but I have to share him now, with Charlotte. Which is fine.'

Jameela sat back and admired her pot and as she did she saw out of the corner of her eye Sheila quickly stuff something familiar into one of the rugby socks to be burned – a small pair of lacy black knickers.

48

Louise

Louise and Danny were inside one of the tents, laying out their sleeping bags. Danny was acting oddly. He couldn't quite look into Louise's eyes.

'Sweetheart, you've been really quiet all day, are you OK?' she asked him.

Her stomach churned – she'd had a feeling of foreboding all day, as if something bad was going to happen.

'I've messed up Louise, I'm an idiot,' he said quietly. He sat down from his crouching position and pulled his rucksack closer to him. He fiddled with the zip as though it was a worry bead.

'Danny, what have you done? It can't be that bad, can it?'

She searched his face. What had he done? She wasn't prepared for some huge confession – here, in the middle of a field with a long night stretching ahead of them. God, he picked his moments. 'Danny? You're scaring me, What've you done?' Still he looked down at the bag. 'Danny!' She was shouting now, and the chattering outside the tent died down on hearing her raised voice.

Danny spoke in a slow whisper, 'I've been hiding something, and I'm so sorry.' He slowly unzipped the bag and pulled out a thick cream envelope. She knew immediately who it was from.

Danny handed her the envelope, and sure enough there was Dawber's Gallery stamped in gold lettering on the front.

Louise was confused. 'I don't understand,' she stuttered. 'When did this arrive? I've been waiting for days. Why have you got it here with you?'

Danny looked ashamed. 'Because I'm an idiot,' he said, matter-of-factly. 'It only came this morning – I hid it. I knew you were really excited about tonight, and if that envelope contains bad news . . . well I didn't want it ruining your whole night, so I just shoved it in my bag. I panicked.' He pulled at his top lip, pinching the pink flesh between finger and thumb.

Louise felt physically sick. 'Jesus Danny, you freaked me out then!' She felt as if she could breathe again. 'I don't care that you hid it, but I wish you hadn't brought it here. What am I supposed to do now?'

She looked down at the envelope and then back up at him.

Danny shrugged, eyes wide in the gloom of the tent.

'I dunno,' he whispered. 'Open it?'

She took a deep breath. 'Look, if I've not got it, I'll be disappointed but I'll be OK – I mean . . .' she trailed off. Why even try to lie? She'd be devastated. The job had been the first and last thing she'd thought about each day since the interview.

'What the hell!' She ripped open the envelope. Inside was a postcard – she slid it out. On one side was Bridget Riley's *Serpentine*, on the other, swirly writing in black ink.

Her eyes blurred with tears as she read it silently.

'Oh sweetheart,' she heard Danny say, 'I'm so sorry.'

She looked up at him, tears now coursing down her face. 'I've got it Danny. I've bloody got it!'

Danny screamed and threw his arms open; she fell into him and he rolled backwards onto the sleeping mats, laughing. She lay in his arms in the tent and read out the best bits to him: 'They were "impressed with my knowledge", "charmed by my passion", and they end saying they'd like to "offer me the position as gallery assistant".'

49

Becky

It was dusk by the time Becky arrived, picking her way through the semi-darkness of the field towards the orange flames. She saw Jack and Pearl first and gave a little wave; in the gleam of the flames they looked like a sculpture, arms entwined, faces glowing copper.

Sasha was on his haunches in a low blanket of smoke, poking at the smouldering wood in the pits, the occasional spark lighting his face fleetingly. Buried deep in the bowels of the burning piles of wood were the pots, each piece bundled up like a foundling in fabric, paper, string, lace and wire, a sprinkle here and there of oxide to add colour. He stood up and looked into the distance, scanning the horizon.

'Hello,' Becky said, beside him.

Sasha jumped. ' It's you! I've been looking for you all night! Are you OK?'

'I'm OK, I'm looking for Elliot really. I can't get hold of him, and I'm paranoid he's upset with me for going AWOL this morning on a mad goose chase.'

She took the plastic cup of red wine from his hand and had a sip.

'Hair of the dog.' He nodded at the cup, 'Keep it,' and he grabbed another plastic cup and sloshed some wine into it. 'How's your head? This morning I felt like I'd repeatedly slammed mine in a truck door.'

She smiled. 'I've felt better. Some parts of last night are a little foggy.'

'Ah,' he smiled, looking embarrassed, 'well you obviously remember me making you promise you'd come here? 'Cos here you are.'

'Yes I do. I also remember your rousing rendition of Craig David's "7 days",' she laughed.

'Noooo,' he shouted. 'Oh my God, I totally forgot that.'

'Well I didn't – it's crystal clear in my mind – you rehashed the lyrics for the "pottery remix" . . . "Came to the community centre on Monday, made a coil pot on Tuesday . . ."'

'Stop it please,' he groaned, then gave her a hug. 'I'm so happy you came.'

Becky nodded, biting her lip. 'Me too Sasha. It's just . . . I feel terrible I wasn't there for Elliot, and we didn't even find the ring. I think he must be really upset with me – I presume he knows about the burglary, and now he's avoiding me . . .'

Sasha nodded grimly. 'Look Becky, the truth, is Elliot IS avoiding you.' Her stomach dropped. 'But he's not cross.' Sasha smiled nervously. Becky was confused. 'He made me swear not to tell you on the phone. He wanted you to find me, so I could be the one to give you this.'

Sasha reached into his coat pocket and pulled out a small black box. Becky took the box and slowly opened it. Inside, sparkling in the light from the campfire was her nana's sapphire ring.

She choked back a sob and covered her mouth. She threw her arms around Sasha in a grateful, disbelieving hug. The potters stopped their chat around the fire and, watched the drama unfold.

'But how . . . where . . .' She was shaking.

'Come on,' he said, 'sit down.' and they perched on a bale by the warmth of the fire.

'When Elliot came home I told him about the ring being stolen and he . . . laughed. I thought he was in shock – he'd had a terrible welcome home – no mum (sorry) then hearing about his prized possessions being nicked, all from some hungover bloke he'd only met a couple of times . . .' Sasha paused, took a sip of wine. 'But then Elliot said he wanted to show me something. I followed him up to his room and he went over to his chest of drawers. I didn't know what he was doing, then he picks up one of those cans of body sprays he has on display, shakes it and, well – it rattled. He took off the lid and tipped something out, and there, in the palm of his hand, was the ring. I couldn't believe it!' Sasha laughed. 'He told me that on the night Tony came back, he just had an instinct to hide it. He'd sneaked into your room and retrieved the ring from, as he put it, "Mum's basic hiding place", and stashed it away himself. He then went off to Ayia Napa and forgot about it, until of course he came home and heard from me that his instincts about his deadbeat dad were spot on.' Sasha paused, smiling at Becky. 'Quite a clever lad you have there. Anyway, we called you right away, but heard your phone ringing in the bedroom. That's when he came up with the plot for me to give you the ring. "It'll be a moment Sash!" He was pretty excited about it, so I didn't have the heart to not go along with his plan.'

Becky had been listening to the whole tale, completely gobsmacked. She looked down at the ring and slid it onto her finger and felt a rush of love and gratitude for her bright and brilliant son. She felt an energy from the ring, as if she was reconnecting with past generations, her own flesh and blood.

'It feels like a gift from Mum – just in time for the thirtieth anniversary of her passing. I feel like she's here with us.'

Sasha hugged her close.

Becky looked back up at his face and kissed him. 'Thank you,' she said. Sasha kissed her back, and they didn't even notice they had a small rapt audience watching them.

As the kiss ended, a small round of applause came from the potters. Sasha laughed. 'All right, all right, get on with your pit fires, you bunch of perverts,' he said.

Becky saw in the distance a woman walking with a torch in the semi darkness. As she approached, there was something familiar in the way she moved, and her long hair.

She made her way around the bales to Jameela, who looked thrilled to see her. They hugged, and the woman, who Becky presumed must be Jameela's sister, produced a bottle of wine and a huge bag of marshmallows to toast on the fire.

As Jameela topped up everyone's drinks, Sasha stood on a bale. The potters were silhouetted in front of the last burst of a beautiful sunset that had turned the sky a light plum colour. He gazed down at them all, and winked at Louise, who looked around her at the potters, once strangers, but now all standing with arms slung around each other, grinning.

'A toast,' said Sasha to the small gathering before him, 'firstly to absent friends,' he looked at Becky and she welled up, picturing her mum's smiling face, which came to her clearly in the firelight. The potters nodded and raised their glasses silently. 'And to tonight! This is the purest kind of pottery, and I'm thrilled we're here to experience it together. Earth, air, fire and water. All the elements. It's been a joy teaching you, watching you grow. Thank you for your time and your passion. Here's to you, the Lennington potters, and may the clay gods keep a watchful eye on our pots tonight.'

A loud 'Cheers!' went up as the potters hugged and clapped.

Becky and Sasha sat on the bales watching the flames. She felt a strange warmth inside her that wasn't just the wine. She felt, what was it? It was unfamiliar to her; it was something close to complete contentment.

Even though she and Sasha had been pretty drunk the night before, it was a relief to have let off steam. Bolstered with Dutch courage, they had each confessed their love for the other and had agreed they wanted to give it a go, to be together. Seeing each other now, more sober, it was clear they'd meant every word they'd slurred the night before. The way Sasha looked at her with such warmth and love made her melt.

Her phone buzzed – a text from Elliot, replying to hers: 'Yayyy! So glad you're happy mumski. Give the hot Scot a kiss from me lol. Love you.'

Becky curled her hand in her pocket and stroked the sapphire ring on her finger with her thumb, and smiled. As she did, her phone buzzed again. *Probably Elliot.* She was wrong.

It was a text from Sergeant Garvey. It simply said: 'Call me'.

Oh God, thought Becky, *what now?*

She moved away from the group and felt the temperature drop as she stepped away from the fire and into the darkness of the night. She shivered.

Joan answered on the first ring and sounded jubilant 'At last!!' she shouted over the noise in the background – it sounded as if she was in a pub. 'You did not hear this from me Becky, but the drugs bust was a biggie – eight kilos of heroin found at The Jesters, plus hundreds of pills – they got the whole gang. Six people arrested in the UK so far, and four detained in Thailand, including . . .' the line broke up.

'What?' Becky shouted down the phone. 'You broke up, I missed that last bit.'

'Including Tony. They got him Becky. He's in Thailand, seems he was over there helping some couple who are at the centre of it all – we'll get him extradited to face charges – imagine he needed the extra cash towards his plane ticket, so robbed you. He won't be bothering you again for a long time. I'm just sorry about the ring,' she shouted. There was raucous cheering in the background as someone made a boozy toast.

'Don't worry about the ring,' Becky replied, 'it's all good – I'll call you tomorrow,' and Joan was gone.

Becky put the phone in her pocket and walked back to the fire. She slipped her arm around Sasha's waist. He looked at her and smiled, his handsome face all aglow.

'All OK?' he said.

'Yes,' she replied. 'Everything is great.'

He pulled her to him, and together they stood and watched the dancing flames.

Acknowledgements

The first thing I should acknowledge in the acknowledgements is that it is actually quite hard writing a novel. I came swanning into the whole experience with a confidence and enthusiasm that far outweighed any actual skill. I'd written a memoir that'd done quite well, surely a novel would be, if not exactly a piece of cake to knock up, then at least a large gâteau – messy, complicated but just about do-able.

Fast forward through a year of writing that coincided with a pesky global pandemic (and children at home who needed regular feeding) and my editor, the legendary Hannah Black, sent back my first draft with the news that a second person was coming on board to help with the edit.

She'd basically called in back-up.

Suddenly my novel was beginning to feel like a dangerous dog that needed specialist training before it could be released from the pound.

Back-up editor Katie Brown sent back the edit with what felt like a thousand notes that December. The story was there, it just needed a character cull and some serious rejigging.

It felt like I'd built a snowman with the small ball at the bottom, the biggest ball on top balancing precariously on the carrot nose, the pieces of coal pressed in at random points like spots on a Dalmatian and the snowman's twig arms being chewed by an actual Dalmatian a few feet away.

On seeing all the notes, I cried. Then I replied angrily to the email saying Christmas was ruined and I couldn't do it and I hated writing.

Then I immediately wrote another email apologising for the last email saying I would give it a go.

Then I texted my good friend and fellow writer Jeremy Vine who gave me some great advice: 'Don't panic. The worst thing you can do is kick off then back down and do it.'

Ah. Awkward.

So I'd like to thank Jeremy for his kindness, empathy and words of wisdom even though they came too late.

A huge thank you to Hannah and Katie who saw through my huffing and puffing and whose advice I followed – turns out they were right about absolutely everything.

Thank you to all the team at Coronet for their time and hard work.

A special mention to proofreader extraordinaire Jackie Williams – AKA my mum – who read the first copy and spotted a few little errors. Thank you, Mum, you're the best.

Thanks to Annie Mac who, having written her (bestselling) debut novel the year before, was always on hand with calm encouragement.

Thanks to my agent and friend, the frankly bloody ace Melanie Rockcliffe and the ever-patient Rebekka Taylor at YMU for the support.

As ever, a thank you to my awesome offspring Lola, Isaac and Renee. We were getting under each other's feet and up each other's noses whilst I was writing this book and I'm so proud of how they handled being locked down with a grumpy mum largely hiding at the bottom of the garden with a computer and some biscuits.

Thank you to my husband and best friend Ben for always making me laugh and without whom I wouldn't have had the confidence, time or basic tech knowledge to get this book done.

A special mention to Valeria who looks after the dogs, cats, house, children, plants – basically everything – and makes it all run like clockwork so I can do fun stuff like write books.

My biggest thank you is reserved for the brilliant ceramic artist Kate Malone MBE. Since working together on the first two series of *The Great Pottery Throwdown*, alongside the lovely Keith Brymer Jones, we've stayed pals.

With Kate's boundless enthusiasm, passion for pottery and rich use of language when talking all things clay, I knew she'd be the perfect person to turn to for help with the pottery elements of the book. I will be forever grateful for her time and meticulous eye for detail...and for not minding when I texted her with random questions about kiln temperatures. Sasha's teaching style is inspired by Kate – the roguish love life not so much!

Right, that's it I think. It's been exciting and knee-knocking in equal measure sharing *Thrown* with you. Thank you so much for reading it. I absolutely loved spending so much time with these four formidable women and I hope you did too.